THE ULTIMATE TRUTH

D0964108

THE ULTIMATE TRUTH

WITHDRAWN

KEVIN BROOKS

TRAVIS DELANEY

MACMILLAN CHILDREN'S BOOKS

First published 2014 by Macmillan Children's Books
a division of Macmillan Publishers Limited
20 New Wharf Road, London N1 9RR
Basingstoke and Oxford
Associated companies throughout the world
www.panmacmillan.com

ISBN 978-1-4472-3896-6

1 3 5 7 9 8 6 4 2

A CIP catalogue record for this book is available from
the British Library.

Printed and bound by CPI Group (UK) Ltd, Croydon, CR0 4YY

For Eugenie – my friend, my belief.

1

I only noticed the man with the hidden camera because I couldn't bear to look at the coffins any more. I'd been looking at them for a long time now. From the moment the two wooden boxes had been brought into the church, to the moment they'd been carried out into the graveyard and lowered gently into their freshly dug graves, I'd never taken my eyes off them. But now, as the vicar intoned his sombre words – 'earth to earth, ashes to ashes, dust to dust' – and I gazed down into the graves, the truth hit me again like a sledgehammer. My mum and dad were in those coffins.

My mum and dad were dead.

It was impossible to believe, impossible to imagine, and it hurt so much that I had to look away. As I slowly raised my head and wiped the tears from my eyes, I felt my nan's hand on my arm. I looked at her. She was crying too, her kindly eyes brimming with tears. I squeezed her hand and smiled sadly at her, then turned to Grandad. He was staring straight ahead, his head held high, his craggy old face weighed down with sadness.

The vicar was saying the Lord's Prayer now – 'forgive us our trespasses, as we forgive those who trespass against us' – and some of the other mourners were mumbling along with him. I gazed emptily around at them, vaguely recognising all the familiar faces, and that's when I saw the man with the hidden camera.

I didn't know he had a hidden camera at first. I wasn't even aware that I was looking at him at first. My mind was blank. I was just staring blindly, not really conscious of what I was seeing. It was only when the sun broke through the clouds for a moment, and a tiny glint of light flashed from one of his suit buttons, that I began to pay more attention to him.

He was fairly tall, with short grey hair and steely grey eyes, and he was standing next to some old university friends of my parents. I knew he didn't belong with them. They were all about the same age as my mum and dad – late thirties, early forties – but he was at least fifty, maybe a bit older. And while I knew all my mum and dad's friends, just as I knew everyone else at the funeral, I'd never seen this man before. That wasn't the only thing that set him apart. There was something else too, something about him that just didn't feel right . . .

Then his button caught the light again, glinting like a tiny bead of glass, and all of a sudden I knew what it was. I'd seen a button camera before. My dad had used one a couple of times. He'd shown it to me, he'd let me try it out. My dad had liked showing me how stuff works.

My dad . . .

My mum.

The memory of them welled up inside me, filling my eyes with tears again, and for the next few minutes everything was just a blur.

The service was over now, the prayers finished, the graveyard tranquil and quiet. A light summer rain had begun to fall, and people were starting to leave, shuffling awkwardly away from the graves and making their way back to their cars.

Grandad put his hand on my shoulder.

I wiped my eyes and looked at him.

'Is there anything you want to say, Travis?' he asked softly.

I couldn't think. My mind had gone blank. I gazed around, looking for the man with the steely grey eyes, but there was no sign of him anywhere.

I stared down at the graves, the two coffins resting in the ground. There were so many things I wanted to say, but the words wouldn't come to me. I closed my eyes, imagining the inscriptions on the gravestones:

JACK DELANEY
BELOVED SON, HUSBAND AND FATHER
DIED 16 JULY 2013 AGED 38 YEARS
REST IN PEACE

ISABEL DELANEY
BELOVED DAUGHTER, WIFE AND MOTHER
DIED 16 JULY 2013 AGED 37 YEARS
REST IN PEACE

What else was there to say?

I saw the man with the grey eyes again as we headed across the church car park towards Grandad's car. He was standing next to a black BMW with tinted windows, talking on a mobile phone. By the time we reached Grandad's car, the man had finished his phone call and was opening the boot of the BMW and taking out a coat. As Grandad searched through his pockets for his car keys, I took out my mobile, turned it on, and opened up the camera function. The man had put on his coat now and was reaching up to close the boot. As I held up my phone and zoomed in on him, I saw him glance over at me. He froze for a moment, his cold eyes staring out at me from the mobile screen, and I quickly took his picture. A second after the camera clicked, I thought I saw him nod his head at me.

'What are you doing, Trav?' I heard Grandad say.

'Nothing,' I muttered, putting my mobile away.

Grandad looked across at the BMW, but there was nothing to see now. The man had got in the car and shut the door, his face indistinct behind the tinted glass. Grandad carried on staring at the BMW for a moment or two, a slight frown on his face, then he turned back to me.

'Come on, son,' he said, opening the back door of his car. 'Let's go home.'

2

My mum and dad ran a small private investigation business called Delaney & Co. Grandad had set up the agency on his own in 1994, and Mum and Dad had started working for him two years later, straight after leaving university. Grandad retired from the business about ten years ago, and since then my parents had run the agency together. Most of the work they did wasn't all that glamorous or exciting – fraudulent insurance claims, corporate security, tracing witnesses and debtors – and although they sometimes got involved with the shadowy side of life, I'd never been particularly worried about their safety. They were very good at their job. They knew what they were doing. They didn't take unnecessary risks. So it had never really occurred to me that one day they might not come home. They were my mum and dad, they *always* came home.

But two weeks ago, on Tuesday 16 July, they didn't.

I'll never forget that day.

It was the day the world stopped turning.

I'd got home from school at the usual time, around half past four, and after I'd changed out of my uniform and had something to eat, Mum and Dad had told me they were driving down to London that night and they wouldn't be back until tomorrow.

'Sorry, Trav,' Mum had said, glancing at her watch. 'I know it's all a bit sudden, but something's just come up, something really important, and we have to get to London as soon as possible. You'll have to stay with Nan and Grandad tonight.'

'But it's Tuesday,' I said. 'It's my boxing night.'

'You can still go to the club,' Dad said. 'Grandad will take you.'

'He doesn't like boxing,' I said. 'He thinks it's for sissies.'

Dad smiled. 'Go and get your stuff ready, OK? We have to get going in a minute. We'll drop you off at Nan and Grandad's on the way.'

It's funny how your memory works. I know I must have gone upstairs to my bedroom and thrown a few things into my rucksack – toothbrush, pyjamas, boxing gloves, shorts – but I have no recollection of actually doing it. What I *can* remember is that when I came downstairs and went outside to put my rucksack in the car, Mum and Dad were standing in the driveway having an argument. They weren't shouting at each other or anything. They never did that. In fact, it wasn't even an argument really, just a minor disagreement. Mum wanted to take her car to London, and Dad wanted to go in his. Mum's car was an automatic, a Volvo, and more comfortable than Dad's old Saab. But Mum's car was parked in the garage, and Dad's was in the driveway. So if they went in Mum's

Volvo, Dad would have to reverse the Saab out of the way, wait for Mum to back the Volvo out of the garage, then drive the Saab back in again.

'It's just a waste of time,' he said.

Mum shook her head. 'I'm not driving all the way to London in that heap of yours.'

'It might be a heap,' Dad replied, 'but at least it's a sensible colour.'

Mum's car was bright yellow, her favourite colour, and Dad was forever teasing her about how ridiculous it looked.

'I'll be doing the driving anyway,' Dad said. 'All you have to do is sit there and look out of the window.'

'The passenger seat gives me backache.'

'It's not far. We'll be there in a couple of hours.'

'I don't want to spend all night in London with an aching back.'

Dad sighed. 'All right, we'll go in yours.'

After he'd moved his car, and Mum had driven hers out, and Dad had reversed his into the garage, they'd had another disagreement. This time it was about Dad's sat nav. Dad had no sense of direction at all, and he always used a sat nav when he was driving, even for local journeys. But Mum hated them, and she never used one wherever she was going. So when Mum saw that Dad was bringing his sat nav with him, she told him to put it back.

'I'm not having that thing in my car,' she said firmly.

'We're driving into the middle of London,' Dad said. 'You know what the roads are like—'

'I don't care,' Mum told him. 'I'd rather get lost than use one of those.'

'But I've already keyed in the address,' he said. 'All we have to do when we get to London is turn it on—'

'No,' Mum said.

Dad looked at her, about to say something else, but when he saw the expression on her face, he changed his mind. He sighed again, turned round, and took his sat nav back to the garage.

The garage is only just big enough for a car, and Dad was over six feet tall, so rather than shuffling his way into the garage to put the sat nav back in the car, he just dropped it into a cardboard box full of odds and ends that was sitting on a shelf inside the door.

And that was it really.

There was nothing to it. By the time we'd all got in Mum's car and were driving off down our street, the whole thing had been forgotten. Mum was smiling and joking about something, Dad was fiddling with the car radio, singing along to some pathetic old pop song, and I was just sitting in the back seat looking forward to my regular Tuesday-night trip to the boxing club.

I remember it all quite vividly.

After that, my memory goes blank again. I can't remember anything between the time we left the house and the moment Grandad's mobile rang. I can't remember what Mum and Dad said to me when they dropped me off at Nan and Grandad's house. I can't remember what I said to them. I can't remember anything between five o'clock, when I left the house with Mum and Dad, and five to seven, when Grandad's mobile rang just as he was pulling his car into a parking space outside the boxing club.

He turned off the engine, I remember, then took out his phone, glanced at the screen, and answered the call.

'Nancy?' he said into the phone. Nancy is my nan's name. 'Nancy,' he said urgently, 'what's the matter?'

Then his face went pale.

Mum and Dad's car had come off the road and crashed into a tree about ten kilometres from Barton. The accident happened on a slip road just off the A12. Dad was killed instantly, Mum died on the way to the hospital. According to the police, the car was travelling at approximately 65 mph when it veered suddenly to the left, went into a 180-degree spin, then flipped up into the air and flew off the verge into an oak tree. Driving conditions were good, the car was mechanically sound, and no other vehicles were involved.

3

The two weeks between the car crash and the funeral were the longest two weeks of my life. The days passed by in a haze of confusion and emptiness. I didn't understand anything. I didn't know what to do, what to think, what to feel. At first I simply couldn't believe that Mum and Dad were dead. I couldn't comprehend it. How could they be dead? They were my mum and dad . . . they *couldn't* be dead. I kept thinking that it had to be some kind of huge mistake. It wasn't my mum's car that had crashed, it was someone else's car . . . the same make as Mum's, the same model, the same colour. The people who'd died in the crash weren't Mum and Dad, they were two other people, a man and a woman who looked just like Mum and Dad . . .

But I knew I was just kidding myself.

It wasn't a mistake.

Grandad had identified the bodies.

I was living at Nan and Grandad's house now. I'd gone a bit crazy the day after the car crash, insisting that I wanted to go home, I wanted to go back to *my* house, I wanted to be there in case Mum and Dad came back. It was hard for Nan and Grandad, of course. They couldn't let me go home on my own. I was thirteen years old, my parents had just died. They had to look after me. I knew that. I knew I was acting irrationally and making everything really awkward for them, but I couldn't help it. My craziness didn't last very long though, and once I'd calmed down and apologised, we all just tried to get on with things as best as we could.

Grandad made a trip back to my house to pick up some of my stuff – clothes, my bike, my laptop, a few other bits and pieces – and although I really missed my own house, my own room, I'd spent so much time at Nan and Grandad's over the years that it kind of felt like my second home anyway. Their house wasn't far from ours. We live – or we used to live – in a place called Kell Cross, a village on the outskirts of Barton, and Nan and Grandad live about two kilometres away on Long Barton Road, the main road between Kell Cross and Barton.

Their house was a nice old place, and I'd always felt really comfortable there. There were three bedrooms upstairs. One was Nan and Grandad's, one was the room I always stayed in, and the third one was Granny Nora's room. She's my great-grandmother, Grandad's mum. She's eighty-six now, and she doesn't get out much any more. She has chronic arthritis, bad legs, bad hips. On good days she can just about walk with the aid of a stick, but when her arthritis is really bad she can only get about in a wheelchair. She's deaf in one ear too, and the other ear's getting worse all the time. Her mind though – and her attitude – is as sharp as a pin.

I spent a lot of time thinking about things during

those endless two weeks. There wasn't much else to do. I didn't want to go anywhere or talk to anyone – friends, kids from school – I didn't want to do anything. What was the point? So I just kind of hung around most of the time. In my room, in the sitting room downstairs, sometimes out in the garden.

I don't think I meant to start asking myself questions about the car crash. It was just that I had nothing else to do, and the only other questions in my mind were too heartbreaking. Why did my mum and dad have to die? Why them? They were the best people in the world. Why did *they* have to die?

There were no answers to those questions.

So I found myself asking others.

How did the crash happen? If there were no other vehicles involved, and driving conditions were fine, and there was nothing wrong with the car, why had it come off the road? Mum and Dad were excellent drivers. Because of their investigation work, they'd taken an advanced driving course, and they were very proud of their driving skills. They drove carefully, not too fast, not too slow. They didn't use their phones when they were driving. They didn't take risks. So what had happened? Why had Mum lost control of the car at 65 mph and careered off the road into a tree?

It didn't make sense.

I also couldn't understand why they were only ten kilometres from Barton when they crashed. They'd left the house at around five o'clock, and according to the police, the crash had occurred just over an hour later, at five past six. It doesn't take an hour to drive ten kilometres. So where had they been? And why hadn't they driven directly to London?

Again, I couldn't think of an answer.

Another thing I couldn't work out was that if they were driving to London, why would they take a slip road off the A12? The A12 is the direct route from Barton to London. Unless you're going somewhere else, you don't need to turn off it.

Questions . . .

I couldn't stop asking them.

Over and over and over again.

Even though I knew the answers didn't matter.

Whatever the answers were, Mum and Dad were never coming home.

4

Everything felt really strange after the funeral. It was as if we'd been waiting for ever for the day to come, and now that it had, and the funeral was over, there was nothing left to wait for. There was just nothing left. The whole world felt empty and dull.

I was still troubled by the unanswered questions about the car crash, and since the day of the funeral I hadn't been able to get the man with the hidden camera out of my mind either. Who was he? Why was he secretly filming my parents' funeral? Normally I would have gone to Grandad and asked him about it, and normally he would have welcomed me and done his best to help. He probably would have come up with some answers too.

My grandad is a very experienced and very smart man. Before running Delaney & Co on his own for nearly ten years, he'd spent five years in the Royal Military Police and twelve years as an officer in the Army Intelligence Corps. So he knows pretty much everything there is to know about investigation work. Unfortunately though, he's always been prone to very dark moods, and ever since the car crash he'd been suffering really badly – moping around all day, not sleeping, getting irritable, not wanting to talk to anyone.

'He'll get over it,' Nan assured me when I asked her

about him. 'He always does. He'll never get over the loss of Jack and Izzy, of course, none of us will. We've lost our son and daughter-in-law, you've lost your mum and dad . . .' She put her arms around me. 'The thing you have to remember, Trav,' she said gently, 'is that you don't *have* to get over it. It wouldn't be right if you did. All you have to do is let your grief become part of you. Do you understand?'

'I think so,' I said.

She smiled sadly at me. 'Don't worry too much about Grandad. He's a tough old boot. He won't stay down in the dumps for ever. This has just hit him really hard, that's all. It's brought back too many bad memories.'

Grandad saw some terrible things in the army, and he went through a lot of terrible things himself. He almost lost his life in a car-bomb explosion when he was stationed in Northern Ireland. It put him in hospital for six months, and even now he still has bits of shrapnel left in his body. But I think it's the memories that haunt him the most. He has nightmares sometimes, he wakes up screaming. I've heard him.

So that's why I didn't ask him about the car crash or the man with the hidden camera. He was suffering too much. The last thing he needed was me pestering him with questions.

But that didn't mean I had to stop pestering myself.

It wasn't as if I had anything else to do.

School was finished for the summer now, and in the

past I'd always spent the holidays helping out Mum and Dad at Delaney & Co. They'd never let me get involved with any serious investigation work, but they'd always been happy to let me hang around the office, doing whatever I could. Filing, writing letters, basic enquiries on the Internet. Sometimes they'd let me tag along with them on a routine surveillance case, an insurance fraud stake-out or something . . .

But that wasn't going to happen this summer.

Two days after the funeral, I downloaded the photograph of the man with the hidden camera to my laptop. The image on the laptop screen was a lot clearer than it was on my mobile, and I must have spent a good two or three hours just sitting there staring at it. It was impossible to make out the button camera in the photograph, even after I'd zoomed in as much as I could, but I hadn't really expected to see it anyway. The button camera that Dad had shown me was so small, and so well disguised, that it was virtually invisible to the naked eye. And when I remembered that, I started to wonder if maybe I'd been imagining things. If a button camera is virtually invisible, how could I be sure that the man at the funeral was wearing one? All I'd seen was a brief glint of reflected light. It could have come from anything – a metal button, a pin, a tiny piece of foil . . .

I thought about that for a while, then I leaned forward and peered closely at the man's face. His steely grey eyes were looking directly at me, but I guessed that wasn't unusual. If you see someone taking a picture of you, it's quite normal to stare back at them. But he hadn't just stared back at me, had he? He'd given me a very slight nod of his head, as if he was acknowledging me. As I looked at him now, I could see that same acknowledgement in his eyes. It wasn't a friendly look, but it wasn't unfriendly either. It's hard to describe, but I got the impression that he was trying to share something with me.

I thought about that for a while too, then I zoomed out and studied the whole photograph again. It showed the man just as he was reaching up to close the boot of his BMW. I focused on the boot, enlarging it as much as I could, trying to see inside it, but the picture quality was too grainy to see anything clearly. I scrolled down a bit and stopped when the car's registration plate came into view. It was clearly visible. Easily readable. I stared at it, wondering, thinking . . .

Although it's illegal to trace the owner of a vehicle through its registration number, it's not hard to do if you know the right people. And I knew for a fact that Grandad knew the right people. He knows all kinds of people. I was pretty sure that if I gave him the registration number of the BMW and asked him to find out who owned it, it wouldn't take him too long to come up with a name. But no matter how much I wanted to, I knew I couldn't ask Grandad to do that. Not while he was feeling so bad. It wouldn't be fair.

As Mum once told me, if you do your best to be kind and fair, you'll never go too far wrong.

I leaned back in my chair, stretched my neck and yawned, then rubbed the tiredness from my eyes and went back to studying the photograph.

5

After breakfast the next morning, I asked Nan if it was all right if I went out on my bike for a while.

'Of course it's all right,' she said, a little hesitantly. 'Where are you going?'

'Nowhere really,' I told her. 'I just thought I'd ride around for a bit, you know . . . get some fresh air.'

She looked at me. 'Well, be careful, OK? And make sure you take your phone with you.'

I nodded. 'How's Grandad today?'

'Not too bad. He's having a lie-in at the moment, which is a good sign. He hasn't had much sleep recently.' She smiled cautiously. 'Hopefully he'll feel a bit better if he can get some rest.'

I just nodded again, not sure what to say.

'Go on, then,' she said, ruffling my hair. 'Go and get yourself some fresh air.'

There wasn't much fresh air along Long Barton Road, just the usual choke of exhaust fumes hazing in the heat of the traffic. Not that I minded. The smell of the streets on the way into town always makes me feel like I'm going somewhere. And that's what I needed just now – the feeling that I was going somewhere, the feeling that I was doing something. I wasn't sure why I needed it, and I wasn't really sure what I was doing either, but somehow that didn't seem to matter. All that mattered was having some kind of purpose.

Nan and Grandad's house isn't far from town, about three kilometres at most, and it didn't take long to get to the North Road roundabout, where the town centre really begins. The roundabout was jam-packed with traffic, and it's one of those massive mega-roundabouts that are really hard to cycle round at the best of times, so I got off my bike and wheeled it along the pavement, then crossed over the road at the pelican crossing instead.

The crossing led me into North Walk, a pedestrianised street at the quiet end of town. If you keep going along North Walk, then turn left at the end, you're right in the middle of town where all the big shops are. But I wasn't interested in big shops. All I was interested in was the familiar small office building at 22 North Walk, where Delaney & Co was located.

That morning though, as I wheeled my bike along the pavement, nothing looked very familiar. A lot of the shops were closed, their doors and windows boarded up. Others were still open, but their windows were cracked and shattered. As I passed by a shoe shop and looked inside, I could see that it had been ransacked – shoes and boots strewn all over the place, the walls kicked in, the sales counter smashed up. The street itself was a mess too – litter bins ripped out, signposts bent out of shape, the road covered with broken glass and bits of rubble.

As I stopped and looked around for a moment, I remembered seeing something on the local news about a small-scale riot in Barton. Under normal circumstances, I'm sure I would have paid more attention to it, but these weren't normal circumstances. Although Nan still turned on the TV most evenings, none of us really watched it. Even if we were sitting there looking at it, we weren't actually taking it in. We had other things on our minds, things that really meant something. So all I could remember about the news report was that there'd been some trouble in Barton town centre recently and looters had damaged a number of shops and buildings.

I hurried on down the pavement, hoping the rioters had ignored Mum and Dad's office. But even as I approached the office building I could see that the main door was patched up with a sheet of plywood, and it was clear that it had been kicked in and smashed open. I couldn't understand it at first. It was obvious from the names of the companies listed on a plaque by the door that there was nothing of any great value in the building: *JAKES AND MORTIMER, SOLICITORS* on the second floor; *TANTASTIC TANNING* on the first; *DELANEY & CO, PRIVATE INVESTIGATION SERVICES* on the ground floor. I mean, why would anyone bother looting places like that? What were they hoping to steal – a sunbed and a couple of filing cabinets? But then I realised that rioters and looters probably don't think very rationally, they just break into anywhere and grab whatever they can. Even if

21

there isn't anything worth stealing, there's always going to be something to smash up.

I wheeled my bike through the open door and headed down the corridor towards Mum and Dad's office.

The office door was half open, the pebbled-glass panel smashed out. As I leaned my bike against the corridor wall, I heard a muffled *clonk* from inside the office. I stopped and listened. I couldn't see anyone through the broken door panel, but there was definitely somebody in there. I could hear them – shuffling footsteps, a muted cough, a quiet sniff.

My heart was beating hard now, and for a moment or two I was tempted to play it safe. Just turn round, walk out, and call the police. Let them deal with it. But my heart wasn't just pounding with fear, it was seething with anger too. This was my mum and dad's office. I'd spent half my life in here. It was full of good memories. It was a special place. It was *our* place. No one else had a right to be in our place.

I took a deep breath, let it out slowly, then pushed open the door.

6

The first thing I saw when I went into the office was a young woman picking up piles of papers from the floor. She had bright-red hair, a tattoo on her right shoulder, and she was wearing a tiny black miniskirt, a vest top, and purple Doc Martens. As she heard me come in, she straightened up and smiled at me.

'Hey, Travis,' she said. 'What are you doing here?'

'Hi, Courtney,' I mumbled, feeling pretty stupid.

The main reason I felt stupid was that Courtney Lane had been Mum and Dad's assistant for almost two years, so it should have at least occurred to me that she might have been in the office. But I also felt stupid because Courtney always makes me feel stupid. She's not only stunningly pretty, but she always wears incredibly revealing clothes. And whenever I see her, I never know where to look, which is pretty embarrassing. It's even more embarrassing when she gives me a hug, which she did just then – grabbing hold of me and squeezing tight – because I never know where to put my hands. Despite feeling stupid and embarrassed though, I was still really pleased to see her.

'I'm sorry I didn't talk to you at the funeral,' she said, letting go of me and stepping back. 'I wanted to, but I wasn't sure if you were up to talking or not. I wouldn't have known what to say anyway. I still don't.'

'You don't have to say anything.'

She sighed, shaking her head. 'I still can't believe it.'

'Me neither.'

'One minute everything's all right, and then suddenly . . .'

I just nodded, not really wanting to think about it, but not wanting to appear rude either.

'Sorry,' Courtney said. 'I didn't mean—'

'It's OK,' I told her.

She sighed again, then went over to her desk and put down the pile of papers she was holding.

I looked around the office. The whole place had been trashed. Desk drawers had been emptied, cabinets ripped open, papers and files were scattered all over the floor. All the office equipment was either missing or smashed to pieces – computers, printers, scanners, phones.

'When did it happen?' I asked Courtney.

'Last Saturday night,' she said. 'From what I've read in the local papers it all kicked off around seven o'clock when a gang of kids from the Slade Lane estate broke into the T-Mobile shop at the end of the street. There were about twenty or thirty of them at first, but once they went on the rampage and started looting all the other shops, loads of other people joined in. They all just went crazy, smashing up everything they came across.'

'Did it spread any further?' I asked. 'Did they move on to the High Street or anything?'

She shook her head. 'The police reacted pretty quickly, apparently. They had the High Street blocked off within about half an hour, so most of the damage was limited to North Walk.'

I looked over at Mum and Dad's private office. The door was half hanging off, the wooden panels kicked in.

'Is it just as bad in there?' I asked.

Courtney nodded. 'I haven't had a chance to check what's missing yet. I thought I'd better try to clear up some of the mess first.' She glanced across at me. 'The police didn't notify your grandad about the damage until Monday. He called me on the Wednesday after the funeral and asked if I could pop in sometime to check that the main door had been fixed.' She gazed around at the mess. 'I would have started on all this earlier, but my mum's been in and out of hospital all week and I just haven't had time.'

'You didn't have to come in and clean up,' I told her. 'I'm glad you did, of course. It's really nice of you. But I don't know if . . . well, you know . . .'

I was suddenly feeling embarrassed again, but this time it was because I didn't know how to say what I was trying to say. Thankfully, Courtney had already read my mind.

'I'm not bothered about getting paid or anything, Trav,' she said. 'I mean, I know I don't have to come in to work any more. I'm not doing this because I have to, I'm doing it because I want to. Your mum and dad were always really good to me.' She wiped her eyes and smiled at me. 'Besides, someone's got to get this mess cleaned up. And I don't suppose you came armed with a dustpan and brush, did you?'

'No,' I admitted.

She turned back to the desk and started sorting through the piles of papers. 'So what *are* you doing here, Travis?'

'I'm not really sure, to be honest,' I told her. 'I suppose I'm just wondering what Mum and Dad were working on when they died. I know they were going to London to meet someone, and I know they'd been working on a new case, but I don't know what it was about.' I went over to a filing cabinet and started looking through the drawers. 'I thought I might find their case notes or something . . .'

'I've already checked that cabinet,' Courtney said. 'It's empty. All the files are on the floor.'

I looked at her. 'Do *you* know what Mum and Dad were working on?'

'Not really,' she said. 'I was on holiday for the first two weeks of July, and I only came back on the Monday before the crash. Your mum and dad weren't in the office that day, and I only saw your mum for a couple of minutes on the Tuesday, so I never got round to catching up with their current cases. The last case I know about was a missing persons enquiry that came through on the Friday before I went away. I passed on the details to your dad at the time, but I don't know if he actually took the case or not.'

'Do you remember who made the enquiry?'

'It was a man called John Ruddy. He said he was an old friend of your dad's.'

'Have you still got his contact details?'

'Well, I entered them into a new-client file on the office computer, as usual. But as you can see . . .' She gestured at the empty space on the desk where the office PC used to be. 'I also printed out two hard copies of his file. One copy went in the filing cabinet, the other went in the in tray in your mum and dad's office.' She looked down at the piles of paper on the floor. 'They could be anywhere now.'

'So you don't have this John Ruddy's phone number or anything?' I said.

'I can't remember his phone number or his home address, but I remember that he mentioned a boxing club.'

'A boxing club?'

'It wasn't the one you go to, it was the other one. The one near Slade Lane, down by the docks.'

'Wonford Boxing Club?'

'That's it. I think Mr Ruddy said he was the club's manager, or maybe the owner. He said your dad knew the club.'

'Dad used to train there when he was boxing,' I told her. 'It's a pretty rough place, but it's got a good reputation for producing pro fighters. Did Mr Ruddy give you any more details about the case?'

'He just said it was a missing persons enquiry and he'd like to talk to your dad about it.' She looked at me. 'What's going on, Travis? Why do you want to know all this?'

I paused for a second, thinking things through, then I sat down and started to talk.

7

When I'd finished telling Courtney everything – my doubts about the car crash, my suspicions about the man at the funeral – she didn't say anything for a while, she just sat at her desk, thinking quietly.

Eventually she said, 'I'm not sure we'll ever know the truth about the car crash, Travis. I've been asking myself exactly the same questions as you. How did it happen? Why did it happen? Why were your mum and dad turning off the A12? None of it made sense to me at first. There didn't seem to be any logical answers. But then I reminded myself that life isn't logical, it doesn't always make sense. Sometimes stuff just happens. Maybe your mum was distracted by something when she was driving, a wasp or a bee, something like that. Or she could have sneezed at the wrong time . . . I don't know. It could have been anything.'

'Yeah, OK,' I said, 'but why were they on the slip road? And why were they only ten kilometres from Barton? Where had they been before then?'

'Perhaps they called in here first. I would have gone home by then. They might have forgotten some paperwork or something, called in here to pick it up, got delayed by a phone call . . .' She shrugged. 'Maybe they were turning off the A12 to find a service station. I know it doesn't sound very likely, but unlikely things happen, Travis.'

I nodded, accepting her point. But I still wasn't convinced. And I didn't think she was either.

'What about the man at the funeral?' I said.

'Let me see the picture you took of him.'

I took out my mobile, found the photograph, and passed the phone to Courtney. She studied the man in the picture.

'Yeah,' she said, 'I remember seeing him. I wondered who he was. I thought he might be one of your grandad's old friends.'

'What made you think that?'

'I don't know . . . he just had that look about him, you know. Like he was ex-military or secret services or something. Did you ask your grandad about him?'

I shook my head. 'He's not feeling too good at the moment. I didn't want to bother him.'

'Is he going through one of his bad patches again?'

I nodded. 'I'm sure he didn't know the man though. He didn't talk to him or anything. Didn't even look at him, as far as I know.'

Courtney glanced at the photograph again. 'Are you sure he was wearing a hidden camera?'

'Fairly sure.'

'Why would anyone want to film your parents' funeral?'

'I don't know. If we knew who he was, we could ask him.'

'But we don't know who he is.'

'We know his car registration number.'

Courtney's eyes narrowed. 'Are you suggesting what I think you're suggesting?'

I smiled at her.

She shook her head. 'It's illegal, Travis. Even if I could do it, and I'm not saying I can, unauthorised access to the DVLA database is against the law.'

'It wouldn't hurt anyone though, would it?'

'That's not the point.'

'No one would have to know.'

'I'd know. And so would you.'

'I can keep a secret.'

She sighed. 'You're not going to let this go, are you?'

'No.'

She pulled out her mobile. 'You don't know I'm doing this, OK?' she said, keying in a number.

'Right.'

She stared at me, apparently waiting for something.

'What?' I said.

'How are you going to *not* know what I'm doing if you carry on sitting there?'

'You want me to leave you alone?'

She smiled. 'If you wouldn't mind.'

'Not at all,' I said, standing up. 'I'll be in the other office if you need me.'

She watched me as I crossed over to Mum and Dad's private office, and she waited until I'd gone inside and shut the door before getting on with her phone call. I didn't know who she was calling, but I'd heard her talking to Dad once about a police officer she knew who owed her a big favour. But like she'd said, it was best if I didn't know.

I looked around Mum and Dad's office, remembering how it used to be, how it was *supposed* to be. Dad's desk against one wall, Mum's on the other side of the room. Dad's desk neat and tidy, everything in its place, Mum's a complete mess, everything piled up in random heaps. The window looking out into an alleyway at the back, the pictures on the walls – framed photos of Mum and Dad and me, a Picasso print, a picture of Millwall FC's 2004 FA Cup Final team. I could see it all in my mind, but now it was all gone – either smashed up and broken, lying in bits on the floor, or just not there any more. Dad's PC was missing, Mum's laptop was nowhere to be seen, the desk drawers had all been emptied.

I could hear Courtney talking on the phone now. I listened hard, trying to make out what she was saying, but she was speaking too softly for me to hear anything. I looked over towards the window. The small wooden table that should have been standing in the corner beneath the window had been kicked across the room. The aspidistra in the brass pot that should have been on the table was lying on the floor, the soil scattered all over the place, the plant itself stomped into the carpet.

I went over to the window, stood there for a moment,

then crouched down and pulled back the carpet from the corner. I paused again, listening to the murmur of Courtney's voice, then I reached down and pulled up a hinged section of floorboard. As I'd hoped, the hidden safe beneath the floorboards hadn't been touched. It was still locked, still safe. I stared at it, remembering the day I'd come across Dad opening it up.

'There's nothing exciting in it,' he'd said, smiling at me. 'It's just boring old business papers – insurance documents, contracts, stuff like that.' He grinned. 'I told Mum it was a waste of money, but you know what she's like. Always worrying about something.' He winked at me. 'Don't tell her I said that.'

I wasn't sure I'd believed him at the time, and I'd always wondered what was really in the safe. But although I knew the code – I'd seen Dad keying it in – I'd never actually looked inside. I'd been tempted a couple of times, but it just hadn't felt like the right thing to do. Even now, as I leaned down and began entering the code, it still didn't feel quite right.

But that didn't stop me.

The four-digit code was the date of my birthday: 3008.

When I punched in the code, the lock beeped and a green light came on. I took hold of the handle, turned it, and pulled. The steel door opened easily. There wasn't much in there – a couple of cardboard files, some A4 envelopes, a handful of papers. I reached in and pulled everything out, then sat down on the floor and began leafing through it all.

It didn't take me long to realise that Dad had been telling the truth about the boring old business papers. The files were crammed with invoices and contracts, the envelopes were stuffed full of insurance papers. There didn't seem to be any case notes. No clues, no secrets. It wasn't until I'd almost reached the bottom of the pile, and almost given up hope, that I came across the photograph.

It wasn't an original, just a computer printout on plain A4 paper. The picture quality wasn't very good either. It looked as if it had been printed off in a hurry. But there was still no mistaking what the photograph showed.

I put the rest of the papers to one side, breathed out slowly, and took a closer look at the picture.

It showed three men standing together outside a building. They were all wearing suits, and it looked as if they were discussing something. One of them had short dark hair and a goatee beard, another one had a shaved head, and the third one was the man from the funeral. There was absolutely no doubt in my mind it was him. He had the grey eyes, the short grey hair, and – Courtney had been right – he did have that ex-military look to him. There were two vehicles parked behind the three men – a black BMW and a black Mercedes van. The registration plates weren't visible. The building in the background was some kind of industrial warehouse. It didn't look as if it was in use, but it didn't look abandoned either. Grey brick walls, blinds in the windows, solid-looking doors. Locked double gates led into a small car park at the front of the warehouse, and the whole place was enclosed behind a high wire-mesh fence.

The time and date was printed in the bottom right-hand corner of the photograph:

16:08 15/07/13

Eight minutes past four, 15 July.

The day before Mum and Dad died.

I sat there studying the picture, trying to work out what it meant. I was fairly sure that either Mum or Dad had taken it – why else would it be in their office safe? – and I was equally sure that it was a surveillance photograph. And that had to mean that the grey-eyed man had something to do with a case that Mum and Dad were investigating.

I looked down at the pile of business papers on the floor, suddenly realising that when I'd taken them out of the safe, I'd inadvertently turned the pile upside down. So the photograph hadn't been at the bottom of the pile after all, it had been at the top. I thought about that, imagining Mum or Dad coming into the office the day before they died, opening the safe and putting the photo inside . . .

Why would they have done that?

There was nothing else in the safe that had anything to do with this or any other investigation. So what was so special about this photograph? Why was it so important?

I turned it over and looked at the back. There was a note scribbled in pencil in the top right-hand corner.

dem 5/8
last day 4th?

There was no doubt it was Dad's handwriting – I'd recognise his spidery scrawl anywhere – but what did it mean? *5/8* could be the fifth of August, and *4th* the day before? But what about *dem* and *last day*? Was *dem* short for something? Demonstration, perhaps? Demand? Or someone's name – Dempster, Dempsey? And what did *last day* mean? The last day of what? Or the last day *for* what?

I took out my mobile and checked the date. Today was the second of August. So if I was right, and the *4th* was the fourth of August, that meant there were only two days to go before the *last day*.

I put the rest of the papers back in the safe, locked it back up, and closed the hinged section of floorboard. I got to my feet, and was just about to go back into the main office to show the picture to Courtney, when I heard her say, quite loudly, 'Who the hell are you?'

I froze, wondering who she was talking to, and then almost immediately I heard another voice, a man's voice.

'Ah, good morning,' I heard him say, his voice deep and confident. 'My name's Owen Smith, I'm here about the insurance. And who might you be, if you don't mind me asking?'

'Have you got some ID?' Courtney said.

'Of course, just one moment.'

I folded the printout into my pocket and went through into the office. The man was standing just inside the doorway, and as I entered the office he was taking a business card from his wallet. He looked over at me, blinked once, then went over to Courtney and passed her his card. I'd never seen him in person before, but there was no mistaking who he was. I'd spent the last few minutes staring at a picture of him with two other men.

The man who called himself Owen Smith was the man with the shaved head from the photograph.

8

My mum once told me that you have to be very careful about judging people by their appearance. 'For example,' she'd said, 'just because the man at your front door is carrying a clipboard and wearing a high-visibility vest and a name badge, that doesn't necessarily mean you can trust him. Anyone can buy a clipboard and a high-visibility vest. And even if someone isn't trying to trick you, it's not always possible to judge their character based on physical appearance alone.' She'd smiled mischievously at me then. 'You only have to look at Courtney to know that.'

There was nothing remotely insulting about what she'd said. In fact, Courtney herself had said much the same thing on countless occasions. All Mum had meant was that because of the way Courtney looked and dressed, a lot of people – especially men – tended to assume she was some kind of brainless bimbo, just a pretty face and a curvy body. And Courtney was quite often happy to let them think that.

'If they think I'm dumb,' she explained, 'I'm already two steps ahead of them. By the time they find out I'm not so dumb, it's already too late for them to do anything about it.'

Courtney Lane wasn't dumb.

She had a first-class degree in mathematics and philosophy from Oxford University, she was fluent in at least four foreign languages, and she knew more about almost everything than anyone I'd ever met. She'd also competed at Under-23 level for the England Athletics Team, running the 200 and 400 metres and the 400-metre relay, and according to Dad she was an absolute genius on the pool table. And that was just the stuff I knew about her. Courtney's one of those people who constantly amaze you with the depth of their hidden talents.

It might seem strange that someone with so much going for them would work as an assistant for a small private investigation company, but Courtney didn't define herself by what she did for a living. Working for Mum and Dad suited her perfectly. Her mother had been the assistant at Delaney & Co for years, and when she was diagnosed with Parkinson's disease, and it got too bad for her to carry on working, Courtney had not only made the decision to stay at home and look after her, she'd also accepted Mum and Dad's offer to take over her mum's job. It didn't pay very much, but it was interesting work, and Mum and Dad let her take as much time off as she needed, plus the office was only five minutes' walk from her house.

In the two years she'd worked for Delaney & Co, Courtney had become very close to my parents, and she was fiercely protective of both them and the company. So when the man with the shaved head began patronising her that morning, talking to her as if she was nothing, I knew he was heading for trouble.

I leaned against the wall, put my hands in my pockets, and settled down to watch the show.

'I need to speak to whoever's in charge here,' he said to her as she studied his business card. 'So if you wouldn't mind—'

'It says here you work for M & G Commercial,' she said, looking up from the card.

'That's right.'

'Who called you?'

'I'm sorry?'

'Who called your company about the insurance claim?'

He hesitated. 'No one called us. We pride ourselves on being proactive in situations such as this.'

Courtney grinned. 'Proactive?'

He gave her a condescending smile. 'It means—'

'I know what it means, Mr Smith. It's just that I've never come across a proactive insurance company before.' She smiled at him. 'No offence, but in my experience it's difficult enough to get a *re*active response from an insurance company.'

'Well, that's as maybe—'

'What position do you hold with M & G?'

He stared hard at her, trying to stay calm. 'I think it's probably best if I speak to someone else about this. Is your manager available?'

'What makes you think I'm not the manager?'

'Are you?'

She stared back at him. 'Your business card doesn't state what position you hold. Are you a loss adjuster?'

He sighed. 'Perhaps it'd be better if I came back another time.'

She nodded thoughtfully. 'That sounds like a good idea. Let me give you a bit of advice though. Before you come back, you might want to check to see who Delaney & Co are actually insured with first.' She passed him back his business card. 'Or at least come up with something better than "M & G Commercial".' She smiled at him. 'I mean, I'm no expert, of course, but if I wanted someone to think that I worked for an insurance company, I'd pick one that actually existed.'

The man glared at her for a moment or two, then he put the business card back in his wallet and said, 'I'll bear that in mind, Ms Lane.' He looked over at me, held my gaze for a second, then turned round and walked out.

'Well, that was interesting,' Courtney said when he'd gone.

'Very interesting,' I agreed, taking the printout from my pocket.

'What have you got there?' she asked.

I went over and gave her the picture. She didn't say anything at first, just quietly studied the photograph, and after a few seconds I saw her raise her eyebrows in surprise.

'That's our friend Mr Smith,' she said, still looking at the picture.

'Exactly.'

'Where did you find this, Trav?'

'It was in Mum and Dad's safe.'

She nodded thoughtfully, then looked at me. 'They were investigating him.'

'And the man with the hidden camera.'

'Do you recognise the other one?'

I shook my head.

She said, 'Smith called me Ms Lane. I didn't tell him my name.'

'I know.'

She sighed. 'I don't understand any of this.'

'There's a note on the back of the photograph,' I told her.

She turned it over and read the scribbled note.

'Your dad wrote this,' she said.

'I know. What do you think it means?'

'Fifth of August . . . the fourth . . .' She scratched her head. 'I don't know . . . "dem" could be an abbreviation.'

'That's what I thought.'

'Or an acronym. D.E.M. – Department of Energy and . . . something? Drug Enforcement Management? It could be anything. And "last day" . . . ?' She shrugged. 'Who knows?'

'Did you get anywhere with the BMW's registration number?' I asked her.

'It's registered to a company called Smith & Co Digital Holdings Ltd.'

'Smith?'

She nodded. 'The company's based in Dundee. I googled them on my mobile but I couldn't find anything.'

'Nothing at all?'

She shook her head, looking concerned. 'Maybe it'd be better if we got in touch with the police about this. There's obviously something going on.'

'The police won't do anything unless a crime's been committed.'

'Well, strictly speaking, Mr Smith is guilty of fraud by false representation. But as he didn't actually try to get anything out of us, I doubt if the police would be interested.'

'So what do we do?' I said.

'*We* don't do anything,' she replied. 'I'll see what else I can find out, and if I come up with anything definite . . . well, we'll deal with that if it happens. But in the meantime, *you* don't do anything, Travis, OK?'

'Why not?'

'You know why not.'

'Because I'm just a kid, I suppose?'

'You *are* just a kid.'

'That doesn't mean I'm an idiot.'

'Yes, it does,' she said, smiling at me. 'All kids are idiots. That's their job.'

I grinned.

'I know you're not stupid, Trav,' she said seriously. 'I know you're perfectly capable of looking after yourself. But you need to let me look after you a bit too, OK?' She smiled again. 'Just humour me, all right? Pretend I'm a responsible adult and I know what I'm talking about.'

I could see the sincerity and determination behind her smile, and I knew she wasn't just thinking of me, she was thinking of Mum and Dad too. And that really meant a lot to me.

But sometimes, no matter how much you *want* to do what you're told, you just can't help yourself.

'OK,' I said.

'OK what?'

'OK, ma'am?'

She laughed.

I said, 'Can I have the printout back?'

'Why?'

'I want to show it to Grandad.'

'I thought you said you didn't want to bother him with any of this?'

'He'll want to know about it when he's feeling better.'

She kept her eyes on me for a while, trying to see into my mind, and then – seemingly satisfied that I was telling the truth – she passed me the picture. 'Promise me that you won't do anything on your own, OK?'

'I promise,' I lied.

9

I don't usually break my promises, and I felt really bad about lying to Courtney, but I would have felt a million times worse if I'd just gone home and done nothing. If there *were* only two days to go before the last day, whatever that meant, I didn't have time to do nothing. I had to find out what was going on. It was as simple as that. I *had* to know.

I texted Nan as I wheeled my bike along North Walk – *wth frnds in twn bak l8r, travx* – then I turned right into Magdalen Hill, got on my bike, and headed off towards Wonford Docks.

It was a hot and humid day, the air thick and heavy, and although it was only a couple of kilometres to the docks, I was covered in sweat by the time I got there. The area known as Wonford Docks is a mixture of old industrial buildings, car repair places, and dingy-looking nightclubs. The nightclubs probably look very different at night-time, but I've only ever seen them during the day, and they always look a bit sad to me, almost as if they're ashamed of themselves.

I rode slowly past them, letting myself cool down a bit, then I turned left into a narrow little lane that sloped down towards the docks. The lane was lined with tall brick buildings that I guessed were old warehouses and mills. They had big wooden doors and soot-stained walls and weather-faded signs hanging on rusty chains. The buildings blocked out most of the sunlight, and as I freewheeled down to the end of the lane, it was so dark and gloomy that it was hard to believe it was the middle of the day.

The boxing club was in a converted warehouse about halfway down the lane. I stopped outside it and gazed up at the sign over the door. *WONFORD BOXING CLUB*, it said simply. Nothing else. No further information, no welcoming words. Just *WONFORD BOXING CLUB*. If they'd added *TAKE IT OR LEAVE IT* to the sign, it wouldn't have looked out of place.

I got off my bike and double-locked it to the railings at the side of the road. I wiped a sheen of sweat from my brow, looked around the deserted street, then crossed over to the wooden door, pushed it open, and went inside.

The gym was bigger inside than I'd imagined, a sprawling brick-walled room with a high ceiling and a concrete floor. Although in some ways it was very different to my boxing club, the overall atmosphere felt pretty much the same. The set-up was fairly basic, to say the least: two boxing rings, both of which had seen better days; a selection of battered old punchbags; an area for weight training, another for general fitness; benches, mats, running machines. There was nothing wrong with it – everything you needed was there – it was just that my club, Barton Boxing Academy, had so much more. Two gymnasiums, state-of-the-art facilities, twice as much equipment, everything bang up to date. My club had loads of other amenities too – a cafe, a swimming pool, central heating, uniformed staff. But my club wasn't five minutes' walk from the Slade Lane estate, it was in a nice quiet area on the other side of town. It wasn't cheap either. Most of its members had reasonably good jobs. The kids who went there had parents with reasonably good jobs. My boxing club was in a different world to this one.

But boxing is boxing, and apart from all the superficial stuff, everything else felt very familiar. The sounds and the smells were the same – the thud of boxing gloves on leather, the squeak of boots on canvas, the grunts and groans of exertion, the smell of sweat – and as I stood there gazing around, I realised that everything looked very familiar too. Men and boys in vests and shorts, some of them working the punchbags, some skipping, some sparring in the ring. Most of them were older than me – tough-looking older kids from the estate – but there were a few around my age.

As far as I could tell, there was only one girl among all the men. She looked about fourteen or fifteen. She was on her own, working on one of the heavy punchbags hanging from the ceiling – dancing around it, throwing good strong punches, her dark eyes burning with fierce concentration . . .

'You want something?' a voice said.

I looked round and saw a hard-looking black guy standing in front of me. He was older than most of the other kids in the gym, in his late twenties at least, and he looked like he'd had plenty of fights. Broken nose, busted-up eyes, scars on his face. He was bare-chested, his hands were wrapped with tape, and a sweaty towel was draped over his shoulder. I guessed he'd just finished a session in the ring.

'I'm looking for John Ruddy,' I told him.

'Yeah?' he said, wiping his nose. 'And who are you?'

'Travis Delaney.'

He paused for a moment, staring hard at me. 'Any relation to Jack Delaney?'

'He was my dad.'

The black guy nodded slowly. 'I saw him fight a couple of times when I was a kid. He was pretty good.' He wiped his nose again and lowered his eyes. 'Sorry to hear about . . . well, you know.'

'Yeah, thanks,' I said.

He looked up. 'You want to see Mr Ruddy, yeah?'

I nodded.

'That's him over there,' he said, turning round and pointing towards the nearest boxing ring. 'The guy with the white hair.'

I looked over and saw a wiry old man with short white

hair. Two kids wearing head guards were sparring in the ring, and the old guy was shouting out instructions to them – '*KEEP YOUR HANDS UP, DWAYNE! WORK THE JAB! USE YOUR FEET, JEZ! DON'T LET HIM BACK YOU UP!*'

'Mr Ruddy!' the black guy called out to him. 'Someone to see you!'

Mr Ruddy looked over. At first he seemed annoyed by the interruption, but when he saw me, his expression changed. I saw a look of recognition in his eyes, then surprise, then something else, something I couldn't read. He turned back to the kids in the ring for a moment, told them to take a break, then waved me over.

10

'You look just like your father,' Mr Ruddy told me. 'That's how I recognised you. You're the spitting image of him.'

We were in his office, a cramped little room at the back of the gym. He was sitting in an old swivel chair behind his desk, and I was sitting in an equally old wooden chair across from him. He was dressed in a tracksuit and trainers. The walls of his office were covered with framed pictures of boxers. I recognised some of them – local fighters who'd gone on to box professionally – but a lot of the photographs were quite old, and I didn't know the boxers in most of them.

'That's your father there,' Mr Ruddy said, pointing proudly to one of the pictures. 'Essex Junior Championship Final 1991.' He smiled. 'Your dad lost by a single point. We found out later that one of the judges was the uncle of the boy who beat him. I was absolutely furious about it. I was going to make an official complaint, but your dad didn't want me to. He said that as long as *we* knew who the real champion was, that's all that mattered.'

I looked up at the photograph. It showed Dad in the boxing ring, throwing a right hook at his opponent. I guessed he was about fifteen or sixteen at the time. Mr

Ruddy was right, he did look a lot like me. Or rather, I looked a lot like him.

'I'm so sorry about your mum and dad,' Mr Ruddy said sadly, shaking his head. 'Such a terrible thing . . .'

I just nodded. I was beginning to get used to the awkwardness of condolences – not really knowing what to say, or how to say it, or whether to say anything at all.

'I still find it hard to believe,' Mr Ruddy went on. 'I mean, it was only a few weeks ago that your dad was sitting where you are, right there, having a cup of tea.' He shook his head again. 'Unbelievable.'

'Was that when he came to see you about your missing persons enquiry?' I asked.

'Did he tell you about that?'

'No, but I'm trying to find out what Mum and Dad were working on when they died. Their assistant remembers you ringing up to make an appointment at the end of June.'

'That's right. Jack came round to see me a few days after I called.'

'Can you remember what date that was?'

He frowned, trying to remember. 'It was a Monday, I know that. The first Monday in July, I think. Whatever date that was.'

'What did you want Mum and Dad to do for you?'

He hesitated for a moment, looking carefully at me. 'Why are you trying to find out what they were working on, Travis? Has it got anything to do with how they died?'

'I don't know,' I admitted. 'There's a couple of things about the crash that I don't understand, that's all. They probably don't mean anything, but I just need to make sure. Otherwise I'll never stop thinking about it.'

Mr Ruddy nodded thoughtfully, looking into my eyes, then he reached into a desk drawer and pulled out a familiar-looking black plastic file. On the front of the file it said *DELANEY & CO*, and underneath that, *PRELIMINARY REPORT*.

He passed me the file and began telling me about a boxer called Bashir Kamal.

Bashir was the best young boxer he'd ever worked with, he told me. He was twenty years old, a light welterweight, and he'd been training with Mr Ruddy for two years. He'd won twenty-six of his twenty-seven amateur fights, twenty-two of them inside the distance, and since the beginning of May he'd been training hard in preparation for his first professional bout.

'Bash was a fanatic about training,' Mr Ruddy said. 'Never missed a session, always on time, never moaned about anything. Just turned up every day and got on with it. Then one day, he didn't show up. Didn't call in sick or anything, didn't leave a message, just didn't turn up. And this was only six days before his first pro fight. I tried calling him, but he didn't answer his phone. He didn't reply to my voicemail messages either. So in the end I went round to his house to see what was going on.'

Bashir lived with his parents in a council house on the Beacon Fields estate, Mr Ruddy told me. He'd moved back in with them a few years ago, after living in London for a while, and he hadn't got round to finding his own place yet.

'When I got there,' Mr Ruddy said, 'his mother wouldn't let me in. She told me that Bashir had gone to Pakistan to look after his grandmother who was seriously ill. I just didn't believe her. Bash wouldn't have gone to Pakistan without letting me know. He's not like that. And there was something about the way his mother was acting anyway, something that didn't feel right. When I asked her how I could contact Bashir, she told me I couldn't. I asked her why not, she wouldn't tell me. It was just really odd, you know?'

'So what did you do?' I asked.

He shrugged. 'What could I do? I couldn't force her to tell me anything, and I had no proof she was lying. There wasn't anything I could do about it.'

'What about reporting it to the police?'

'I tried that, but there was nothing they could do either. Bashir's not a kid, he's twenty years old. He can go wherever he likes, whenever he likes. He doesn't have to tell anyone where he is. If he wants to give up his boxing career to look after his sick grandmother in Pakistan, that's entirely up to him.'

'So you asked my dad to see what he could find out,' I said.

Mr Ruddy nodded. 'After a couple of days he got back to me with that,' he said, indicating the file.

I opened the report and began flipping through the pages.

'Your dad was fairly sure that Bash wasn't at his parents' house,' Mr Ruddy said. 'As far as he could tell, no one had seen or heard from him since he stopped coming to the gym.'

'But Dad hadn't found anything to suggest that Bashir had left the country,' I said, skimming the report.

'That's right. Jack told me that he was happy to carry on looking for Bashir, but that it might take some time, and even though he was giving me a good discount, it could still be fairly expensive. I told him to go ahead.'

'Did he find out anything else?'

'Nothing specific, but he called me a couple of times and said they were making some progress.'

I carried on studying the report. There was a brief summary of the case on the first page, outlining what Mr Ruddy had told Dad, and the next page listed Bashir Kamal's personal details – age, address, phone number, etc. There was also a photograph of him. He had a longish face, short black hair, and hauntingly dark eyes.

I quickly read through the summary.

'What's this about Bashir being preoccupied about something?' I asked Mr Ruddy.

'Your dad asked me all sorts of questions about Bashir, and I remembered that in the week or so before he went missing, Bash wasn't quite as focused as he usually was. He just seemed . . . I don't know, a bit distracted about something. As if he had something else on his mind, you know? Something *other* than the fight.'

'Did you ask him about it?'

'Yeah, but he just shrugged it off. Said it was nothing.'

I thought about that for a few seconds, then said, 'When was the last time you heard from my dad?'

'He called me a couple of days before the crash. He wanted to know if I knew anything about Bashir's life before he came to Barton.' Mr Ruddy shrugged. 'There wasn't much I could tell him really. Bash is a very private person, he doesn't like talking about himself. All he'd ever told me was that he'd lived in the East End of London for a while and that he'd done most of his training at a boxing club somewhere in Stratford.'

'Right,' I said. 'And that was it? You didn't hear from Dad again?'

'No.'

I closed the file and just sat there for a while thinking about everything Mr Ruddy had told me, trying to work out if any of it meant anything. And, if so, what. But I didn't get very far. The truth was, I didn't really have a clue what I was doing.

'Can I keep this?' I asked Mr Ruddy, holding up the file.

'I don't see why not.'

I took out my mobile and showed him the photograph

of the man at the funeral. 'Have you ever seen him before?'

Mr Ruddy shook his head. 'Who is he?'

'I don't know,' I said, taking the printout from my pocket. 'What about these men?' I said, showing him the picture. 'Do you recognise any of them?'

'That's the one from the other photograph, isn't it?' he said, pointing out the man from the funeral.

'Yeah, but what about the others? Have you seen any of them around?'

'No, sorry.'

'Is it all right if I show the pictures round the gym, see if anyone recognises them?'

'Of course, no problem.'

'Did Dad talk to anyone else here about Bashir?'

'He talked to just about everybody. I don't think they were very much help to him though. Like I said, Bashir's a very private person. He keeps himself to himself. Everyone here knows him, of course, and they all respect him as a boxer, but Bash didn't really make friends with anyone. Not that I know of, anyway.'

'OK,' I said, getting to my feet. 'Well, thanks for all your help, Mr Ruddy. I'll let you know if anything turns up.'

He smiled at me. 'I hear you're a pretty good boxer yourself.'

'I don't know about that,' I said.

'Your dad was very proud of you.'

'Was he?'

Mr Ruddy nodded.

I didn't know what else to say. I just stood there looking back at him for a moment or two, feeling the tingle of tears in my eyes, then I took a deep breath, swallowed hard, and went out into the gym.

11

Mr Ruddy was right about the other boxers. None of them knew very much about Bashir. They didn't all want to talk to me – kids from the Slade are naturally suspicious of anyone asking questions – but even those who were happy to talk didn't have much to say. Apart from the fact that he was a brilliant boxer, no one seemed to know anything about Bashir at all. No one recognised any of the men in the pictures either. By the time I'd talked to everyone in the gym except the dark-eyed girl, I'd pretty much given up hope of finding out anything useful.

I'm not sure why I left the girl until last. I suppose, if I'm honest, it was probably a mixture of fear and embarrassment. She was still working out on the heavy punchbag, and the look on her face as she pounded her fists into it was genuinely quite scary. I mean, she was pummelling away at the bag as if she was trying to kill it or something. I'd never seen anything like it. She looked so intense, so driven, that I seriously considered just leaving her to it. But she also looked really nice – those deep dark eyes, that beautiful light-brown skin, that strangely intriguing face – and I just couldn't stop glancing over at her. I knew that I *wanted* to talk to her, but I also knew that I didn't. It was a really weird feeling. Good and bad at the same time. Very confusing.

In the end, I told myself not to be so stupid, and I just went over and introduced myself.

'Hi, I'm Travis Delaney,' I said. 'Do you mind if I ask you a few questions about Bashir Kamal?'

She didn't reply. Didn't even look at me. She just carried on thumping away at the punchbag – *thump*, *thump*, *thump*.

'Excuse me,' I said, raising my voice a little.

She skipped to her right and started hitting the bag even harder – *thump*, *thump*, *THUMP* – still totally ignoring me. It was *really* annoying. I knew I shouldn't let it get to me, and I tried telling myself that it simply wasn't worth getting annoyed about. It was up to her if she wanted to act like a spoiled little kid. But for some reason I didn't seem to want to listen to myself. Instead, I just stood there for a while, watching her batter the punchbag, and then I said quite calmly, 'You need to work on your uppercut.'

That got a reaction.

'You *what*?' she snapped, stopping suddenly and glaring at me.

'Your left uppercut,' I said. 'You need to dip your shoulder a bit more.'

'Yeah?' she sneered.

'Your elbow needs to be nearer your hip.'

'You think I don't know how to throw an uppercut?'

I shrugged. 'I'm only trying to help.'

'*I'm only trying to help,*' she said, mocking me.

I didn't rise to her bait, I just stared at her.

She said, 'What do you know about boxing anyway?'

'I've been boxing since I was a kid.'

'Not here, you haven't.'

'I go to BBA,' I told her.

She grinned. 'Barton Boxing Academy?'

'Yeah.'

'Got a rich mummy and daddy, have you?'

I didn't say anything. I *couldn't* say anything. I was too angry to speak. I just gritted my teeth and stared coldly at her. I think she realised she'd said something she shouldn't have – I could see the flicker of uncertainty in her eyes – and although she didn't take it back or anything, she at least had the decency to change the subject.

'Look,' she said, 'I don't need your help, OK? I know what I'm doing.'

'I didn't say you didn't.'

'Just because I'm a girl—'

'What's that got to do with anything?'

She hesitated for a moment, slightly taken aback. 'I can fight.'

'I know you can.'

'Don't patronise me.'

'I'm not—'

'I could kick *your* ass.'

I didn't mean to laugh, it just came out – a quick snort of laughter. I wasn't laughing at her, I was laughing at the absurdity of the situation. But, of course, she didn't take it like that. She took it as an insult. And I could tell from the way she was looking at me that I was about to pay for it. She was looking at me in the same way she looked at the punchbag.

'Hey, listen,' I said, holding up my hands, 'I didn't mean—'

'You reckon you could take me?'

I shook my head. 'I was just—'

'Well, why don't we find out, eh?' She glanced over her shoulder at the nearest boxing ring, saw that it was empty, then turned back to me. 'What size gloves do you wear?'

'I'm not going to fight you.'

'Why not?' she sneered. 'Scared of getting beaten up by a girl?'

'No. I just . . .'

'You just what?'

I sighed. 'This is ridiculous.'

'Come on, tough guy,' she said with a mocking smile. 'Let's see what you've got. Show me how it *should* be done.'

I was aware that people were watching us now. The gym had gone quiet, and a dozen or so faces were turned our way, looking on with amused curiosity.

'I'll tell you what,' the girl said. 'You get in the ring

with me, and if I *don't* put you on the floor, I'll answer your questions. How's that?'

I looked at her, staring into her eyes, and I knew there was only one thing to do. Fighting her was out of the question. It didn't serve any purpose at all. It was pointless, childish, utterly stupid. So what if she – or anyone else – thought I was scared? I didn't have anything to prove. All I had to do was turn around and walk away. That was the only sensible thing to do. Just turn around, right now, and walk away.

'All right,' I said, smiling at her. 'You want a fight? Let's fight.'

12

By the time someone had found me a pair of boxing gloves, a head guard, and a gum shield, and I'd got myself ready and climbed into the ring, I was already regretting my decision. I should have listened to myself. Fighting her *was* pointless. It *was* childish and utterly stupid. And I had no idea at all why I'd agreed to it.

But it was too late to change my mind now.

We were facing each other in the middle of the ring. Everyone in the gym had stopped what they were doing and had gathered round to watch us, including Mr Ruddy. Some of the younger kids were making the most of it – whooping and laughing, whistling and clapping, cheering on the girl: *COME ON, EVIE! PUT HIM DOWN, GIRL! EE-VIE! EE-VIE! EE-VIE!*

At least I knew her name now.

Evie.

It was a nice name.

'You ready?' she said, looking into my eyes.

'How's this going to work?' I said.

She grinned. 'I'm going to hit you, and you're going to fall down. That's how it's going to work.'

'You know what I mean,' I said. 'How many rounds are we fighting? How long is each round? Who's going to—?'

'Are you going to fight or just stand there yapping?'

I stared at her.

Without taking her eyes off mine, she raised her gloves, dropped into her stance, and started skipping and dancing on the spot. I watched her for a moment, keeping my hands at my side, and then I grudgingly raised my gloves.

'Ready?' she said.

I adjusted my feet and got myself balanced. 'OK, let's go.'

She moved so fast that I didn't have a chance to react. A quick dip of her left shoulder, a half-step towards me, and she hammered her fist into my ribs. The punch knocked all the air out of me, and I sank to one knee, gasping for breath. As I squeezed my eyes shut, trying to breathe, trying to ignore the pain, I was vaguely aware of people cheering and calling out, but it seemed as if they were a long way away. I steadied myself, sucking in a lungful of air, and looked up at Evie.

She was standing over me, smiling.

'How's that for a left uppercut?' she said. 'Do you think I dipped my shoulder enough?'

I took another deep breath, heaved myself back to my feet, and squared up to her.

'You sure you want to go on?' she said, still smiling.

I flicked a left jab at her head. It wasn't much of a punch, and she leaned back just in time to take most of the sting out of it, but it was enough to wipe the smile off her face. She glared at me for a second, then lunged forward and swung a right hook at me. I parried it with my left hand and skipped away to my right. She tried again, this time feinting to throw another left uppercut and then switching to a straight right at the last second. It wasn't a bad move, but I read it a mile off, and just as she was shifting her weight to throw the straight right, I flicked out another left jab. It caught her smack in the face, knocking her off balance. She retaliated instantly, lunging forward with a swinging right hand, but I'd already skipped away from her again, and her punch missed my head by a long way.

For the next few minutes, the fight continued along the same lines. Evie kept barrelling forward, throwing punch after punch at me, and I kept bobbing and weaving, dancing out of her way. Every now and then I'd catch her with a well-aimed jab to the head. Each time I hit her, she'd back off slightly for a while, trying to control her aggression. But as soon as she started punching again, all the aggression came back. It was like fighting a Tasmanian devil. Although most of her punches missed, she did manage to catch me with a couple of good ones, and while I'd been hit harder before, I hadn't been hit *much* harder. I mean, she could *really* punch. There was no doubt she was a pretty good fighter. In fact, she was probably a better fighter than me. But I was the better boxer. Evie might have been bigger and stronger than me, and she was definitely more aggressive, but there's a lot more to boxing than power and aggression.

I could see that she was getting tired now. Throwing punches takes a lot out of you, especially if you've already been pounding away on a heavy punchbag for hours. And when you get tired, you get sloppy. As Evie lunged towards me again and tried to throw a big right hook, I could see that she wasn't balanced properly. Her stance was all wrong, her feet out of position. I knew this was my chance to end the fight. Instead of skipping away from her this time, I stood my ground. I let her get close, letting her put all her weight into the punch, and just as she threw the big right hook, I quickly leaned back. Her right hand just missed my chin, and as the weight of her punch swung her off balance, and she stumbled awkwardly to my left, I twisted round and hit her with a short right cross to the side of her head.

I didn't mean to knock her out or anything, and I didn't actually hit her that hard, but because she was already off balance, and she just happened to turn her head into the punch, it caught her in just the right spot – or the wrong spot, from her point of view – and she dropped to the canvas like a sack of bricks.

Suddenly the gym went very quiet.

I looked down at Evie, breathing hard, and for a second or two I feared the worst. She wasn't moving. She was just lying there, face down, her hands at her sides. I quickly crouched down next to her, and was just reaching out to remove her gum shield, when all of a sudden she pushed herself up off the canvas and sat up straight.

'Whew!' she gasped quietly, blinking her eyes and shaking her head. 'What happened there?'

'Are you OK?' I asked.

''Course I'm OK. I tripped over, that's all. You got lucky.'

I smiled, relieved that she was all right. I held out my hand. She hesitated a second, then took hold of it and let me help her up.

'We'll call that one a draw, OK?' she said.

I nodded.

She grinned. 'But I'm not going to go so easy on you in the next round.'

'The next round?'

'What's the matter? You had enough?'

As I stared at her, dumbfounded, Mr Ruddy climbed into the ring and came up to us. 'I think you've both had enough for now,' he said.

Evie glared at him. 'But we've only just started.'

He gave her a stern look. 'I said, that's enough.'

'Yeah, but—'

'Don't push it, Evie,' he said firmly. 'All right?'

She sighed.

'Now shake hands,' he said to both of us.

I held out my gloves. Evie paused for a second, then reluctantly lifted her hands and tapped my gloves.

'You're a hell of a fighter,' I told her.

'You're not so bad yourself.'

'I just got lucky,' I said, smiling.

She smiled back. 'You want to get a Coke or something?'

13

I assumed we'd be getting a Coke or something from a drinks machine, but instead Evie led me over to a locker room, opened one of the lockers, and took out a rucksack. She pulled a two-litre bottle of Tesco's Value Cola from the rucksack, unscrewed the cap and took a long drink, then passed the bottle to me.

'You want to sit down?' she said, indicating a long wooden bench against the wall.

I sat down and took a drink from the bottle.

'What was your name again?' she said, dropping her rucksack on the floor and sitting down next to me.

'Travis Delaney.'

'I'm Evie Johnson.'

I nodded, passing her the bottle. She screwed the cap back on, put the bottle on the floor, then leaned back and scratched her head with both hands. She wore her hair in short spiky dreadlocks, and in the fluorescent light of the locker room the blackish-brown locks glistened with beads of sweat.

'So, Travis Delaney,' she said, 'how come you're so interested in Bashir Kamal?'

I kept my explanation as brief as possible. I didn't really want to tell her about Mum and Dad, but I couldn't see how to avoid it. So I told her they were private investigators, and I told her they'd been looking into Bashir's disappearance, and then I told her they'd both been killed in a car crash.

'They're both dead?' she said, staring wide-eyed at me. 'When did it happen?'

'A couple of weeks ago.'

'*God*,' she whispered, putting her hand on my arm. 'I'm so sorry. Why didn't you tell me? I wouldn't have put you through all this crap if I'd known—'

'It doesn't matter.'

'Of *course* it matters.' She shook her head. 'How can you even *talk* to me after what I said about having a rich mummy and daddy?'

'You weren't to know, were you?'

She sighed. 'I'm really sorry, Travis.'

She stared silently at the floor for a while.

I rubbed tentatively at my ribs. They still ached.

'I didn't really know Bashir very well,' Evie said thoughtfully. 'He was pretty quiet, you know? Never really said much to anyone.'

'Did you ever talk to him about anything?'

'Not really. I mean, we always said hello to each other, and he gave me a few words of advice about boxing now and then. You know, little tips about footwork and training, stuff like that. But we never talked about anything personal.'

'Did you notice anything unusual about him before he disappeared?'

She looked at me. 'Well, there was *some*thing . . . I mean, I don't if it's "unusual" or not, but I remember thinking it was kind of odd at the time.'

'What was it?'

She rubbed her face, thinking about it. 'It was the Friday before he went missing. I'd spent most of the evening in here, and I'd seen Bash working out earlier on. He was doing a lot of sparring at the time, getting ready for his big fight. By the time I'd finished my training, I noticed that he wasn't in the gym any more. Which was a bit strange, because he was usually the last to leave. But I guessed he was talking to Mr Ruddy about something, going over his tactics maybe, or they might have gone to see a fight together somewhere . . .' Evie shrugged. 'I didn't really give it much thought, to be honest. It was only later, when I was on my way home, and I saw Bash sitting in a parked car with a couple of guys in suits, that I began to wonder what he was doing.'

'He was in a car?' I said.

She nodded. 'In the passenger seat.'

'Where was this?'

'Colehouse Avenue. It's a little side street just off Slade Lane. It's a dead-end road, you know, a cul-de-sac. So nobody uses it much, apart from the people who live there. I was visiting a cousin. She's got a place at the end of the street. I passed the car on the way to her house.'

'And it was definitely Bashir you saw?'

'Definitely. Like I said, he was in the passenger seat.

There was a guy in the driver's seat and another one in the back.'

'What were they doing?'

'Nothing much. Just talking.'

'Did you recognise the two men?'

'Never seen them before.'

I took out my mobile and showed her the picture of the man from the funeral. 'Was he one of them?'

She studied the photograph. 'No.'

I showed her the printout of the other men. 'What about them?'

She had a good look, then shook her head. 'They kind of looked similar, you know, the same *type* of men. But that's probably just because they're all wearing suits.'

'I don't suppose you know what kind of car it was, do you?'

'I'm just a girl,' she said, smiling at me. 'I don't know anything about cars.'

'Right . . .'

She laughed. 'It was a silver Audi S6. Do you want the registration number?'

I couldn't help looking surprised. 'You remember the number?'

She closed her eyes for a moment, then opened them again and reeled off the number. 'Do you want me to write it down for you?' she asked. 'Hold on . . .' She reached into her rucksack, pulled out a pen, then took hold of my hand and wrote the number on my palm.

'How come you remember it?' I said.

She shrugged. 'I'm good at remembering stuff.'

I looked at her, frowning.

'What?' she said. 'Don't you believe me?'

'No . . . I mean, yeah, of course I believe you. It's just . . . well, you know. It's pretty unusual to be able to remember something like that.'

'It's just a few numbers and letters.'

'But you only saw it once, and that was quite a while ago.'

She sighed. 'It's just something I can do, OK? I have a freakishly good memory. It's no big deal.'

I was intrigued, and I wanted to ask her more about it, but I got the feeling that she'd rather I didn't.

'Did you tell my dad about any of this?' I asked her.

'I never saw him.'

'Mr Ruddy said he talked to everyone here.'

'When?'

'About three weeks ago.'

'That was probably when I was sick. I had a really bad stomach bug for three or four days. I was off training for a week.'

'So you haven't told anyone about seeing Bashir in the car?'

'No one's asked me about him.' She looked at me. 'What do you think's happened to him?'

'I don't know. His parents are saying he's in Pakistan.'

'Yeah, that's what I heard.'

'Where did you hear that?'

'Just around, you know – rumours, gossip. Is it true?'

I glanced at my watch and stood up. 'That's what I'm trying to find out.'

'Why?'

'Why what?'

She got to her feet. 'Why are you bothering? I mean, you don't know Bashir, do you?'

'No.'

'So what does it matter to you where he is?'

'It was my mum and dad's last case. It might have something to do with what happened to them.' I sighed. 'I don't know . . . it just feels like something I've got to do.'

Evie put her hand on my arm. 'Well, good luck with it.'

'Thanks.'

'What's your mobile number?' she asked, taking out her phone.

I gave her my number. She keyed it into her phone, waited for my mobile to ring, then ended the call.

'You've got my number now,' she said. 'If you need any help with anything, just call me, OK?'

'Thanks,' I said.

She smiled. 'I'd better get going.'

'Me too.'

'I'll see you later.'

'Yeah.'

14

It was just gone three o'clock when I got back to the office in North Walk. Courtney was still there, still trying to get the place cleaned up, and she didn't seem too surprised to see me.

'I thought you were going home,' she said, giving me a knowing look.

'Well, yeah,' I muttered. 'I was going to, but . . .'

'You changed your mind?'

I smiled sheepishly. 'I just wanted to have a quick word with John Ruddy. You know, the man who hired Mum and Dad?'

'Right,' she said, nodding. 'So you went to the boxing club and talked to him, even though I asked you not to do anything without telling me first.'

'Sorry,' I said. 'I couldn't help it.'

'You couldn't help it?'

I shrugged.

She sighed. 'You'd better tell me all about it then.'

After I'd told her everything I'd found out about Bashir Kamal, and showed her Dad's preliminary report, Courtney spent a few minutes reading through the file, and then she just sat at her desk thinking quietly about things for a while. I didn't interrupt her, I just waited.

Eventually she looked up and said, 'What's the registration number that Evie Johnson gave you?'

I read it off the palm of my hand.

Courtney took out her phone and said, 'Why don't you go and make us a cup of tea?'

I left her to it and went into the kitchen area at the back of the office. The cupboards had been emptied, the kettle was smashed, and all the teabags and coffee and stuff was scattered all over the floor. I crunched my way through the mess and went into the little bathroom at the back of the kitchen. The door had been kicked in, but everything else was still intact.

By the time I'd come out and gone back into the main office, Courtney had finished her phone call and was looking troubled about something.

'What's the matter?' I said.

She sighed heavily. 'That number you just gave me. The silver Audi . . .'

'What about it?'

'The registration record is restricted.'

'What does that mean?'

'All sorts of things, unfortunately.'

'Like what?'

She blew out her cheeks. 'Well, firstly, it means that the Audi isn't registered on any of the normal databases, so it's virtually impossible to find out who owns it. And the most likely reason for that is that it's either a special operations police vehicle or it belongs to one of the security services.'

'Like MI5, you mean?'

'MI5, MI6, Special Branch, a Counter-Terrorism Unit . . . it could be any of them.'

'So just before he went missing, Bashir was seen talking to two men who could be some kind of spies.'

'Well, possibly, yes. But we've only got your friend Evie's word for it that she saw him in the car. We've also only got her word for it that she's got an incredible memory. And even if she *has*, and she *did* see him with the two men in the car, we don't know for sure that they're spooks.' She sighed again. 'The trouble is, if they *are* spooks, they're going to know that someone's been checking out their car.'

'How are they going to know?'

'They monitor everything. If someone's trying to trace one of their vehicles, an alarm's going to go off somewhere, and it's not going to take them long to find out who's been snooping around. And then they're going to start asking questions.' She looked at me. 'The person I called will do his best to bluff his way out of it, but even if he doesn't give up my name, it's possible they'll track me down through the phone records. And then . . . well, I don't know what'll happen then.'

'At least we'll know they're spooks,' I said.

'How's that going to help us?'

'Knowledge is power.'

'Yeah, but it can also get you into a whole load of trouble.'

*

I almost didn't bother asking Courtney if she wanted to go and see Bashir's parents with me. I suppose I just assumed that she'd tell me not to be so stupid, that we'd already got ourselves into enough trouble as it was, and that the only sensible thing to do was leave things alone and forget all about Bashir. But I was wrong. She didn't say anything like that. All she said, after I'd finally summoned up the courage to ask her, was, 'Yeah, why not?'

'You think it's a good idea?' I said, surprised.

'Probably not. But if we're going to do this – and it looks like we are – we might as well do it properly. And besides, whatever I say or do, you're going to go and see them anyway, aren't you?'

'Not necessarily.'

'Liar,' she said, smiling. She picked up the preliminary report file, opened it up, and found Bashir's home address. 'They live at Beacon Fields. We'll have to go in my car.'

Beacon Fields is a housing estate at the west end of Slade Lane. It's not quite as big as the Slade Lane estate, and not quite as rough, but you still wouldn't want to go there on your own.

'Ready then?' Courtney said. 'We'll lock up here and walk over to my place to get my car. You can leave your bike at my house.' She looked at me. 'Is something the matter?'

'No,' I said hesitantly. 'It's just . . . well, I was just thinking . . .'

'About what?'

'Bashir's parents.'

'What about them?'

'Well, they might be . . . I mean, if they're very traditional, you know, they might . . .'

'Travis?' Courtney said impatiently, staring at me with her hands on her hips. 'Just spit it out, OK?'

I sighed, bracing myself for her reaction. 'They might not like the way you're dressed.'

A flash of anger crossed her eyes, and just for a second I thought she was going to start yelling at me, but it only took her a moment to realise that I had a point. The Kamals weren't necessarily Muslim, but there was a fairly good chance they were. And if they were very traditional Muslims, and we wanted to talk to them in their home, it probably wasn't a good idea for Courtney to turn up looking like a dancer in a rap video.

'I'll get changed before we go,' she said.

15

Courtney didn't say a word as we left her house and drove off towards Beacon Fields. She'd changed her clothes and was now wearing a short brown jacket with a brown knee-length skirt and a stuffy-looking light-grey blouse. Her hair was neatly tied back in a ponytail, and she'd even toned down her usually over-the-top make-up. She looked like a different person. And it was quite obvious that she hated it.

I resisted the temptation to say anything for as long as I could, but as we swung round the roundabout at the bottom of Magdalen Hill, I couldn't hold back any longer.

'You look really smart,' I told her.

'Shut up, Travis,' she said, not amused.

'No, really,' I went on. 'It suits you. You should dress like that more often.'

'You're not funny, you know.'

I smiled. 'You should have worn a pair of glasses too. You know, those smart designer frames they're all wearing these days. They'd look *really* good on you.'

'Do you want to walk the rest of the way?' she said, slowing the car.

'All right,' I said, holding up my hands. 'I won't say anything else, I promise.'

As she speeded up again, I could see her trying to hide a smile.

I kept quiet for a while then, just looking out of the window at the passing streets, letting random thoughts float around in my head. It was a pleasant afternoon now. The heaviness and humidity had lifted, the air was clear, and the sky was bright with a pale summer sun. It felt really nice for a minute or two – driving along in the afternoon sunshine, the windows open, the summer streets busy with traffic – but after a while all I could feel was a big hole in my heart where Mum and Dad should have been. I wanted to be in a car with them, enjoying the sunshine with them, going somewhere nice with them. I wanted to *be* with them. I wanted them more than anything else in the world. But they were gone. And there was nothing I could do to bring them back.

Nothing.

The sun would never shine on them again.

'Are you all right, Travis?' Courtney asked quietly.

'I can't stop thinking about Mum and Dad.'

She glanced at me, looking concerned. 'Maybe we'd better leave this for now. We can always—'

'No, it's all right,' I said. 'I'd rather be doing something than just sitting around at home, you know?'

'Sure?'

'Yeah.'

'OK.'

I looked out of the window again. We were heading

along Slade Lane now, about a kilometre or so from Beacon Fields. In the distance up ahead, I could see the grey houses of the estate shimmering in a haze of heat.

'I'd better use the sat nav when we get to the estate,' Courtney said, reaching up to turn it on. 'Driving around Beacon Fields is a nightmare. What's the address again?'

I looked in the file. '42 Roman Way.'

As she keyed it into the sat nav, a memory of Mum and Dad flashed into my mind. It was the day of the car crash. Dad was getting out of his car with his sat nav in his hand, and Mum was saying to him, 'I'm not having that thing in my car.'

'We're driving into the middle of London,' Dad had said. 'You know what the roads are like—'

'I don't care,' Mum had told him. 'I'd rather get lost than use one of those.'

Then Courtney's sat nav piped up – *In 400 metres, turn right* – and the memory faded.

But as I glanced up at the map on the sat nav screen, something else flickered briefly into my mind, something that seemed to mean something. I closed my eyes for a second, trying to get hold of it, but it had already gone. I knew there was no point in trying to get it back. It was one of those elusive feelings that you just have to let go, because the more you chase after them, the further they float away. So I just let it go, hoping it would come back when it was ready, and turned my mind to something else.

'Can I ask you something?' I said to Courtney.

'Of course. What is it?'

'What's going to happen to Delaney & Co now?'

'I'm not sure,' she said. 'It depends what arrangements your mum and dad made. When they took over the agency from your grandad, they insisted that he stay on as a partner, even though he wasn't directly involved in the business any more. So I suppose their share of the business will go to him.'

'Does that mean Grandad owns it?'

'Possibly.'

'So, if he wanted to, he could keep it open.'

'He retired a long time ago, Travis.'

'He still knows what he's doing.'

'I know. But he found it hard enough running the business on his own before, and he was twenty years younger and stronger then.'

'He wouldn't have to run it on his own. You could help him.'

'Me?' she said, taken aback.

'Why not? You're smart, you know the business, you're good at it.'

'Well, that's nice of you to say, but it's not really up to me.'

'You'd like to do it though, wouldn't you?'

'Yeah, of course I would. I'd love it.'

'The only thing is . . .'

'What?' she said.

'Well,' I said seriously, 'Grandad's a bit old-fashioned in his ways.'

'So?'

I looked at her. 'If you worked for him, you'd have to dress like that every day.'

She laughed.

I smiled.

Just for now, everything felt all right again.

16

The Kamals' house was pretty much the same as all the others houses on the estate – grey, pebble-dashed, with net curtains in the windows and a small front yard.

'Let me do the talking, OK?' Courtney said as we went up to the door.

'You're the boss,' I told her.

She gave me a serious look. 'I'm going to have to explain what happened to your mum and dad. Are you going to be all right with that?'

'Yeah.'

'Sure?'

I nodded.

She rang the bell, and after about ten seconds the front door inched open and a woman's face appeared in the gap.

'Yes?' she said warily.

Courtney smiled at her. 'Mrs Kamal?'

'Who are you?'

'My name's Courtney Lane,' she said. 'And this is Travis Delaney. We're from Delaney & Co. I believe you spoke with Mr Delaney recently regarding the whereabouts of your son.'

'He's not here,' she said, starting to close the door. 'I'm sorry. I can't help you.'

'It's all right, Mrs Kamal,' Courtney said gently. 'We're not here about your son.'

Mrs Kamal hesitated. 'What do you want?'

'Well, unfortunately, Mr and Mrs Delaney passed away a few weeks ago,' Courtney said, lowering her voice. 'It was very sudden. A road traffic accident.'

'Oh, my,' Mrs Kamal said, glancing at me. 'How terrible. I'm so sorry.'

Courtney nodded. 'All we're doing at the moment is going through some of their unfinished cases, trying to clear up a few loose ends. It's just routine paperwork, Mrs Kamal. Nothing to worry about. So if you could possibly spare us a few minutes of your time, we'd very much appreciate it.'

Mrs Kamal hesitated again for a moment or two, thinking over what Courtney had just told her. Then she unlatched the security chain on the door and showed us inside.

We followed her into a small front room, and she asked us to sit down. It was a neat and tidy little place, everything spotless and clean, but it felt peculiarly lifeless. The net curtains filtered out most of the sunlight, and as I looked around, my eyes adjusting to the gloom, I realised that everything was old and worn out – the furniture, the wallpaper, the carpet. Even the net curtains were yellowed with age.

As Courtney took out a small notepad and a pen and began asking some questions, I sat there quietly and concentrated on Mrs Kamal. She was about forty, I guessed. Dark eyes, dark hair, a tired-looking face. She was wearing a traditional Pakistani dress and silky trousers.

Although she'd become a little less wary since Courtney had assured her that we weren't here to talk about her son, she was still far from relaxed, and I could tell she was worried about something. Courtney was aware of her anxiety too, and she was being very careful not to push her too hard. When she asked her what Dad had been to see her about, and Mrs Kamal told her that it was all a misunderstanding, and that Bashir wasn't missing at all but had simply gone to Pakistan to look after his grandmother, Courtney didn't take it any further. She just made a few notes and pretended to accept Mrs Kamal's story.

'I see,' she said. 'So in this case there wasn't actually anything to investigate.'

'Nothing at all,' Mrs Kamal said. 'As I said, it was just a misunderstanding.'

Courtney smiled. 'Was that the only time Mr Delaney came to see you?'

'Yes.'

'He didn't contact you again?'

'No.'

'What about your husband?'

'What about him?'

'Was he here when Mr Delaney talked to you?'

'Yes.'

'Where is he now?'

'At work.'

Courtney made another note in her pad. 'Do you know if Mr Delaney ever contacted him again?'

'No, he didn't.'

'OK,' Courtney said, nodding. 'Well, I think that's about all for now, Mrs Kamal . . . oh, just one more thing.' She turned to me. 'Have you got those pictures, Travis?'

I gave her the printout, then took out my mobile, opened up the photo of the man at the funeral, and passed her the phone.

Courtney turned back to Mrs Kamal. 'If you wouldn't mind having a quick look,' she said casually, holding out the phone for her to see.

'What is this?' Mrs Kamal said, looking cautiously at Courtney.

'Please?' Courtney said. 'It won't take a second.'

Mrs Kamal sighed, then lowered her eyes and looked at the photograph of the man at the funeral. She tried very hard to hide her surprise, but it was immediately obvious that she recognised him. Her mouth opened then closed, her eyes went still, and her shoulders tensed.

'I'm sorry,' she said, avoiding Courtney's eyes as she passed back the phone. 'I can't help you. Now, if you don't mind—'

'What about the men in this picture?' Courtney said,

showing her the printout. 'Do you recognise any of them?'

'No,' Mrs Kamal muttered, shaking her head. 'I've never seen them before.'

She hadn't even looked at the picture. She was very edgy now – sitting up straight, her eyes darting all over the place. She wasn't just nervous, I realised, she was frightened.

'Well, thank you very much for your time, Mrs Kamal,' Courtney said, passing me the phone and the printout. 'You've been very helpful. And I'm sorry about the misunderstanding.' She smiled. 'We'll leave you in peace now.'

Mrs Kamal nodded.

Courtney looked at me. 'OK, Travis?'

'Yeah,' I said, grimacing slightly. 'I just need to . . .'

'What's the matter?'

'Nothing. It's just . . .' I turned shyly to Mrs Kamal. 'Would you mind very much if I used your bathroom before we go?'

She hesitated, clearly desperate for us to leave, but at the same time not wanting to be ill-mannered. 'Up the stairs,' she said, smiling awkwardly. 'At the end of the landing.'

'Thank you,' I said, getting to my feet.

As I left the room I heard Courtney say, 'It sounds like you have a wonderful son, Mrs Kamal. He must be a very caring young man.'

'Bashir has a good heart,' she said. 'I couldn't ask for any more in a son.'

There were only three rooms upstairs. A main bedroom on the left, a smaller bedroom on the right, and the bathroom at the end of the landing. I hurried down to the bathroom, opened and closed the door without going in, then quietly went into the smaller bedroom. There was no doubt it was Bashir's room. There was a weight machine on the floor, a punchbag in one corner, and a poster of Amir Khan on the wall. It was a very small room, and the weight machine took up about half of it, so there wasn't much space for anything else. There was a single bed, a chest of drawers, a bedside cabinet, and that was it.

I went over to the chest of drawers and started searching through it. I wasn't looking for anything in particular, I was just looking, hoping to find something that might throw some light on whatever was going on. I went through the drawers as quickly and quietly as possible, but I didn't come across anything useful. There was nothing in there except clothes.

As I went over to the bedside cabinet, I heard Courtney calling out from downstairs. '*Travis! Hurry up, Trav! We need to get a move on!*'

It was a warning. She'd guessed what I was doing, and she was trying to tell me that Mrs Kamal was getting suspicious and it was time for me to come back down.

I hesitated for a moment, knowing that I should heed her warning, but I was at the bedside cabinet now, and it only had two drawers . . . it would only take a couple of seconds to go through them.

I leaned down and opened the bottom drawer. It was full of bits and pieces: an old iPod, headphones, bootlaces, a pack of playing cards, a can of shoe polish . . .

'*Travis!*'

Courtney's voice again. Louder now, more urgent.

I opened the top drawer. It was jam-packed with boxing magazines. *Boxing Monthly*, *Boxing News*, *The Ring* . . .

'Damn,' I muttered.

'*TRAVIS!*'

As I went to close the drawer, something caught my eye. There was something poking out from between the pages of one of the magazines, a little booklet or something. I reached in and pulled it out.

It was a passport.

I heard footsteps then. The sound of someone coming up the stairs. It didn't sound like Courtney. With my heart thumping hard, I opened the passport and scanned the details, then I dropped it back in the drawer and tiptoed quickly out of the room and along the landing to the bathroom. As I went in and closed the door, I heard Mrs Kamal's voice from the top of the stairs, 'Excuse me? Are you all right in there? What are you doing?'

I flushed the toilet, ran the taps, turned them off

again, and opened the door. Mrs Kamal was standing on the landing.

'Sorry,' I said, holding my belly and looking embarrassed. 'I think I must have eaten something bad . . . I'm really sorry.'

She frowned at me, not sure whether to believe me or not, and I saw her glance over at Bashir's room.

'Are you all right, Travis?' Courtney called out from the bottom of the stairs.

'Yeah,' I told her. 'I'm OK. I'm just coming.'

As I moved off along the landing, and Mrs Kamal stepped aside to let me pass, I could tell from the way she was looking at me that she guessed I'd been up to something. She didn't say anything though. And I knew that she wouldn't. Because I knew now, without a shadow of doubt, that she was lying about her son.

17

I told Courtney about Bashir's passport as we drove back to her house.

'Are you sure it was his?' she asked.

'It was in his name, and it had his photograph in it. It wasn't an old one either. The expiry date was September 2021.'

'He can't have left the country then.'

'No.'

'So why are his parents lying?'

'His mother's definitely scared of something.'

'And she definitely knew the man in the photograph.'

I looked at Courtney. 'What do you think's going on?'

She shook her head. 'I don't know, Travis. But whatever it is, I'm beginning to think that your mum and dad were on to it. Everything seems to revolve round them. They were investigating Bashir. Bashir's mother knows the man you saw at their funeral. The man at the funeral knows the man who showed up at the office today pretending to be someone else.' She took a deep breath and let it out slowly. 'There's more to this than just a missing boxer, I'm pretty sure of that.'

When I didn't answer, she looked across at me.

I was leaning to one side, angling my head to get a better view in the wing mirror.

'What are you doing?' Courtney said.

'I think we're being followed.'

She immediately looked up at the rear-view mirror.

'Three cars back,' I told her.

'The silver Audi?' she said, raising her eyebrows.

'It's been behind us since we left the Kamals' house.'

'Are you sure?'

'It was parked at the end of Roman Way. It didn't follow us immediately when we went past it, but it was behind us when we left the estate.'

'Did you get the registration number?'

I shook my head. 'It was blocked by another parked car in Roman Way. And now it's too far back to see it.'

Courtney looked in the rear-view mirror again, narrowing her eyes to get a better look. 'Is it an S6?'

'Yep.'

'Damn,' she said quietly.

It went without saying that we were both thinking the same thing – that the car behind us was the same silver Audi S6 that Evie Johnson had told me about, the one with the restricted registration number . . . the one that in all likelihood was either a special operations police vehicle or a security services car.

Courtney didn't say anything for a while, she just carried on driving, staring straight ahead, thinking things through. Then, after another quick look in the mirror, she flicked the indicator switch, slowed the car, and pulled up in a bus lay-by at the side of the road. She reached into her pocket and passed me a pen.

'Get the registration number when it goes past,' she told me. 'I'll see if I can get a look at the driver.'

Moments later the Audi sped past us. I read off the registration number and wrote it down on the back of my hand. By the time I looked up again, the Audi was disappearing into the distance.

'Did you get it?' Courtney asked.

I showed her the number.

She frowned. 'That's not the same, is it?'

'Not quite,' I said, turning my hand over and showing her the number that Evie had written on my palm.

The first five characters matched, the last two were different.

'What do you think it means?' I asked.

'I'm not sure,' Courtney said. 'It could just be a coincidence.'

I gave her a doubtful look.

'Strange things happen, Trav.'

'You've said that before.'

'Well, it's true.'

'It's more likely that the two cars *are* somehow connected though, isn't it?'

'There's a pretty good chance,' she agreed.

'Did you get a look at the driver?'

'Not really. He turned his head away as he went past. All I could really see was that he had black hair.'

'Was he wearing a suit?'

'I couldn't tell.' She reached into her pocket and took out her notepad. 'Let me see the number again.'

I showed her the back of my hand. She took the pen from my other hand, copied down the number, then put the notepad back in her pocket.

'Aren't you going to check it out?' I asked.

'I'll do it later.'

'Why not now?'

'We need to go home now.'

'Go home?'

'Look, we don't know for sure that the guy in the Audi *was* tailing us, OK? But if he was, and if he knows what he's doing – which he will if he's police or security services – he'll have realised that we're on to him. He won't carry on following us if he knows we're looking out for him. Not for a while, anyway. So the best thing for us to do right now is go home, get some rest, and start again in the morning.'

'Yeah, but—'

'It's been a long day, Travis. I need to get back and make sure my mum's OK, and you need to get home before your nan and grandad start worrying. We both need time to think things through. All right?'

'I suppose so.'

She looked at me. 'We're a good team, Travis. You and me, we can do this together.'

'Yeah.'

She put her hand on my shoulder. 'But not right now,

OK? Right now we both need to go home.'

'But we'll start again tomorrow?'

'First thing in the morning,' she said, putting the car into gear.

'First thing?'

'I'll meet you in the office at nine o'clock. Is that all right with you?'

'Perfect.'

She looked over her shoulder, waited for a gap in the traffic, then pulled out of the lay-by and drove off.

The plan was to drive back to Courtney's place to pick up my bike and then she'd give me a lift back home. When we arrived at Courtney's house though, her mum was in a bit of a bad way. She'd fallen over in the kitchen, and although she wasn't seriously hurt, she was pretty shaken up, and obviously Courtney didn't want to leave her on her own. I asked if there was anything I could do to help, but Courtney said her mum just needed to get some rest. So I told Courtney not to worry about me, and I got on my bike and started riding back to Nan and Grandad's.

I'd kept my eyes open for the silver Audi on the drive back to Courtney's house. I hadn't seen it anywhere, and I hadn't seen any obvious signs that anyone else was following us either, but I carried on looking as I cycled out of town and along Long Barton Road – watching out for parked Audis, checking every vehicle that went past me, glancing over my shoulder every fifty metres or so.

I didn't see anything to worry about though, and by the time I'd reached the top of the hill that leads down to Nan and Grandad's house, I'd begun to relax a bit. I hadn't stopped looking over my shoulder or anything, I just wasn't doing it all the time any more. So when a car horn beeped right behind me, and I looked round and saw a white Nissan Skyline creeping along on my tail, I was kind of taken by surprise.

It was a boy-racer car – alloy wheels, rear spoiler, a big noisy exhaust system. The sun was in my eyes, and the car had a tinted windscreen, so it was hard to make out who was in it. There were definitely two people in the front, and I got the impression that there were more in the back, but I wasn't hanging around to find out. I stood up in the saddle, hit the pedals, and hurtled off down the hill.

The car horn beeped again as I raced away, and I thought I heard someone call out my name, but I didn't stop. Moments later I heard the Nissan coming after me – tyres screeching as it picked up speed, gears changing rapidly, the roar of a souped-up engine . . .

It was catching up fast.

I didn't have time to think.

I veered out into the middle of the road, waited for an oncoming lorry to pass, then swung the bike sharply to the right and launched myself across the road . . .

Straight into the path of a Tesco van.

18

The Tesco van only just missed me, its front bumper millimetres away from clipping my back wheel, and as the van zoomed past me – with its horn blaring and the furious driver yelling out four-letter words – the sudden rush of air almost knocked me off my bike. I just managed to keep my balance though, and as the adrenalin rushed through me, tingling in my veins, I hopped the bike up onto the pavement and kept going as fast as I could – along the pavement, a skidding right turn into a steep downhill lane, then across the lane and through an open gate into the relative safety of a single-track footpath.

The path was far too narrow for a car, so I knew the Nissan couldn't follow me any more, but I still wanted to get as far away from the road as I could. So I just kept my head down and kept pumping away on the pedals.

The footpath ran parallel to Long Barton Road, and Nan and Grandad's house was less than a kilometre away. Their back garden backed onto the path, and I knew I could get into it without having to go out onto the road.

All I had to do was keep going.

I glanced over my shoulder, expecting to see the Nissan parked in the lane, and maybe the driver and his passengers standing at the gate, looking dejectedly in my direction, resigned to the fact that I'd given them the slip. But the lane was empty. No parked Nissan, no one standing at the gate. Which I thought was a bit strange. They must have seen me cutting across the road and turning right into the lane. So why hadn't they followed me? It didn't make sense.

I thought about that for a moment or two, and then I realised there was something else that didn't make sense. Why would someone be following me in such a noticeable car? And why would they beep their horn at me and call out my name? That didn't make sense at *all*.

Forget it, I told myself. *Now's not the time for questions. The only thing that matters now is getting back to Nan and Grandad's.*

There wasn't far to go. I was coming up to a gap in the path where a road cuts across it at a right angle. All I had to do was cross over the road and carry on down the footpath on the other side, and I'd be at Nan and Grandad's in minutes.

I slowed down as I approached the crossing, and I was just about to swing my leg over the saddle and get off when I heard the sound of a souped-up engine speeding down the road. I tried telling myself that it wasn't necessarily the Nissan, that there were plenty of other boy racers around with big noisy exhausts, but I knew in my heart that I was kidding myself. I jammed on my brakes, skidded to a halt, and started to turn the bike around. But the path was so narrow there wasn't enough room to manoeuvre. I yanked on the handlebars, trying to hop the front wheel over a tree stump at the side of the path, but the spokes of the wheel got caught in a broken branch. I was completely stuck now. I looked over at the crossing, listening to the rapidly approaching car, wondering if I should get off my bike and run, but even as I was thinking about it, I heard a squeal of tyres and I saw the Nissan pulling up at the side of the road. Before I had a chance to do anything, the car doors opened and two figures got out.

One of them was a tough-looking kid, about sixteen years old, wearing a black hoodie and black trackpants. The other one was an absolute giant – well over six feet tall, with the body of a heavyweight boxer, shoulders like an ox, and a massive head that looked as if it was carved out of stone.

'Hey, Travis,' the tough-looking kid called out. 'What are you doing, man?'

'Bloody hell, Mason,' I said, letting out a sigh of relief. 'You nearly scared me to death.'

19

Most people probably wouldn't think much of Mason Yusuf. They'd take one look at him and think – street kid, gang kid, hoodie, criminal. They'd assume he was just another council-estate kid, another uneducated teenager from another broken family, just another lost kid with no future and no hope. And in some ways, they'd be right. Mason *is* an estate kid. He was born and raised on the Slade, he's lived there all his life, he grew up with the gang kids who run the estate. He knows them, hangs around with them, he *is* one of them. And although I've never witnessed him breaking the law, I'd be very surprised if he hasn't broken a few in his time. The way Mason sees it though, as he explained to me once, is that if you live on the Slade, and you want to survive, the only law that matters is the law of the estate. 'And our laws aren't always compatible with yours,' I remember him telling me, with a roguish grin.

But whatever the rights and wrongs of his way of life, there's a lot more to Mason than meets the eye. A whole lot more.

I first got to know him about a year ago after an incident with his younger sister Jaydie. I didn't actually know Jaydie at the time, I'd just met her one day when I was riding my bike across this little park near the Beacon

Fields estate. She was riding her bike across the park too, but she'd run into a gang of kids who'd blocked her way and wouldn't let her pass. I don't think they meant any serious harm, they were just 'having a bit of fun' with her – calling her names, teasing her, just messing around really. But she was only eleven at the time, and she was on her own, and there were at least half a dozen of them, and they were all about fourteen or fifteen. It wasn't right. I knew I had to do something to help her. So I just rode up to them and told them to leave her alone. And they did. Because now they had me to pick on. And because I was a bit older than Jaydie, and I wasn't a girl, they didn't have to hold back with me. And they didn't.

I managed to fight them off long enough for Jaydie to get away, and as far as I can remember I put at least two of them down, but I was never going to beat them all. There were just too many of them. Within a few minutes they had me on the ground and were giving me a pretty good kicking. The last thing I remember is looking up at a circle of grinning faces, wondering how much this was going to hurt, and then – BOOM! – my head exploded and everything went black.

I wasn't too badly hurt, no broken bones or anything, and after a couple of days I was up and about again. I don't know how Mason found out who I was, but on the day I went back to school after the beating, he was waiting for me at the school gates at the end of the day.

'Travis Delaney?' he said.

I just looked at him, a tough-looking fifteen-year-old Slade kid, and wondered what the hell he wanted with me.

'Mason Yusuf,' he said, holding out his hand. 'You helped my sister.'

'Oh, right,' I said, shaking his hand. 'How is she?'

Mason grinned. 'She can't stop talking about you. You're her hero.'

I shrugged, embarrassed. 'I didn't really do anything.'

'Yeah, you did. You stood up to six Beacon Boys and took a beating for her.'

'I got a couple of them.'

'So I heard.' He glanced to one side, then looked back at me. 'Anyway, I just wanted to let you know they've been taken care of.'

'What do you mean?'

'The kids who beat you up, the ones who were messing with Jaydie. They've been dealt with. They won't bother you again.'

'Right . . .' I said, not quite sure what he meant.

He took a scrap of paper from his pocket and passed it to me. 'That's my address and mobile number. Any problems, anything you want, anything at all, just get in touch, OK?'

'Thanks,' I mumbled.

'You looked out for Jaydie,' he said simply. 'Now I'm looking out for you.'

'You don't have to do that. I mean, there's no need—'

'I've got to go,' he said, ignoring my protest and walking off. 'Next time you're passing the Slade, call in and see us.' He grinned over his shoulder at me. 'You'll make Jaydie's day.'

Since then, Mason has been true to his word. He's looked out for me, kept his eye on me, helped me out whenever I needed it. And although we come from completely different backgrounds, and our lives are worlds apart, we've become really good friends. I've got to know Jaydie pretty well too. She's twelve now, and she's still got a bit of a crush on me, which can sometimes make things a bit awkward between us. But we manage to get round it most of the time. We're friends. We work it out. That's what friends do.

I could see Jaydie getting out of the back of the Nissan now. She smiled at me and followed Mason and the other guy over to where I was standing. I'd got off my bike now and was trying to disentangle the front wheel from the tree roots.

The guy with Mason was Big Lenny. I don't know if Lenny's his real name or not, but that's what everyone calls him. He's Mason's minder. He goes almost everywhere with him. Some people make the mistake of thinking Lenny's a bit dim-witted. Partly because he's freakishly big, partly because he very rarely says anything, and partly because he always wears slightly odd clothes. Today, for example, he was wearing cheap denim jeans with six-inch turn-ups, a V-neck jumper with no shirt, and a second-hand suit jacket that was at least two sizes too small for him. Which, admittedly, did make him look a bit odd. And maybe Lenny *is* a bit odd. But there's nothing wrong with that. And as for being dim-witted . . . well, he might not say very much, and he might not be the world's greatest thinker, but he always seems perfectly content with his life, and in my book that's a pretty smart way to be.

'Hey, Lenny,' I said, looking up at him. 'Good to see you.'

He didn't reply, just nodded his enormous head.

Jaydie came up to me then and gave me a hug, putting her arms round my waist and pressing her head into my chest. 'I'm really sorry about your mum and dad, Travis. If there's anything I can do . . . I mean, if you want to talk about anything . . . well, you know where I am.'

'Thanks,' I mumbled, feeling a little bit embarrassed, but kind of good too.

She let go of me and stepped back, and I stood there smiling at the three of them. They looked like a bunch of misfits and outlaws, and I suppose in a way they were. But as we stood there together that day, baking in the afternoon sun, there was no one else I'd rather have been with.

20

'So what are you doing here, Mason?' I said, tugging at my front wheel again.

'Looking for you,' he replied, helping me with the wheel. 'I heard you were living with your nan and grandad now. We were on our way out to see you. Why the hell did you ride off when you saw us?'

'I didn't know it was you, did I?'

'Who did you it think it was? Is someone after you?'

'Possibly . . .'

'Who?'

'Well, it's kind of a long story.'

I gave the wheel another hard yank and it finally came free. I straightened up, getting my breath back, and glanced over at the Nissan. Rap music was thudding quietly from inside, and a skinny young guy was sitting in the driver's seat smoking a cigarette and nodding his head to the music. I realised now that when I'd shot off down the hill and turned right into the lane, Mason must have guessed I was heading for Nan and Grandad's along the footpath, and rather than following me down the lane he'd told the driver to carry on along Long Barton Road and then take a right to cut me off at the crossing.

'Who's the guy in the car?' I asked Mason.

'They call him Toot,' Mason said. 'He's all right. Not

that sharp, but he's a good driver.'

'Nice car,' I said, grinning. 'Really classy.'

Mason shrugged. 'It's a car.' He looked at me. 'So what's this long story all about then, Trav? Who do you think's been following you?'

I didn't tell them the whole story, but I told them enough to put them in the picture. I wasn't surprised to find out that Mason knew all about Bashir Kamal – there's very little that Mason doesn't know – and when I mentioned Evie Johnson, it turned out that he knew her too. He'd known her since she was a kid.

'Evie's cool,' he said, nodding his head. 'You can trust her. If she said she saw Bashir with a couple of suits in a car, that's what she saw.'

'Have you heard anything about Bashir?' I asked. 'Any rumours or anything?'

'The word on the Slade is he's in Pakistan. Something to do with a sick grandmother.'

'Do you believe it?'

'It's possible, I suppose. Kind of odd that he'd just pack up and go so quickly though, especially with his big fight coming up. There was something a bit weird about the way the word spread so fast as well. I mean, usually when a rumour goes round the estate, it starts off pretty slowly, with just a couple of people knowing about it, and then it gradually gets bigger and bigger, until eventually it reaches a certain point, and then it just kind of explodes, and *everybody* knows about it. But this rumour about Bash going to Pakistan was different. It was like one minute no one knew anything, and then – BAM! – the next minute it was all over the estate. Do you know what I mean?'

I nodded. 'I'm pretty sure he's not in Pakistan.'

'Really?'

I told Mason about finding Bashir's passport.

'Doesn't necessarily mean he's still in the country,' Mason said. 'It's not hard to get a false passport.'

'Why would he travel on a false passport?'

'You tell me. You're the detective.' He paused for a moment, thinking about something. 'Let me see those pictures you told me about.'

I showed him the printout and the photo of the man at the funeral.

'This is the guy,' he said, tapping the printout.

'What guy?'

'This one,' he said, pointing to the man with short dark hair and a goatee beard. 'That's the guy I came here to tell you about.'

21

Mason hadn't taken part in the riot that had smashed up all the shops and offices in North Walk. He'd known it was going to happen, he told me, and he knew just about everyone who *had* taken part in it, but he hadn't been there himself.

'I knew your mum and dad's place was probably going to get looted,' he told me, 'and although I couldn't do anything to stop it, I didn't want to be part of it. I thought about letting you know it was going to happen, but I couldn't really see what good it would do. I guessed you had more important stuff to deal with anyway. I mean, you'd only just lost your mum and dad . . . I thought it was best to leave you alone, you know?'

The four of us were sitting together on a wooden bench just down the road from the crossing. I'd asked them if they wanted to come back to Nan and Grandad's place with me, but Mason said he had to get going quite soon as he had 'a bit of business' to sort out back at the Slade.

'I thought the whole thing was a stupid idea anyway,' he went on. 'I mean, if you're going to go looting and ransacking, at least make sure you're doing it somewhere that's got something worth stealing.' He shook his head. 'I mean, there's nothing *in* North Walk. It's just little shops and offices and stuff. Why bother smashing them up? There's no point. It's just mindless vandalism, isn't it?'

'I suppose so,' I said, not really sure what he was trying to say.

Mason looked at me. 'It was *organised*, Travis. Everyone on the Slade knew exactly when and where it was going to kick off. It was all planned. You don't *plan* mindless vandalism, do you?'

'I don't get it,' I said, shaking my head.

'Neither did I at first,' Mason told me. 'That's why I started asking around. That's how I heard about this guy, the one in the picture.' Mason took out his mobile, tapped the screen, then held it out for me to see. The photograph showed a man in a suit coming out of a low-rise block of flats. It was the dark-haired man with the goatee beard. 'That was taken on the Slade two days before the riot,' Mason told me. 'From what I've been told, the guy in the suit was just coming out of a meeting with a guy called Drew Devon. They call him Dee Dee.' Mason looked at me. 'Have you heard of him?'

'No.'

'Dee Dee runs pretty much everything on the Slade. He's a *very* powerful guy.'

'I still don't get it,' I said, frowning. 'What's all this got to do with the riot?'

'The word on the street is that the guy in the suit paid Dee Dee to arrange it.'

'Arrange what?'

'The riot.'

'He *paid* for a riot?'

Mason nodded. 'I mean, I can't prove it or anything, but that's what it looks like to me. One of the kids who was there that night told me he'd only gone along with it because Dee Dee's guys told him to. I'm pretty sure that some of the older kids were paid good money to make sure the riot went ahead.'

'You think they were paid by Dee Dee?'

Mason smiled ruefully. 'Well, he wouldn't have paid them from his own pocket personally, he would have got someone else to do it. But, yeah, I think Dee Dee was probably behind it. The guy in the suit paid him, he paid his guys, and they sorted it out.'

'Why would the guy in the suit *want* a riot?' I said, looking at Mason. 'Why would *anyone* want a riot? It doesn't make sense, does it?'

'It didn't until I saw this,' Mason said, studying the printout of the photo again. 'Now I'm beginning to think it makes perfect sense.' He held his mobile over the printout, positioning it so that the photograph of the man on his phone was right next to the image of the man in the printout. 'It's definitely the same guy, isn't it?'

'Yeah,' I agreed.

'And your dad took this picture when he was trying to find Bashir Kamal?'

'Yeah.'

'So the men in your dad's picture have got something

to do with Bashir going missing, and one of them paid Dee Dee to organise the riot in North Walk, which just happens to be where your mum and dad's office is.' He looked at me. 'Do you see what I'm saying?'

'No,' I admitted.

He looked at Jaydie. 'Do you get it yet, Jay?'

She nodded.

He smiled at her, then turned back to me. 'What if your mum and dad had some kind of proof that these guys in suits were involved in whatever happened to Bashir? And what if the suit guys *knew* your mum and dad had proof, and they guessed it was in their office, but they didn't want to just break in and steal it because eventually someone might notice it was missing, and that might look suspicious.'

'Right,' I said, getting it now, 'but if it went missing with a load of other stuff when the office was smashed up and ransacked during a street riot, no one would ever know.'

'Exactly,' Jaydie said.

I looked at her.

She smiled.

I turned back to Mason. 'So who's the guy who paid Dee Dee?'

'No idea,' he said. 'I've asked around, but no one knows anything about him.'

'Dee Dee knows who he is,' I said. 'Why not ask him?

Jaydie stifled a giggle.

'What?' I said to her. 'What's wrong with that?'

'He's Dee Dee,' she said simply. 'You can't just knock on his door and start asking him questions.'

'Why not?'

'Because you can't,' she said, frowning at me as if it was the most obvious thing in the world.

I looked at Mason. 'You know all the right people, don't you? I mean, surely you could get to see him.'

'My influence only goes so far, Travis. I mean, yeah, I know a lot of people, and a lot of people know me. But asking me to call in on Dee Dee is like asking you to call in on the prime minister or the Pope or something.' He shrugged. 'It's just never going to happen.'

'Maybe I could try talking to him?' I suggested.

'Yeah, right,' Mason said dismissively. 'And while you're at it, you could try growing some wings and flying to the moon as well.'

We carried on talking things over for a while, trying to work out who the men in the pictures could be, and if they were connected to the men in the Audi. But by the time Mason said he had to get going, we hadn't really got anywhere.

'I'll keep asking around, OK?' he said, getting to his feet. 'I'll let you know if I hear anything.'

'Thanks,' I told him.

'Keep in touch, yeah?'

'Yeah.'

'Anything you need, any problems, just call me.'

I nodded.

Jaydie hugged me again before she went, and then Big Lenny gave me a pat on the shoulder – which almost knocked me off the bench – and the three of them walked back to the Nissan and got in. The engine revved loudly, the big exhaust roaring like a jet, and the car pulled away and sped off down the road. I watched it go, then got back on my bike and headed off towards Nan and Grandad's house.

22

After I'd had tea with Nan and Grandad and Granny Nora – who was well enough to come downstairs for once – I went to my room, lay down on my bed and tried to make sense of everything I'd found out. It was really difficult. I had so much information in my head, so many things that people had told me, so many thoughts and feelings and possibilities . . . it was just too much. I knew that it all meant something, that everything was somehow connected, but I just couldn't fit the pieces together. It felt like I had a jumbled-up jigsaw puzzle floating around in my mind – a three-dimensional jigsaw puzzle with some of the bits missing. Every time I thought I was getting somewhere with it, fitting a couple of pieces together, I'd suddenly realise that the colours didn't match or the bits didn't really fit together or something, and then I'd have to start all over again.

I lay there for a long time, just staring at the ceiling, lost in the puzzles inside my head.

I don't know what time it was when Grandad came up to see me, but I remember realising that it was getting dark outside, the night sky streaked with a crimson sunset, so it must have been around nine o'clock, maybe nine thirty. I'd given up trying to think about things by then, and for the last half-hour or so I'd been sitting on my bed playing chess on my laptop. I'd thought about playing something else, but I didn't really feel up to shooting people or managing a football team, and although I'm not much good at chess, it always seems to help me when I'm trying to sort out stuff in my head. Chess takes your mind away to another place. And while you're in that place, focusing on the complexities of the game, the rest of your mind is free to concentrate on the stuff that needs sorting out.

That's how I see it anyway.

I was just about to lose the game I was playing when Grandad knocked on my door. I had a queen and a rook left, but my opponent had a queen and two rooks, and it was only a matter of time before the extra rook got the better of me. So when I heard Grandad knock on my door and call out softly – 'Are you awake, Trav?' – I was quite happy to close the game without saving it, telling myself that I hadn't really lost, I'd just been interrupted.

I'd already noticed at teatime that Grandad was looking a lot better, and as he came into my room that night I could tell from the way he was walking that he was almost back to himself again. He wasn't shuffling any more, his shoulders weren't stooped. He had an air of confidence about him.

'How's it going?' he said, crossing over to the window.

'Well, you know . . .'

He looked at me, nodding slowly. 'Yeah, I know.'

'How are you?' I asked him.

'Not too bad, thanks.' He sighed and looked out of the window. 'Listen, Travis,' he said solemnly, 'I'm sorry I haven't been here for you over these last couple of weeks. It's not because I didn't want to—'

'It's all right, Grandad,' I said. 'You don't have to explain.'

'No, it's not all right,' he said sadly, shaking his head. 'This is the worst time in the world for you. It's the worst time for all of us, but I should have *been* with you. Every day, every hour, every minute. But I wasn't. That's unforgivable.'

'Nothing's unforgivable, Grandad,' I said. 'Dad told me once that if you really love someone, nothing's unforgivable.'

Grandad smiled. It was the first time I'd seen him smile in weeks. 'Your dad always did have a way with words, didn't he? Even when he was a little kid he could talk his way out of almost anything. It used to drive his mother mad sometimes.' He grinned at the memory. 'I remember once, when your dad came home from school one day with his clothes all ripped up and covered in mud . . . this must have been when he was about six or seven, maybe a little older . . .'

We spent the next few hours just talking to each other. While I stayed slumped on the bed, Grandad made himself comfortable in an armchair in the corner and told me stories about Dad when he was a kid – growing up in south London, getting into trouble sometimes, going to see Millwall play. As the sun went down and the night turned dark, the talk gradually turned to more personal stuff. How was I *really* feeling? Grandad wanted to know. What did I have in my head? My heart? Was there anything I wanted to tell him? Anything I wanted to talk about? Did I have any questions about anything, anything at all?

I didn't know what to say at first. My head and my heart were full of stuff about Mum and Dad – feelings, questions, confusion – but I didn't know how to put any of it into words. It was just *there*. Inside me. Part of me. No matter how much I wanted to express it, it didn't seem to want to come out. It was somehow as if it just wasn't ready yet. The other stuff though, the jigsaw-puzzle stuff, that *was* ready to come out. And although I knew it wasn't the kind of stuff that Grandad had in mind, I also knew that I just *had* to tell him about it.

'Do you remember the man in the car park at the funeral?' I said to him. 'The one I took a picture of on my mobile?'

Grandad frowned for a moment. 'The man with the black BMW?'

I nodded, glad that he remembered.

Then I started telling him everything.

23

They say that the eyes are the window to the soul, and as I sat in my room with Grandad that night, telling him everything I'd found out about Bashir Kamal and the mysterious men, it was pretty obvious from the look in Grandad's eyes that his soul couldn't make up its mind what to think. He was clearly intrigued by what I was telling him, and no matter how much he tried to hide it, I could see an instinctive curiosity twinkling in his eyes. But the more I told him, the darker the twinkle became, and gradually his eyes took on a hard-edged look of growing concern and suspicion. He was worried about me, frightened for me. And that almost made me wish I'd kept my mouth shut about everything.

But it was already too late by then.

Besides, however much I wished I hadn't told him anything, I was still incredibly relieved that I had. I felt so much lighter now. It was as if I'd been walking around all day with a boulder strapped to my shoulders, and now suddenly the boulder was gone.

'You should have told someone about all this, Travis,' Grandad said sternly. 'You should have let someone know what you were doing.'

'I did,' I said. 'I told Courtney. She came to see Mrs Kamal with me.'

'You should have told Nan.'

'I didn't want to bother her.'

He sighed sadly. 'I suppose that's why you didn't come to me, is it? You didn't want to bother me.'

It was a hard question to answer, and I wasn't sure how to do it. I didn't want to lie to him, but I didn't want to make him feel bad about himself either. He felt bad enough as it was. So I didn't say anything for a while, I just looked at him, trying to let him see that I didn't blame him for anything, that I knew he couldn't help sinking down into his dark moods, and that everything was OK now anyway. He was better again, we were talking, and that was all that mattered.

After we'd both sat there for a minute or two, looking at each other in the moonlit darkness of my room, Grandad eventually just nodded his head. It wasn't much – a brief silent nod – but it was all either of us needed. I smiled quietly to myself, nodded back, and then we got on with it.

I thought he'd want to see the pictures first – the photo on my mobile and the printout I'd taken from the safe – but instead he started asking me questions. Questions about the two Audis, questions about the man at the funeral and the man with the shaved head, questions about everything. What kind of men were they? Calm? Angry? Clever? Agitated? How did they speak? Did they have accents? What exactly did they say? Are you sure the

Audi was following you? Did Evie Johnson give you a description of the men she saw in the Audi with Bashir?

It was surprisingly difficult to remember the details, and I was kind of annoyed with myself for having to say 'I don't know' or 'I can't remember' all the time. Grandad assured me it was nothing to worry about. He said that almost everyone struggles to remember the little things, and that most people, when asked to describe someone they've only seen once, can't even recall the most basic details – hair colour, height, clothing.

'I've interviewed a lot of eyewitnesses in my time, Trav,' he said. 'And, believe me, you're better than most of them.'

'They must have been pretty useless then.'

'Don't put yourself down. You know a lot more than you think.'

I wasn't sure he was right about that, but I was happy enough to accept it.

'Right,' he said, 'let's see those pictures you told me about.'

I went over to the armchair and passed him the printout. He took a pair of reading glasses from his cardigan pocket, cleaned them on his shirt, then put them on and looked at the picture. While he was doing that, I took out my phone and opened up the photo of the man at the funeral. Grandad was studying the printout very closely, taking his time, examining every little detail in concentrated silence. I watched quietly as he took off his glasses and held them over the image of the three men, squinting through the lenses to get a better view. He didn't seem too pleased with the result though, and after a while he shook his head and put his glasses back on again.

'Dad wrote a note on the back,' I told him.

He turned over the printout and read the scribbled note.

'What do you think?' I asked him.

He carried on studying the note for a while, then he looked up slowly, took off his glasses, and stared straight ahead, his brow furrowed in concentration. After a good minute or so, he let out a sigh of frustration and shook his head. 'It's obviously got *something* to do with the fourth and fifth of August, but I'm damned if I can figure out what.' He looked at me. 'Have you got any ideas?'

We spent the next five minutes discussing what 'dem' and 'last day' might mean, but we didn't come up with anything useful. In the end, Grandad suggested that we leave it for now and put it to the back of our minds.

'You never know,' he said. 'Sometimes the best way of solving a puzzle is by *not* thinking consciously about it.' He turned over the printout, put his glasses back on, and looked at the picture of the three men again. 'Which one was it who came to the office?' he asked.

'Him,' I said, pointing out the man with the shaved head.

'And this one?' he said, indicating the man with the

goatee beard. 'He's the one your friend says paid for the riot?'

I nodded.

'And this is the man from the funeral,' he said, indicating the man with the steely grey eyes.

'Yeah.' I passed Grandad my phone. 'This is the picture I took of him in the car park.'

Grandad took the phone and studied the photograph. He stared hard at the man in the picture, and after a while I saw his eyes narrow to a frown. He brought the phone closer to his eyes, trying to focus on something, then he moved it away again and held it at arm's length, angling his head and squinting over the top of his glasses at it. Still not satisfied, he took off his glasses again, held the phone in his left hand, and with the thumb and index finger of his right hand he began adjusting the size and position of the photo on the screen. It took him a while to get it how he wanted it, but eventually he stopped fiddling around, and then he just sat there for a while staring thoughtfully at the image he'd ended up with. He'd zoomed in quite a lot, so the image was a bit blurred, but I could still just about make out that it was a close-up view of the man's left arm, showing his hand on the boot of the BMW just as he was about to close it.

'Can you see it?' Grandad asked quietly, still staring at the image.

'See what?' I said.

He passed me the phone. 'Look at his wrist.'

I gazed at the screen, focusing on the man's left wrist. He was wearing a watch. It wasn't very clear, but from what I could see of it, it seemed perfectly ordinary. Just a plain, silver-coloured watch, with an expanding metal strap.

'It's just a watch,' I said, shaking my head.

Grandad leaned over and carefully pointed to a darkish smudge on the back of the man's wrist, just above the watch.

'See that?' he said.

I looked closer. It wasn't just a smudge. It was a tattoo.

I brought the phone closer to my eyes. It wasn't a very big tattoo, about two centimetres across at most, and it was really hard to make out what it was. It looked a bit like the letter O, with a bit missing at the bottom and two little feet.

Like this: Ω

'His watch strap is loose,' Grandad muttered, almost as if he was talking to himself. 'That's why you can see it. If the strap wasn't loose, the tattoo would be covered up by the watch. But when he reached up to close the boot –' Grandad raised his arm, mimicking the man's pose '– the watch slipped down his wrist, revealing the tattoo underneath.'

'What is it?' I asked Grandad, staring hard at the tattoo. 'It looks vaguely familiar, but I don't know why.'

'It's a Greek letter,' he said, looking at me. 'Omega. The last letter of the Greek alphabet.'

I frowned. 'What does it mean?'

'I'm not sure,' he said, sighing. 'It might not mean anything. It might be that this man, whoever he is, just happens to have an Omega symbol tattooed on his wrist. On the other hand . . .'

'What?'

'Well, if it means what I think it might mean, I'm not sure I want to believe it.'

24

Although I knew a little bit about Grandad's career in the Army Intelligence Corps, he'd never really told me exactly what he did as an intelligence officer, and he'd always been particularly reluctant to talk about the work he'd done in Northern Ireland during the 1980s. I'd assumed this was because his memories of that time were overshadowed by the trauma of the car bomb that almost killed him, but as we sat together in my room that night, and Grandad began telling me what he knew about an organisation known as Omega, I realised that it wasn't just the car bomb he was trying to forget.

'Between 1982 and 1990,' he told me, 'I was an officer with a covert military intelligence squad based in Belfast called the FRU – the Force Research Unit. Our main job was to recruit informants from the paramilitary forces and run them as undercover agents. Most of the assets we handled were either members or supporters of the IRA, but we also recruited agents from some of the Loyalist groups.' Grandad looked at me. 'You know enough about the Troubles in Northern Ireland to know what I'm talking about, don't you?'

I nodded. My history teacher had told us a bit about the conflict in Northern Ireland, and although I didn't understand everything about it, I knew that it was basically a war between the Nationalist and Unionist communities over the status of Northern Ireland. The Nationalists, or Republicans, were Catholic; the Unionists, or Loyalists, were Protestant. The Nationalists wanted a united Ireland and an end to British rule, the Unionists wanted Northern Ireland to remain as part of the United Kingdom. Both sides used paramilitary forces to fight for their cause. The IRA was the main Republican force, and for almost thirty years they'd fought a guerrilla campaign against both the Loyalist forces and the British people, who they saw as their enemy. The Troubles claimed the lives of thousands of people on both sides – soldiers, paramilitaries, police, civilians – and many more thousands were seriously injured and maimed.

'It was a long and dirty war, Travis,' Grandad said quietly, 'and a lot of really bad stuff happened. It always does in a war, of course. People get killed and terribly wounded, lives are shattered, everything changes. Wars always bring out the worst in the human race.' He sighed. 'But as well as the hell that everyone knows about, there's another kind of hell that goes on during a war, a hidden hell. And that's where I spent most of my time.'

His eyes darkened as he went on to tell me about his work with the FRU, and I could see that it pained him to talk about it.

'We had to recruit informants who had inside information,' he explained, 'and that meant working with people who were still active members of terrorist groups. So we knew they were personally involved in the planning and execution of all kinds of atrocities – bombings, murders, assassinations – but most of the time we couldn't do anything about it. Because if we did, we'd be putting our informant at risk, and in the long term that could lead to the loss of more lives. So sometimes we just had to accept that we were dealing with killers, paying them for information, looking after them, keeping them safe.' Grandad shook his head. 'It wasn't an easy situation to live with. What made it even worse was that we didn't have any control over what we were doing. We were soldiers, we worked for the army. We did what we were told. The army did what it was told by the British government. And the government was constantly being influenced by other forces – MI5, Special Branch, counter-intelligence services, the Royal Ulster Constabulary. There were so many different organisations involved, all of them with different strategies and different motives, that sometimes it was almost impossible to get anything done.' Grandad looked at me again. 'I know it all sounds a bit complicated and confusing, Trav, but the point I'm trying to make is that it was *so* complicated and confusing that after a while a lot of us became totally disillusioned with it all. There were people like me who just hated what we were doing and didn't want to be part of it any more, and there were others who really believed in it, but were sick of being constrained by all the rules and politics of intelligence work. They wanted the freedom to do their job properly, and to them that meant no rules, no restrictions, and no accountability.' Grandad got up then and began pacing quietly around the room. 'I first heard the rumours about an organised group of disaffected intelligence officers in the mid-1980s,' he continued. 'There was no real substance to the rumours, no evidence to back them up, and the so-called facts about this secret organisation kept changing all the time, depending on who you listened to. But the basic story was always the same – a small group of intelligence officers had got together and formed an unofficial security service. Some of them were still active in their official units, others had resigned or retired, and they came from all kinds of different backgrounds. Army Intelligence, FRU, MI5, MI6, Special Forces . . .' Grandad stopped at the window and gazed out into the night. 'There was a lot of speculation about this rogue security service – who was involved, how big the organisation was, where they got their funding from – but no one really knew anything. Even when people began referring to the group as Omega, there was no way of telling if that's what *they* called themselves, or if it was just another rumour.'

'What did people think this group was actually doing?' I asked.

Grandad turned from the window. 'The general consensus has always been that Omega works for the good of the country. They do the same kind of work that all the official security services do – counter-intelligence, counter-terrorism, internal and external national security – but they do it on their terms.'

'What does that mean?'

'They do what they think has to be done,' Grandad said. 'No rules, no restrictions, no accountability. Whatever it takes to get the job done, they'll do it. No matter what.'

'So you think Omega really exists?'

He shrugged. 'I've never been able to make up my mind. Sometimes I think it's all a myth, just one of those stories that people like to talk about, especially people in the security services. But strange things have happened over the years, things that can't easily be explained unless you accept that Omega *does* exist, or at least an off-the-grid organisation like Omega.'

I looked at the photo on my mobile, staring at the Omega symbol tattooed on the man's wrist. 'Is that how they identify themselves?' I asked Grandad. 'With the tattoos?'

'I honestly don't know, Travis,' he said. 'Someone once told me they'd seen an Omega symbol tattooed on the wrist of a man whose body was found at the scene of an attack on a suspected terrorist cell in Glasgow. When the official report into the attack came out, there was no mention of this body, and no conclusive evidence was found as to who carried out the attack.'

'Is that the kind of thing Omega would do?' I asked.

'I mean, would they carry out an attack on suspected terrorists?'

'Well, from what I've heard, they'd definitely carry out an attack on *confirmed* terrorists. They wouldn't care how they got their evidence either.'

'So if Omega *is* real . . .' I said slowly, turning my attention to the photograph again. 'If it really exists, and this man is part of it . . .' I shook my head, unable to finish the question. I was so confused now that I didn't even know what to ask any more.

'I need to make a phone call,' Grandad said abruptly. 'And I need those registration numbers you've got.'

'Which ones?'

'All of them.'

I found a scrap of paper and copied down the numbers of the two Audis from my hand, then I looked at the photo on my mobile and wrote down the registration of the black BMW. I passed the piece of paper to Grandad.

'Tell me again what Courtney found out,' he said, studying the numbers.

'The BMW is registered to a company called Smith & Co Digital Holdings Ltd. They're supposedly based in Dundee, but she couldn't find anything about them on the Internet.'

Grandad nodded. 'And she couldn't get anything at all on the first Audi.'

'Her contact told her the registration record was

restricted. She said she was going to try checking the other Audi's number tonight.'

'Right,' Grandad said. 'Well, let's see what I can find out.'

'Do you want to use my mobile?' I asked him.

He shook his head. 'I'm going to use the phone box across the street.'

'The phone box?'

'Modern technology is all well and good, Trav, but sometimes the old ways are still the best.'

25

I didn't know who Grandad was calling, but the only time I'd known him use a phone box before was when he'd had to get in touch with one of his old army intelligence contacts, so I guessed he was doing something similar now. And I assumed from what he'd said about the old ways still being the best that he felt safer using a public phone than a mobile or a landline because there was less chance of the call being bugged.

As I sat on the bed waiting for him to come back, it suddenly struck me how weird everything had become. Here I was, sitting in my room at eleven o'clock on a Friday night, while my grandad was outside making clandestine phone calls from a telephone box, trying to find out the connection between a seemingly straightforward missing persons case and a shadowy security organisation known as Omega whose agents might or might not have arranged a riot to cover up a break-in at my mum and dad's office . . .

How had it all come to this? I wondered.

And where was it all going to end?

It was still too much for me to think about. I tried for a while, going back over everything Grandad had told me – trying to understand the bits I hadn't understood the first time round, and trying to make sense of the bits that I had understood – but there was just too much of everything again. Too much information for my brain to digest.

I looked at my watch. Grandad had been gone for about twenty minutes now. I got up off the bed, went over to the window, and looked down the street. The telephone box was about thirty metres away, outside a pub called the Live and Let Live. I could see that Grandad was still in the phone box, and I could also see a bunch of young thugs hanging around outside the pub, shouting and laughing, making a lot of noise. They looked like trouble, but I wasn't worried for Grandad's safety. He might be getting on a bit now, and he's certainly not as fit and strong as he used to be, but he's still more than capable of looking after himself. He's a *very* tough man, my grandad. He's not aggressive or anything, and I've never seen him lose his temper, but I've seen him in action a couple of times. Once when he helped a woman who was getting mugged in the street, and another time when a fight broke out at a football match. Grandad in action is an awesome thing to see. It's not nice – he fights hard, and he fights dirty – but it gets the job done, and sometimes that's all that matters. 'If you have to fight someone, Travis,' he once told me, 'and I don't mean in the boxing ring, I mean a real, life-or-death fight, you can't afford to mess around. You have to hit your opponent before they hit you, you have to hit them as hard as you can – preferably with something other than your fists – and you have to hit them wherever it'll do the most damage. That's all you've got to remember, OK? You put them down as quickly as possible, and you make sure they stay down.'

He was coming out of the phone box now, and even from a distance I could tell that he was deep in thought – walking briskly, his eyes fixed straight ahead, his grizzled old face determined and grim. As he passed by the group of thugs, one of them – a mean-looking guy in a tracksuit – made some kind of stupid remark, laughing and pointing at Grandad. Grandad didn't even glance at him, just carried on walking as if he wasn't there.

I was sitting on my bed again when Grandad came back into the bedroom. He didn't say anything at first, he just quietly closed the door, went over to the window, and stood there with his back to me, gazing out at the night. I was desperate to ask him who he'd just called and what he'd found out, but I guessed he was still thinking things through, and I knew better than to disturb him when he was thinking. So I forced myself to keep quiet and wait. After a minute or two I saw him straighten his back, take a deep breath, and let it out slowly, and I knew then that he was ready to talk.

26

The only thing Grandad would tell me about the person he'd called was that he'd known him a long time, that he was still an active agent with one of the national security services, and that he trusted him as much as he trusted anyone in the security business.

'Which isn't much,' he admitted, lowering himself into the armchair. 'Not that you can blame them for lying all the time. I mean, they're spies, they tell lies for a living. If you spend your whole life lying and cheating and twisting the truth, you get so used to it that you don't even know you're doing it most of the time.' Grandad looked at me. 'That's part of the reason I got out when I did. I didn't want to end up as cold-hearted as the rest of them.' He paused for a moment, thinking about something, then carried on. 'Anyway, I'm pretty sure my contact didn't tell me everything he knows, but I'm also reasonably certain that he didn't lie to me either. That's usually how it works with him. If there's something he doesn't want to tell me, or something he *can't* tell me, he doesn't lie about it, he just doesn't tell me. So the stuff he *does* tell me is almost always the truth.'

'Almost always?' I said.

Grandad smiled ruefully. 'Never trust a spook, Trav.'

'You used to be one,' I said, grinning. 'Does that mean I shouldn't trust you?'

'It's pointless asking someone if you can trust them.'

'Why?'

'Because if you trust them in the first place, there's no need to ask. And if you don't trust them in the first place, you're not going to believe what they tell you. So either way there's no point in asking the question, is there?'

'I suppose not . . .' I muttered, scratching my head.

He watched me for a moment, quietly amused by my confusion, then he lowered his eyes and his face became serious again.

'Do you remember those spy stories I used to read to you when you were little?' he said.

'Yeah . . .'

'Well,' he sighed, 'I've got another one for you. Only this time it's real.'

On 6 April 2009, two days after Bashir Kamal's sixteenth birthday, his older brother Saeed was killed in a suicide bombing in Islamabad, the capital of Pakistan. Saeed had been on holiday at the time – seeing the sights, visiting his parents' birthplace – and as far as anyone knows, he just happened to be in the wrong place at the wrong time. The place was a street market, the time three o'clock in the afternoon. The suicide bomber was a twelve-year-old boy dressed in school uniform. The intended target was unknown. Twenty-one people were killed in the blast, ninety-eight others were seriously injured. Taliban insurgents claimed responsibly for the attack, but according to CIA sources it bore all the hallmarks of an al-Qaeda operation.

'Although I don't suppose it mattered to Bashir and his parents who actually did it,' Grandad said bitterly. 'All that mattered to them was that Saeed was dead. An innocent victim of a pointless atrocity.'

I stared at the floor, my mind numbed. I tried to imagine a twelve-year-old boy, walking through a market place at three o'clock in the afternoon with explosives strapped to his body . . . a *twelve-year-old boy*, just a year younger than me . . . knowing that he was about to die . . . knowing that he was about to kill and maim dozens of people. How could he possibly *do* that? And why? Was he forced, threatened, brainwashed? What was in his head? How did he feel? What did he think about what he was doing?

I couldn't even begin to imagine it. It was so far beyond me, so utterly incomprehensible, that I just couldn't get my head round it.

'I don't know for sure how MI5 got to Bashir,' Grandad continued, 'but knowing the way they work, I'd be willing to bet they started watching him pretty soon after his brother was killed.'

'Why would they watch him?' I asked.

'Well, first of all, they'd want to make sure that Saeed really was just an innocent bystander. They'd have already checked out his background, so they were probably fairly sure that he didn't have anything to do with the bombing. But after all the mistakes they've made in the past, MI5 always double- and triple-check everything these days, just to be on the safe side. Once they were satisfied that Bashir was clean, they would have started working out how to use him.'

'Use him for what?'

'His brother had been murdered. He was angry, vengeful, eaten up with hatred and bitterness. He despised the people who'd caused his brother's death. He'd do anything to strike back at them. At least, that's how MI5 would have seen him. Even if he wasn't angry and vengeful, it wouldn't take much persuading to make him that way. He was vulnerable. Vulnerable people are easy to persuade. All MI5 had to do was convince him that if he worked for them, he'd be hitting back at the people who killed his brother.'

'So Bashir was working for MI5?'

'They recruited him as an informant, and within a year he'd infiltrated a home-grown terrorist cell in London. The members of this group were mostly British-born Pakistanis. MI5 had been watching them for some time, so they knew they'd been visiting al-Qaeda training camps in Iraq and Yemen, and they knew they were planning an attack somewhere in the UK, but they didn't know where or when. Bashir not only managed to get in with the terrorists, he actually ended up living in the same house as them in Stratford. That's how he eventually found out that they were planning to attack the American Embassy in London. Apparently it was a very sophisticated plan, and if it had gone ahead . . . well, thank God it didn't.'

'What happened?'

'The details are a bit sketchy, but it seems like it was a very close thing. From what I can tell, Bashir only just managed to warn MI5 in time for them to stop it. When counter-terrorism officers raided the house in Stratford, the bombers were already making their final preparations. Fortunately they were all there at the time, and every one of them was safely apprehended and arrested, including Bashir.'

'To prevent his cover being blown,' I said.

Grandad nodded. 'He'd done an excellent job, and MI5 were hoping to use him again. And apparently Bashir was quite happy to carry on working for them. But he never got the chance.'

'Why not?'

Grandad sighed. 'Well, this is where it gets a bit complicated. It seems that when MI5 found out that the terrorists were targeting the American Embassy, they decided *not* to share this information with their American counterparts, the CIA. I'm not sure why they wanted to keep it quiet, but I can't say I'm surprised. Security services the world over are notorious for keeping things to themselves. But, of course, the CIA eventually found out about the planned attack, and because it was the American Embassy that had been targeted, they immediately started pressing the British government to release all the details of the thwarted bombing and the arrested terrorists. The way they saw it, because the bombers had planned to attack the US Embassy and US civilians, they should be tried and sentenced in the USA.'

'That would have blown Bashir's cover,' I said.

'Exactly. And MI5 didn't want that to happen. They didn't want the USA to kick up a big fuss about it either. Mainly because that would bring everything out into the open, which they wanted to avoid. But also because the UK needs all the help it can get from the US, and a flat refusal to give them what they wanted wouldn't have been good for international relations. So in the end, MI5 did what they always do. They didn't agree or disagree to anything, they just let their lawyers take over and hoped they could drag things out for as long as possible.'

'Did the CIA know about Bashir?' I asked. 'I mean, would MI5 have told them that one of the arrested terrorists was actually an informant?'

'I don't know,' Grandad said thoughtfully. 'But if you asked me to guess, I'd say no. From their point of view, the fewer people who knew about Bashir, the better.'

'So if the CIA did find out about him, they might actually think he *was* a terrorist?'

'Quite possibly.' Grandad looked at me. 'Are you

following all this so far, Trav? I mean, I know it's all a bit confusing . . .'

I nodded. Although I didn't understand everything he'd told me, I was beginning to see where the story was going. Bashir had tried to do the right thing . . . he'd *done* the right thing. But he'd ended up being an innocent pawn in a sinister game of chess.

I remembered what Grandad had told me about the rivalries between different intelligence agencies. *There were so many different organisations involved, all of them with different strategies and different motives, that sometimes it was almost impossible to get anything done . . . it was* so *complicated and confusing that after a while a lot of us became totally disillusioned.* And that's where Omega had come in, I recalled. A group of intelligence officers who really believed in what they were doing *but were sick of being constrained by all the rules and politics of intelligence work.*

I thought about that for a while, then looked at Grandad and said, 'What happened to Bashir? I mean, what did MI5 do with him?'

'Well, that's the thing,' Grandad said. 'That's where it all went wrong.'

27

It was getting late now, almost midnight, and I could see that Grandad was getting tired. I was kind of worn out myself – physically and mentally – but despite feeling drained and exhausted, there was a part of me that felt strangely buzzy and excited. It was an odd feeling, not unpleasant in itself, but somehow it just didn't feel *right* to be excited about any of this. My mum and dad were dead, and there was a distinct possibility that all this stuff about Bashir and spies and terrorists was somehow connected to what had happened to them. And there was absolutely nothing *exciting* about that at all, not in a million years. Losing Mum and Dad had ripped out my heart. It was *the* worst thing in the world. How *dare* I feel anything other than emptiness and despair? How *could* I? How could I even *think* of anything else?

It was hard to work it out.

Too hard for me.

I wiped my eyes and turned my attention to Grandad.

'Are you OK?' he asked me.

I nodded. 'You were telling me about Bashir,' I reminded him.

'Right . . .' he said hesitantly, a worried look on his face.

'What happened to him after the arrests in London?'
I asked.

Grandad cleared his throat. 'Well, he *should* have
been looked after by his MI5 handler, the agent who'd
recruited him in the first place. The agent should have
made sure that Bashir was safe, and kept him under
wraps until all the wrangling with the CIA and the US
government was over. But that didn't happen.'

'Why not?'

Grandad rolled his eyes. 'Because, believe it or not,
the agent was fired by MI5 after a Sunday newspaper
ran a story about his wife's involvement in some stupid
political scandal. Apparently she was paid a *lot* of money
for some incriminating photographs she took of a so-
called Very Important Person. It's not clear whether her
husband was actually involved in the scandal himself, or
whether he was just duped by his wife into providing
her with sensitive information. Either way it was acutely
embarrassing for both MI5 and the government.'

'MI5 sacked him because he was an *embarrassment* to
them?'

'They not only sacked him,' Grandad said, 'they
also closed down all the cases he was working on and
terminated the contracts of his undercover assets. They
basically washed their hands of him.'

'So where did that leave Bashir?'

'He was given assurances that his undercover work
wouldn't be revealed to anyone, and that his name would

be kept out of everything, but apart from that . . . well, he was pretty much left on his own.'

'They just let him go?'

'So it seems.'

'Is that why he left London and moved to Barton?'

'Probably. From what I can gather, it seems as if MI5 were true to their word. Because for a couple of years everything went OK for Bashir. He moved back in with his parents, concentrated on his boxing, and just got on with his life. No one bothered him, no one was looking for him, no one seemed to know who he was or what he'd done. But then . . .' Grandad shook his head. 'I don't know how it happened. Maybe someone in MI5 slipped up and mentioned Bashir's name by mistake. Or it could be that they've got a leak somewhere. But somehow the CIA found out about his involvement with the Embassy bombers. Once they had his name, it wouldn't have been hard to find out where he was.'

'He wasn't actually *involved* with the bombers though, was he? I mean, just because he lived in the same house as them, that doesn't make him a terrorist.'

'The CIA wouldn't see it like that. When they're dealing with potential terrorists, their principle is guilty until proven innocent. Bashir knew the bombers, he lived with them . . . that's more than enough for the CIA to assume he was one of them.'

'Do you think they've got him?'

'It's possible, I suppose. Anything's possible. I mean,

he might have gone into hiding himself.' Grandad paused for a moment, thinking. 'If the CIA *have* got him though, I don't understand why MI5 agents are still sniffing around. If the CIA already had Bashir, he wouldn't be in Barton any more. He'd be locked up in a cell somewhere in the USA. Or worse.'

'If Evie Johnson's right about seeing Bashir in the Audi,' I said, 'and the Audis are MI5 vehicles, that means that Bashir was meeting with MI5 agents *before* he disappeared.'

'It also means that MI5 are interested in you.'

'Or Courtney. It was her car they followed.'

'They're probably keeping an eye on both of you.' Grandad paused, thinking. 'The way I see it, that can only be because you've been looking into your mum and dad's investigation into Bashir.'

'Why would MI5 suddenly be interested in Bashir again?' I asked. 'I mean, they didn't want to know him two years ago, did they? What changed their minds?'

Grandad shook his head. 'That's one of the things my contact wouldn't tell me. It could be a simple matter of not wanting to let the CIA get their way. Or maybe someone at MI5 realised that letting Bashir go was a big mistake. Or maybe they just needed him again for another undercover operation.' He shrugged. 'I really don't know, Trav. But if MI5 agents are still in Barton, which they obviously are, and they're still interested in anyone or anything to do with Bashir, it's a pretty good bet they don't know where he is.'

'What about the CIA? Do you think they're still here too?'

Grandad looked at me for a moment, then he got up and went over to the window. He casually gazed out, and then without turning round he said to me, 'Come over here.'

I went over and stood beside him.

'Don't make it obvious,' he told me, 'but if you take a look down the street you'll see a white van parked behind a red Mondeo.'

Without turning my head, I glanced down the street. 'The van with the writing on the side?' I said. 'The one that says *J. Block & Sons Plumbing Solutions*?'

Grandad nodded. 'It's been there for a couple of days now. I haven't had a chance to take a really good look at it, but I'm fairly sure it's not a plumber's van.'

'What makes you think that?'

'Well, firstly, as I said, it's been there for two days – all day and all night – and I know it doesn't belong to anyone who lives round here. And even in emergencies, plumbers don't work round the clock. Secondly, if you watch the van for long enough, you'll see that it moves very slightly every now and then. Parked vans don't move unless someone's inside them. And thirdly . . .' Grandad smiled at me. 'I asked my contact to check the registration number. He didn't actually say it *was* a CIA vehicle, but he didn't say it wasn't either.'

I flicked another quick look at the van. 'You really think there are CIA agents in there?'

Grandad put his arm round my shoulder and guided me away from the window. 'It'll just be a surveillance team. There's nothing to worry about. They'll just be keeping an eye on us. I wouldn't be surprised if they've had us under surveillance ever since your mum and dad started looking for Bashir.'

'Do you think Mum and Dad knew about any of this?'

'I honestly don't know, Travis. They didn't usually discuss their cases with me – we had an agreement about that – but I would have thought they'd have said something to me if they'd known that the CIA and MI5 were involved. So I'm guessing that they didn't know.'

I sat down on the bed. 'You don't think . . . ?'

'What?'

'Well, you know, the accident . . .' I looked at him. 'I mean, it *was* an accident, wasn't it?'

Grandad put his hand on my shoulder. 'There's nothing to say it wasn't, Travis,' he said quietly. 'I've seen the official police report, I've spoken to the accident investigators. There's absolutely no evidence to suggest that anyone else was involved in the crash.' He crouched down in front of me and looked into my eyes. 'Even if the CIA or MI5 were following your mum and dad, they had no reason to harm them. Your parents were quite possibly their only leads to Bashir Kamal. So, if anything, they'd want to keep them as safe as possible.'

'But the CIA and MI5 aren't the only ones mixed up in all this, are they?' I said. 'There's Omega too. You said yourself that they'll do whatever it takes to get the job done, no matter what.'

'Well, yes, but—'

'"No rules, no restrictions, no accountability." That's what you *said*, Grandad.'

'I know,' he sighed. 'But at the moment we don't know where Omega fits in to all this. We don't even know for sure that the men in the photographs *are* Omega. So there's no point in jumping to conclusions about anything. We just need to calm down and—'

'Did you ask your contact about Omega?'

He nodded. 'No one knows anything about them. Or if they do, they're not talking.'

'What about the company in Dundee that owns the BMW? Can't Omega be traced through them?'

'The address in Dundee is just a mailing address. There's no actual office or anything there. Smith & Co Digital Holdings Ltd *is* a legitimate company, but it's a subsidiary of a company based in Dublin, and *that* company is owned by a South African corporation, which in turn is a subsidiary of yet another company . . . it's an endless trail, Travis. It doesn't lead anywhere. We don't even know that the BMW has got anything to do with Omega anyway.'

'But we know that the men in the pictures have got something to do with what's going on, don't we? I mean, one of them was at the funeral, one of them came into the office, another one set up the riot—'

'All right, Trav,' Grandad said softly, trying to calm me down.

'Dad wouldn't have taken a picture of them if they didn't have anything to do with Bashir—'

'I know, Travis, OK?' He put his hand on my shoulder again. 'I *know*. And I'm going to do everything I can to get to the bottom of this, all right?'

I breathed out, suddenly realising that for the last minute or so I'd been jabbering away like a lunatic.

'You're tired,' Grandad said gently. 'It's gone midnight, and you've had a long day. You need to get some sleep.'

'But what about—?'

'Listen, Travis,' he said, looking into my eyes again. 'There's nothing we can do right now, OK? We're perfectly safe where we are. The people in the van outside aren't going to do anything. They're just going to sit there all night getting bored out of their minds. In fact, if you think about it, we're actually safer now than we usually are.' He grinned. 'I mean, we've got a van full of CIA agents watching our house. That's not a bad security system, is it? So just forget about them, all right? Forget about everything for now. Tomorrow morning I'll make some more phone calls and see what else I can find out, and when I've done that I'll go and have a look round the office just in case you missed something when you were there.'

'I'll come with you,' I said. 'I told Courtney I'd meet her there at nine o'clock.'

He shook his head. 'You need to stay here tomorrow.'

'Why?'

'Because I don't know if any of us are at risk at the moment, and until I find out, I'm not taking any chances.'

'That's not fair—'

'Fair's got nothing to do with it,' he said firmly. 'You need to understand that, OK? I know it's difficult, but just for now you have to leave everything to me. Do you think you can do that?'

Part of me wanted to argue with him, to remind him that if it wasn't for me he wouldn't even know that anything was wrong. I mean, I'd done all right so far, hadn't I? Why should I have to stay home and leave everything to him? It *wasn't* fair.

But as I looked into Grandad's eyes I could see the depth of his concern. And although he was trying to hide it, I could also see his terrible sense of loss. I knew in my heart that it wasn't right to do anything that would make him feel even worse. So, like it or not, I swallowed my selfish feelings and told him what he wanted to hear.

'Yeah,' I said quietly, 'I can do that.'

'Good,' he said, smiling sadly. 'I promise I won't let you down, OK?'

I nodded, still looking at him. I knew he'd had enough of talking now – I could tell by the weariness in his eyes –

but there was something else I wanted to ask him, and no matter how tired he was, I just had to do it now.

'What's going to happen to Delaney & Co now, Grandad?' I said tentatively.

He frowned, momentarily taken aback. 'Well . . . I don't know. I haven't really thought about it, to be honest. Why do you ask?'

I shrugged. 'No reason . . . it's just . . . well, I was talking to Courtney about it earlier on, and she said she'd be happy to help you out if you wanted to keep the agency going.'

'Keep it going?' he said, surprised.

'I could help you as well. I mean, I know I'd be at school during the week, but I'd still have plenty of time—'

'I've been retired for ten years, Travis,' he said. 'You know that.'

'Yeah, but—'

'I'm too old for it now,' he went on. 'Too old and too useless. I mean, sometimes the shrapnel in my legs hurts so much that I can barely get down the stairs. And you know what I'm like when I get depressed about things . . .' He lowered his eyes. 'I couldn't even talk to you when you needed me the most, could I? What good would *I* be as a private detective these days?'

'You've done pretty well tonight,' I reminded him.

He shrugged. 'All I did was make a phone call.'

'Yeah, but you knew who to call, didn't you? You knew what to do with the information he gave you. *And* you spotted the CIA van—'

'Anyone could have done that.'

'No, they couldn't.' I looked at him. 'You've still got what it takes, Grandad. You could keep Delaney & Co going, I *know* you could.'

He shook his head. 'It's a nice idea, Trav, but I really don't think I'm up to it.'

'You don't have to decide right now. Why don't you just think about it for a while?'

He sighed.

'Please?' I said.

He looked at me. 'Well, all right . . . I'll think about it.'

'Thanks, Grandad.'

'But I'm not going to change my mind.'

'We'll see,' I said, smiling at him.

He smiled back, but it was a tired smile, and as he said goodnight and made his way out of the room, I got the feeling that he was struggling with all kinds of conflicts.

28

I didn't get much sleep that night. There was so much stuff in my head, so many facts and theories and puzzles and possibilities, that no matter how much I wanted to forget about everything, I just couldn't. All I could do was lie there in the darkness, trying to make sense of the chaos in my mind. Where was Bashir? Did the CIA have him? Did MI5 know where he was? Why would they be interested in me and Courtney if they knew where he was? And what about Omega? Did they really exist? If they did, whose side were they on? Were they the good guys or the bad guys? Were Omega looking for Bashir too? Was that why they'd come to the office and staged the riot in North Walk? What did they think my parents knew about Bashir? What *did* my parents know about Bashir? What did 'dem' and 'last day 4th?' mean? And why were Omega after Bashir anyway? What did they want with him?

I kept asking myself the same basic questions over and over again – why? who? what? where? CIA? MI5? Omega? – and I kept coming up with the same empty answers: I don't know. It doesn't make sense. I have no idea what any of this means.

Eventually though, in the early hours of the morning, when my brain had just about had it, it suddenly struck me that I'd been wasting my time all along. The simple truth was that I didn't need to answer *all* the questions. I just needed to answer one. Where was Bashir? If I could work that out, if I could actually find him, I'd have all the answers I needed. It was so obvious that I felt like an idiot for not thinking of it before.

The trouble was, I didn't have a clue where to start looking for him.

Or so I thought.

I'm not sure what time it was when I finally drifted off into a fitful sleep. I remember noticing that the faint light of dawn was beginning to show through the curtained window, so I suppose it must have been around 4.30 a.m. And I'm as sure as I can be that the last thing I was thinking about before I fell asleep was the photograph of the Omega men outside the warehouse. I could see the picture quite clearly in my mind. The men in suits, the BMW and the black Mercedes van parked behind them, the wire-mesh fence, the warehouse. It was the warehouse I was concentrating on. The grey brick walls, the blinds in the windows, the solid-looking doors. Where could it be? I was wondering. Was it in Barton? How many buildings were there like that in Barton? If I could find out where it was, and what the Omega men were doing there . . .

I was almost asleep now. The picture in my mind was fading. The men in suits were no longer there, the warehouse was just a memory, and all that was left of the photograph was the time and date printed in the bottom right-hand corner:

16:08 15/07/13

Eight minutes past four, 15 July.

The day before Mum and Dad died.

I've never really believed that dreams actually mean anything. I think they're just the by-product of a tidying-up process in your brain. You go to sleep, your brain goes into standby mode, and then the tidying-up mechanism goes to work and starts sorting things out in your mind – clearing out all the unnecessary rubbish, sorting stuff out, putting things back where they belong. It's an automatic process, so most of the time you're not consciously aware of it, but sometimes your sleeping mind catches brief glimpses of what's going on. You might see some of the rubbish that's being thrown out, for example, and you might even recognise a few bits and pieces. But your sleeping senses are usually so jumbled up that most of it doesn't make sense.

Sometimes, though, the tidying-up process actually helps you to see things *more* clearly. By clearing away all the clutter in your brain, it allows you to see things that have been hidden away beneath all the rubbish. It's a bit like clearing up your bedroom and finally finding that book or DVD you've been looking for all day. You knew it was in there somewhere, but your bedroom was in such a mess – piles of stuff all over the place – you just couldn't find it.

I could be completely wrong about all this, of course. I mean, what do I know about the human brain? But that night, as my dreams tumbled around in my head, I know for a fact that I found something.

The dream began on the footpath. I was running. Dream-running . . . *running as fast as I can . . . someone's chasing me . . . I don't know who it is . . . I'm scared, desperate to get away . . . my legs are pounding, my arms pumping, but I'm not getting anywhere . . . the dream footpath is moving beneath my feet, like an escalator going the wrong way . . . the faster I run, the faster it moves . . . I can't get anywhere . . . I look over my shoulder to find out who's chasing me and I see Evie Johnson . . . she's wearing boxing gloves and a black suit . . . I smile at her . . . she smiles back . . . and then suddenly she changes into the man at the funeral, the man with the hidden camera, the man with the steely grey eyes . . . Omega man . . . and I'm not on the footpath any more, I'm at the funeral . . . the service is over, the prayers finished, the graveyard tranquil and quiet . . . a light summer rain has begun to fall and people are starting to leave, shuffling awkwardly away from the graves and making their way back to their cars . . . Grandad puts his hand on my shoulder . . . I look at him . . . he's staring straight ahead, his head held high, his craggy old face weighed down with sadness . . . and then he changes . . . his face gets younger . . . he smiles at me . . .*

'Hey, Dad,' I say to him.

. . . I can't think . . . my mind is blank . . . I look over at the man with the hidden camera but he's not the man with the hidden camera any more . . . he's Dad . . .

'Is there anything you want to say, Travis?' he asks softly.

. . . I glance around, trying to work out what's going on . . . I look down at the graves, the two coffins resting in the ground . . . Mum's sitting on one of them . . . she's smiling at me . . . there are so many things I want to say to her, but the words won't come to me . . . I stare at her . . . she looks over at Dad . . .

'I'm not having that thing in my car,' she says, frowning at him.

. . . I turn back to Dad and see him getting out of his car and heading over to Mum with his sat nav in his hands . . .

'We're driving into the middle of London,' he says to Mum. 'You know what the roads are like—'

'I don't care,' Mum says. 'I'd rather get lost than use one of those.'

'But I've already keyed in the address. All we have to do when we get to London is turn it on—'

'No.'

. . . Dad looks at her, about to say something else, but when he sees the expression on her face, he changes his mind . . . he sighs, turns round, takes his sat nav back to the garage

and drops it into a cardboard box full of odds and ends that's sitting on a shelf inside the door . . . and now we're driving off down our street . . . Mum smiling and joking about something . . . Dad fiddling with the car radio, singing along to some pathetic old pop song . . . and I'm sitting in the back seat talking to myself . . .

'Dad's got no sense of direction at all,' I say.

'I know,' I reply.

'He always uses a sat nav when he's driving,' I say.

'I know,' I reply.

'Even for local journeys.'

. . . I look at myself . . .

'Do you understand what I'm saying?'

'Yes,' I tell myself. 'I understand.'

29

I don't know if I woke up immediately after the dream or if I carried on sleeping for a while and then woke up. All I know for sure is that as soon as I opened my eyes, I knew exactly what I had to do. And I knew I had to do it right now.

It was just gone six o'clock. The sun was already streaming in through the curtains, and as I got out of bed and began to get dressed, I could hear birds singing outside. The house was silent, and I was pretty sure that everyone else was still asleep, but I wasn't taking any chances. I dressed as quietly as I could – easing open drawers, tiptoeing around in bare feet, trying not to make a sound. I was also trying to ignore the voice in my head that kept telling me to think about what I was doing. But no matter how hard I tried to dismiss it, it just wouldn't stop nagging away at me. *You know Grandad told you to stay at home today, don't you? You know he'll go ballistic if he finds out what you're doing. Why do you have to do this on your own anyway? Why don't you just wait for Grandad to wake up, and then tell him all about it? Or if you can't wait, just go and wake him up right now. Wake him up and explain everything to him. He'll know what to do.*

There was no arguing with the voice's logic. Grandad *had* told me to stay at home. There *was* no reason to do this on my own. I *should* just leave it to Grandad. It was the only sensible thing to do.

And I was fairly sensible, wasn't I?

I wasn't thoughtless or stupid. I usually did what I was told.

I definitely wasn't the kind of kid who sneaks out of his bedroom at six o'clock in the morning, creeps along the landing in his socks, tiptoes down the stairs, puts on his trainers, grabs a key off the rack in the kitchen, then quietly opens the back door, steps out into the morning light, and hurries down to the shed to get his bike.

That wasn't like me at all.

So why did I do it?

Because today was the third of August, the last day before the 'last day'. And although I still didn't know what 'last day 4th?' meant, I knew it had to mean something. If it wasn't important, Dad wouldn't have written it down. So if I was going to find Bashir and get all the answers I needed, it had to be done today. There just wasn't time to wait for Grandad and explain everything to him. And what's more, if I did leave everything to him, as I'd said I would, he might take too long deciding what to do. He might even decide not to do anything at all. *I don't know if any of us are at risk at the moment*, he'd told me, *and until I find out, I'm not taking any chances.*

The way I saw it, I didn't have a choice.

I had to do what I was doing.

I just *had* to.

Besides, if everything went as planned – and there was no reason it shouldn't – I was only going to be gone for an hour or two. I should be back by seven thirty, eight o'clock at the latest. With a bit of luck, Nan and Grandad would still be in bed then, and Granny Nora wouldn't hear me coming in even if she was awake. So hopefully I could just sneak back into my room without anyone knowing I'd been anywhere.

But what if you are *gone for more than a couple of hours?* the voice in my head said. *What if you're delayed or something? Or what if Nan or Grandad* do *get up before you get back? They're not going to know where you are, are they? They're going to be* really *worried . . .*

'All right, all right,' I muttered, wheeling my bike out of the shed.

Having a conscience can be really annoying sometimes.

I leaned my bike against the shed and went back into the kitchen. I paused for a moment, listening hard, but I didn't hear anything. Everyone was still asleep. I tiptoed over to the message board on the wall, wiped off all the old messages – *GET SPAGHETTI! CALL JOAN. DENTIST WED 2PM* – and quickly wrote out a new one. **NAN, GRANDAD**, I scrawled in big black capital letters. **I'VE HAD TO GO OUT SOMEWHERE. SORRY, I KNOW I SHOULD HAVE WAITED, BUT IT'S REALLY REALLY IMPORTANT. I'LL EXPLAIN EVERYTHING WHEN I GET BACK. LOVE, TRAVIS.**

'Satisfied now?' I asked my conscience.

Not really, it said. *But I suppose it's better than nothing.*

The CIA surveillance team were bound to see me if I went out the front way, so I wheeled my bike down the garden path and left by the back gate instead. The gate leads directly to the footpath, and if you turn left along the path and carry on for about fifty metres, you come to another little path that takes you back up to Long Barton Road.

There was no one around as I cycled along the path, and when I came out onto Long Barton Road, there was hardly any traffic at all.

I glanced at my watch.

It was still only 6.20.

I looked over to my left, gazing back along the road towards the house, trying to spot the white van. I was quite a long way from it now, and I could only just make it out among all the other cars and vans parked along the road. Hopefully that meant that I couldn't be seen from the van either.

I spent a while just sitting there on my bike, checking to see if anyone else might be watching me. Mum and Dad had taught me what to look for – anyone who seems out of place, anyone trying too hard to appear casual, anyone who goes out of their way not to look at you.

I didn't see anyone to worry about. In fact, apart from

the few early-risers driving past in their cars, I didn't see anyone at all.

I looked at my watch.

6.24.

Time to go.

It's not too late to change your mind, my conscience said. *If you turn round right now, just turn round and go back to the house, no one will ever know.*

I pulled out across the road, turned right, and headed off towards Kell Cross.

30

Although some of the older inhabitants of Kell Cross still refer to it as 'the village', it's not really a village any more. It's still got a few old-fashioned village shops, and there's a patch of grass near the bus stop that's officially known as the village green, but the vast majority of Kell Cross is taken up by a massive retail park and a sprawling housing estate that backs onto the Barton bypass. Not everyone likes the park and the estate. There's always someone complaining about something – the village isn't what it used to be, the housing estate 'lowers the tone' of the neighbourhood, there's too much out-of-town traffic these days, the local shops can't compete with the megastores. But, to me, Kell Cross is simply the place where I've always lived. I was born there, I grew up there. I know every inch of it – every street, every lane, every field, every shop. Whether I *like* it or not is kind of irrelevant.

It's where I live.

Simple as that.

Except I *didn't* live there any more.

As I cycled into Kell Cross that morning, following the all-too-familiar route to my house – left off Long Barton Road, left again into Broad Avenue, then right into Dane Street – I realised that things weren't quite so simple any more. I suppose I'd just assumed that everything would be the same. I was going back to *my* house, riding my bike along *my* street . . . why shouldn't everything be the same? And in some ways, it was. The bumps and potholes in the street hadn't changed, the drain covers were still in the same place, the broken kerb where I hopped my bike onto the pavement was still there, and as I pulled up and stopped at my front gate, my house looked exactly the same as it always had too. The white walls, the grey-tiled roof, the cherry tree in the front garden . . .

Nothing had changed.

But nothing felt the same any more. The street I'd walked a thousand times, the house I'd lived in all my life . . .

They'd gone.

All that remained were lifeless replicas.

It was a very weird feeling, and I didn't really understand it, but as I opened the gate and wheeled my bike up the driveway, the sense that I no longer belonged here grew stronger and stronger with every step. It was like being in some kind of parallel universe, a world in which everything is both familiar and unfamiliar at the same time – the sound of the gravel crunching under my feet, the scratches on the wall where I leaned my bike, the brush marks in the paintwork on the front door. I knew it all, but I was a stranger to it all.

When I opened the front door – with the key I'd taken from Nan and Grandad's – and went inside the house, the intensity of that familiar-yet-unfamiliar feeling was so bewildering that I very nearly turned round and left. It was all I could do to shut the door and stay where I was. For a minute or two I just stood there in the hallway, staring at the floor, listening to the absolute silence of the house.

It was *so* quiet.

So empty, so still . . .

So lifeless.

It felt like a house that hadn't been lived in for years.

I didn't like it.

And I hated not liking it. It wasn't right. It wasn't fair to the house. I mean, it wasn't *its* fault that it felt like this. It was just . . .

It was just the way it was.

But I couldn't let it get to me.

I had things to do.

I closed my eyes for a moment, took a few deep breaths, then moved off down the hallway.

There were no obvious signs that the house had been searched, and to an unacquainted eye it probably would have looked perfectly normal, but as soon as I went into the sitting room I knew that someone had been in there. It was just a feeling at first, an instinctive sense that something wasn't right, and it wasn't until I started looking around and examining things more closely that my instincts were confirmed. It was mostly just little things – an ornament slightly out of place, Dad's DVDs lined up in the wrong order, the curtains tied back incorrectly, a settee cushion the wrong way up. I was perfectly aware that on their own these things didn't necessarily prove anything, and it did occur to me that maybe Grandad had moved things around when he'd come here to pick up my stuff. But the more I looked, the more things I found out of place. By the time I'd been through all the rooms, upstairs and down, there was absolutely no doubt in my mind that the house been searched.

I tried to deal with it rationally. I went into my bedroom, sat down at my desk, and did my best to stay calm and think logically. Who could have done it? The CIA, MI5, Omega? And why? What were they looking for? Did they find it? I gazed around my room, trying to stay focused, trying to control my emotions, trying to convince myself that whoever had been in here and gone through my stuff, they'd just been doing their job. It wasn't personal. It wasn't worth getting angry about. Just because someone had been in here and opened the little wooden box where I keep all my special things – the funny little notes from Mum, a photo of Dad when he was a kid, the tiny brass frog with jewels for eyes that Mum's mother had left me in her will.

They'd opened it . . . they'd opened my box.

I could tell.

It wasn't closed properly. The lid gets stuck, and you have to squeeze the sides of the box in just the right place to get it to close. I always close it properly.

Always.

I stared at the box now, my heart pounding, my fists clenched, my head bursting with fury and hate.

Not personal?

Like hell it wasn't personal.

It took a while for the worst of the anger to leave me, and although I was still seething when I left my bedroom and went downstairs, I was composed enough to remember why I'd come here in the first place. I hadn't just come here out of sentiment or curiosity, I'd come for a reason. I'd come here to get something.

The answer to everything.

31

There hadn't always been a door from our hallway into the garage. But a few years ago I'd been sitting with Dad watching *The Simpsons* on TV, and at the end of the opening sequence – the bit where Marge's car chases Homer through the garage into the sitting room – Dad had suddenly pointed at the TV and said, 'We should get one of those.'

'One of what?' I'd asked him.

'A door from the garage into the house.' He grinned at me. 'What do you think, Trav? It'd be pretty cool, wouldn't it?'

I gave him a look. 'Pretty cool?'

'What?' he said. 'What's wrong with that?'

'It's a *door*, Dad,' I said, shaking my head. 'There's nothing *cool* about a door.'

I didn't like to admit it at the time, but when he finally got round to putting the door in, it actually *was* pretty cool. Not that I went into the garage all that much, but somehow it just felt kind of nice having a door at the end of the hallway that led into the garage.

As I unlocked and unbolted the door that morning, then opened it up and paused, peering into the windowless gloom, the memories of Dad came flooding back to me. I gave myself a moment or two, breathing in the familiar garage smells and letting the memories soak in, and then I did what I knew Dad would want me to do – I got on with the job in hand.

When I turned on the garage light, everything was just as I remembered it. Dad's car was still there – his beloved Saab 900 – and it was still surrounded by the kind of stuff that always gets piled up in garages: shelves stacked with tools, cardboard boxes full of God-knows-what, the remains of my old bike, a never-used exercise machine, unwanted books, rolls of wallpaper, cans of paint . . .

There was just enough room for the car to fit in among all the clutter, and Dad had always made sure there was a clutter-free gap on the right-hand side so he could open the car door and get out. It was still a tight squeeze for him to get out of the garage, and the only way he could do it was by edging along sideways with his back to the wall. I was probably about half Dad's size, so it wasn't quite as awkward for me, but it still took me a while to shuffle my way along the wall to the front of the garage. I kept looking around as I went, checking for any signs that the garage had been searched. I hadn't been in there for quite a long time though, and it was all in such a mess anyway that it was hard to tell if anything had been disturbed or not. But if the people who'd searched the house were professionals – and I was pretty sure that they were – I couldn't see how they *wouldn't* have searched the garage, if only to check Dad's car. I just had to hope that they hadn't had the time or the inclination to go through everything that was piled up in here.

I'd reached the front of the garage now.

I closed my eyes for a second and took myself back to the day of the car crash. I pictured the scene outside the house again, the scene from last night's dream – Mum and Dad arguing about the sat nav, Dad sighing, turning round, taking his sat nav back to the garage. And then rather than squeezing his way back into the car to put the sat nav away, he'd just dropped it into a cardboard box full of odds and ends that was sitting on the shelf inside the door.

I opened my eyes and looked at the shelf.

The cardboard box was still there.

I leaned over and looked into the box.

The sat nav was still there.

Dad's got no sense of direction at all.

He always uses a sat nav when he's driving.

Even for local journeys.

I reached into the box, pulled out the sat nav, and turned it on. As I watched the screen start up, I wondered how much battery was left. The sat nav had been lying in the box for almost three weeks now . . .

The sat nav chimed quietly – *bing-bong* – and the opening screen lit up.

The battery icon showed two bars. Good enough.

I pressed the NAVIGATION icon, then MENU, then GO TO.

I paused for a second, mentally crossing my fingers,

then selected RECENT DESTINATIONS and held my breath. A second later, a list of addresses appeared on the screen. As I read the one at the top, I recalled Mum and Dad arguing about the sat nav again.

I'm not having that thing in my car.

We're driving into the middle of London. You know what the roads are like—

I don't care. I'd rather get lost than use one of those.

But I've already keyed in the address. All we have to do when we get to London is turn it on . . .

He'd already keyed in the address. The address they were going to in London. He'd already keyed it into the sat nav.

I was looking at it right now.

Thames House, 11 Millbank, London SW1

It took me a moment to work out why the address seemed so familiar, and even then I wasn't sure if it meant anything or not. The reason I recognised the address, I realised, was that I'd seen it on TV. It was always being shown on *Spooks*, the BBC series about MI5 agents. In the TV programme, when the spies are in their HQ in London, the location comes up on the screen to let us know where they are: *Thames House*, it says. *London MI5 Central HQ.* Of course, that didn't necessarily mean the *real* MI5 was based at Thames House, but it didn't take me long to find out. I took out my mobile, opened up

Google, and typed in *MI5 HQ*.

The entry at the top of the list was from Wikipedia. It read:

> **Thames House** is an office development in <u>Millbank</u>, <u>London</u>, on the north bank of the <u>River Thames</u> adjacent to <u>Lambeth Bridge</u>, designed originally as commercial head offices. Since December 1994, it has served as the headquarters of the <u>UK</u> Security Service (commonly known as <u>MI5</u>).

So now I knew that on the day they died, Mum and Dad were driving down to London to meet with someone at MI5. But what did that mean? Did Mum and Dad know about Bashir's undercover work? Had they found out where he was? Were they meeting with MI5 to let them know they'd found him? Or maybe they *didn't* know anything about Bashir's MI5 connection. Maybe someone at MI5 had requested a meeting with them, possibly to warn them off, and Mum and Dad had agreed to go, but they'd had no idea what the meeting was about.

It seemed as if I'd answered one question – why were Mum and Dad going to London? – but in doing so I'd uncovered a dozen more. None of which I could answer.

'Great,' I muttered to myself, turning back to the sat nav. 'More unanswered questions . . . *just* what I need.'

I wasn't too despondent though, because hopefully I was going to find the answer to everything in one of the other addresses in the RECENT DESTINATIONS list. I didn't know which one it was yet – I was guessing it'd be the second or third – and I wouldn't really know until I'd done some more checking. But for now I just wanted to make sure the addresses were there. I wanted to know where Dad had been the day before he died.

I studied the list.

They were all fairly local addresses, and most of them were in or around Barton. I looked at the most recent entry first, the second address on the list.

Sowton Lane, Barton BR10 6GG

It didn't ring any bells. As far as I knew, I'd never heard of Sowton Lane.

But I recognised the next entry.

42 Roman Way, Beacon Fields, Barton BR11 8TW

The Kamals lived at 42 Roman Way.

I already knew that Dad had been to the Kamals' house, but had he been there more than once?

I started fiddling around with the sat nav menu, looking for anything that would tell me the time and date of a saved destination. If I could find out exactly when Dad had entered the addresses into the sat nav, I'd know which one to concentrate on.

I selected the Sowton Lane address and tried holding it down, hoping for some kind of menu to appear, but nothing happened. I studied the screen again, looking for other options, but I couldn't see anything useful.

It was at that point, just as I was about to go back to the main search menu, that I heard the front door opening.

32

In the second or two between the sound of the front door opening and the sound of it being closed, a whirlwind of thoughts raced through my head. Who could it be? Grandad? Courtney? The police? A neighbour? Whoever it was, they'd opened the door with a key. I'd taken Nan and Grandad's door key. Did they have another one? Why would Grandad be here? Did Courtney have a key? What about the neighbours? Would the police have a key?

I heard voices then.

Muttered voices from the hallway.

I froze, barely breathing, and listened hard.

The voices were low and muffled, and I couldn't quite make out what they were saying, but I was fairly sure there were two of them. And from the sound of it, they were both American.

American? I thought.

CIA?

The surveillance team from the white van?

The footsteps were moving along the hallway now.

Did they know I was in the garage? I wondered. Did they know I was in the house at all? Had they followed me from Nan and Grandad's? Even if they hadn't, they must have seen my bike outside. They must know I was here somewhere. I looked over at the door to see if I'd closed it or not. It was shut. But the garage light was on, and I knew the light was visible from the other side of the door. You could see it shining through the gap at the bottom. So even if they didn't know I was in here, they'd know *someone* was in here when they saw the light.

Should I turn it off?

I reached out for the light switch . . . then stopped.

I could hear them approaching the door now. They could probably see the light already, which meant they'd see it being turned off. Then they'd *definitely* know someone was in here.

What should I do?

Think!

Turn off the light? Leave it on and hope they didn't see it?

I was still trying to make up my mind, my finger poised over the light switch, when I saw the door starting to open. Without really thinking about it, I hit the light switch, quickly slipped the sat nav in my pocket, and began edging round to the front of the car. As the light went off, plunging the garage into darkness, the door swung open and I saw two figures silhouetted in the doorway. The one on the left immediately reached round for the switch by the door, and as the light came back on again, I could see them both quite clearly. The one who'd switched the light back on was a well-built man in his mid-twenties wearing a dark-grey suit. The other one was a short-haired black woman in a leather jacket and jeans.

The woman was pointing a gun at me.

It was a pistol, a handgun. A matt-black automatic.

I couldn't take my eyes off it.

The woman was standing perfectly still. She was holding the gun in her right hand, supporting her wrist with her other hand, her elbows tucked in close to her body.

I was too stunned to do anything. I couldn't move, couldn't speak, couldn't think. I didn't even feel scared, just numbed to the bone. All I could do was stand there like a zombie, staring dumbly at the barrel of the gun.

It was probably only a second or two before the woman lowered the pistol and secured it in a holster on her belt, but it didn't *feel* like a second or two. It felt like for ever.

'It's all right, Travis,' the woman said, holding up her hands to show me they were empty. She smiled, trying to reassure me. 'We just want to talk to you, OK?'

I still couldn't speak. I just stared at her.

She smiled again, trying to look friendly, but the smile didn't reach her eyes. Her eyes were cold and calculating.

'Hey, come on, Travis,' she said breezily, her American accent soft and unthreatening, 'why don't you just—'

'Who are you?' I said, surprised at the steadiness in my voice. 'What are you doing in my house?'

The woman hesitated for just a second, then reached into her jacket pocket. 'We're with the CIA, Travis,' she said, taking out a wallet. 'I'm Special Agent Zanetti, and this –' she indicated her colleague '– this is Special Agent Gough.'

Gough took a wallet from his pocket, and they both opened them up and held them out, showing me their CIA identity cards. Which was kind of pointless. Because even if I could have seen them from where I was standing – which I couldn't – I had no idea what a genuine CIA identity card looks like anyway.

'So can we talk now?' Special Agent Zanetti said, putting her wallet away. 'All we want—'

'How did you get in here?' I said.

She sighed. 'Listen, Travis—'

'You can't just break into my house and point a gun at me,' I said, taking out my mobile. 'I don't care *who* you are. I'm calling the police.'

Zanetti glanced quickly at Gough, and I saw him nod his head and put his hand in his pocket. I thought he might be reaching for a gun, but he didn't take anything out. I held up my mobile, my thumb poised over the screen, letting them know that I meant what I said. Zanetti just looked at me and shrugged, as if to say, *Go on then, call the police, see if I care.* I wondered if she was calling my bluff, just pretending she didn't care, but then Gough took something out of his pocket and held it up for me to see. It was a small handheld device with three stubby little aerials sticking out at the top. I was pretty sure I knew what it was – Dad had shown me something similar once – and when I glanced at my mobile and saw that I didn't have a signal, I knew I was right.

'Mobile phone jammer?' I said to Gough.

He nodded, looking bored, and put the device back in his pocket.

They both started moving towards me then – Zanetti edging her way along the right-hand side of the car, Gough squeezing through the clutter on the left. I instinctively began backing away from them, but there was so little room between the bonnet of Dad's car and the garage door that I simply had nowhere to go.

'There's no need for this, Travis,' Zanetti said, pushing past a pile of boxes. 'We're only trying to help you.'

Ignoring her, I turned round to the garage door and tried the handle. I didn't remember Dad locking the door after he'd put the sat nav in here, but either I'd misremembered or someone else had locked it since, because it was definitely locked now. I yanked the handle a couple of times, just to make sure, but I knew I was wasting my time.

I turned back and looked at Zanetti and Gough. They were getting closer, both of them passing the car doors and heading towards the front wheels. There was absolutely no way I could get past them. And I couldn't run *away* from them . . .

There was nowhere to go.

I was trapped.

They'd reached the front wheels of the car now. A few more steps, and they'd have me.

I saw Zanetti glance across at Gough – *You ready?*

Gough nodded – *I'm ready.*

They both turned back, looked at me, and started moving again – up to the front wings of the car, around the bonnet . . .

I waited until they'd almost reached me, and then I made my move.

33

Using the front bumper as a step, I leaped up onto the bonnet of the car, then straddled up over the windscreen, rolled onto the roof, and started sliding myself towards the back of the car. Gough made a lunge for me, reaching out for my trailing foot, but I was too fast for him. I could hear Zanetti barking out orders as she shoved her way back along the garage wall, and then I felt the car shift beneath me, and I guessed that Gough had climbed up onto the bonnet and was coming after me. I knew he wasn't going to catch me though. I'd taken them by surprise. I'd given myself the head start I needed. All I had to do now was keep going, keep sliding – down the rear windscreen and over the boot – and there was no way they were going to stop me getting to the door.

They didn't even get close.

As I slid off the car boot and sprinted for the door, I glanced over my shoulder and saw that Zanetti was stuck about halfway along the garage wall. She'd got herself tangled up in the folds of a deckchair that had slipped off the wall in front of her. Gough, meanwhile, was crawling clumsily across the roof of the car. When he saw me looking back at him, and realised how close I was to getting away, he heaved himself up onto his hands and knees – in an effort to crawl faster, I suppose – and promptly cracked his head against a metal strut in the garage roof. As he swore loudly and clutched at his head, I gave him a quick smile, then stepped through the garage door into the hallway and shut the door behind me. I slid the bolts shut, top and bottom, then locked the door and removed the key.

I instinctively started to run then, heading along the hallway towards the front door, but after a second or two I stopped. I thought for a moment, then turned round, went back to the garage door, and just stood there, listening and thinking, taking my time . . .

There was no need to rush now, I realised. Zanetti and Gough were safely locked in the garage. The locked door wouldn't hold them for ever, of course, but they weren't going to get through it in a hurry. I had time enough to think things through.

I put my ear to the door and listened. I could hear Zanetti talking, her voice calm and controlled, but I couldn't make out what she was saying. Whatever it was though, Gough wasn't saying anything in reply. All I could hear was a metallic *dong* followed by a dull thump – which I guessed was the sound of Gough jumping or sliding off the car boot – and then another muttered curse of pain.

'Get the door open,' I heard Zanetti tell him.

There was still no reply from Gough, but a few seconds later the door handle turned and the door rattled in its frame. I imagined Gough on the other side, yanking on the handle, trying the door, assessing its strength. I knew it wouldn't be long before he started trying to smash it open.

Every cell in my body was telling me to run, just turn round right now and get out of here as quickly as possible, but I forced myself to resist the urge. *Just think about things for a second*, I told myself. *Think about what you're doing. Do you really need to run away? What's going to happen if you don't? Are Zanetti and Gough going to hurt you?*

Something heavy thumped against the door then, and I saw it bend outwards, straining against the frame. Gough had obviously found something to use as a battering ram.

Time was running out.

Maybe you shouldn't run? I said to myself. *Maybe you should stay here and talk to them after all? You never know, you might get some answers . . .*

Gough hammered the door again, and this time it bent even further.

Can you trust them? I asked myself.

I remembered what Grandad had told me. *Never trust a spook, Trav.*

As the door took another pounding, and I heard the sound of cracking wood, I turned and ran for the front door.

I suppose I should have realised that Zanetti and Gough would have a contingency plan, and I probably should have realised what Zanetti was doing when I'd heard her talking in the garage, her voice calm and controlled. I should have known that she wasn't just talking to Gough. I should have at least considered that she'd told him to switch off the jammer and then used her mobile to call for back-up.

If I'd thought about that, I wouldn't have been quite so surprised when I opened the front door and found myself facing a giant-sized man wearing a black suit and wrap-around sunglasses.

34

One of the first things Dad taught me about boxing was that speed is more important than size. 'It doesn't matter how big your opponent is,' he told me. 'If you're fast enough to hit them without getting hit yourself, you're going to beat them every time.' And he was right. It was how I'd beaten Evie Johnson and countless other kids over the years. But none of those kids was anywhere near the size of the CIA agent standing in front of me. I mean, he was just *massive*. At least six and a half feet tall, huge shoulders, a great solid barrel of a chest, arms as thick as my waist, hands the size of shovels. He was so big that he completely filled the doorway. And the instant I saw him, I knew straight away that it *did* matter how big he was. It was obvious. He was simply too big to punch. Even if I could reach his head, which I doubted, my little fists wouldn't make any impression on that giant-sized skull. And a punch to his belly would be about as effective as punching a whale.

Not that I actually *thought* about any of this.

I just opened the door, saw this man-mountain on the step, and in a split second my instincts told me what to do. *Do what Grandad would do*, they told me. *Fight dirty. He might be big, but he's still just a man. Every man's got a weak spot.*

I backed away, making sure I looked really scared of him – which wasn't difficult – then I turned round and started running down the hallway. As soon I heard him stumbling after me, I quickly changed direction – stopping on the spot, spinning round, and running back towards him. His sunglasses had mirrored lenses, so I couldn't actually see the look of surprise in his eyes, but I was pretty sure he wasn't expecting me to turn on him. Which was why, just for a second, he hesitated.

A second was all I needed.

As he lumbered to a halt and just stood there staring at me, not quite sure what I was doing, I ran up to him, feinted to one side, then dipped my shoulder the other way and kicked him as hard as I could between his legs. I put all my weight and momentum into it, imagining that I was volleying a football into the top corner of the net, and from the sound the big man made as he doubled over and fell to his knees – a deep, breathless, pitiful groan of agony – I knew I'd put him out of action.

He didn't do anything to stop me as I squeezed past him and ran for the door. He was too busy trying to breathe.

My bike was just where I'd left it, leaning against the wall. As I sprinted over to it, my head was spinning with a crazy mixture of relief, disbelief, and sheer exhilaration. I couldn't quite believe that I'd done it. I'd actually *done* it. I'd outmanoeuvred Zanetti and Gough,

I'd neutralised their giant-sized back-up . . .

I'd beaten the CIA.

I mean, how mad was that?

I'd beaten the CIA!

All I had to do now was get on my bike and get going.

But that was the last positive thought I had.

Because as I reached my bike and grabbed hold of the handlebars, I saw that both of the tyres had been slashed to ribbons, and all of a sudden I was back in the real world again. Of *course* I hadn't beaten the CIA. Who the hell did I think I was? They were the CIA. I was just a kid. They knew every trick in the book. I was making things up as I went along. They didn't just have contingency plans, they had contingency plans for their contingency plans . . .

Pull yourself together, I told myself. *So they slashed your tyres. So what? You can still run, can't you? You can still beat them.*

I started to run.

Just as I got going I heard a crash of wood from inside the house, and I guessed that Gough had succeeded in smashing down the garage door. I ran faster, pelting along the driveway towards the gate, hoping to get out of sight before Zanetti and Gough came out of the house. If they didn't know which way I'd gone, I might still have a chance of getting away. I knew the streets round here like the back of my hand. I knew all the little tracks and lanes, the shortcuts and pathways, the places where cars couldn't go. I was already picturing them in my mind as I got to the gate. I was already planning out my escape route – turn right at the gate, along Dane Street, left at the end, then over the road and cut down the cycle path into the kids' playground . . .

I saw the men getting out of the Range Rover just as I was turning right out of the gate. Two more black-suited men, undoubtedly CIA agents, their eyes fixed on me as they got out of their car and started walking along the street towards me. I turned round and started running in the opposite direction . . . then stopped again. Another two CIA agents were blocking the pavement up ahead, about twenty metres away. As I stood there staring at them, they began walking towards me as well.

I glanced back at the other two. They were fifteen metres away.

I heard a shout, looked over my shoulder, and saw Zanetti and Gough coming out of the house.

I was trapped again.

Two men to my left, two to my right, Zanetti and Gough behind me.

Nowhere to go.

And they were all closing fast.

Fifteen metres away . . . twelve . . .

My only option was to just go for it. Just run. Right or left, it didn't matter. Just run at them, get past them, and keep going.

Ten metres . . .

Could I get past them?

Nine . . .

Probably not. Almost definitely not.

Eight . . .

And even if I did . . .

Seven . . .

Don't think. Just do it.

I took a breath, got ready to run . . . and then stopped at the sound of a speeding car. I looked down the road to my right and saw a black BMW with tinted windows racing up the street. It didn't slow down as it approached the two CIA agents, and if they hadn't leaped out of the way at the last moment, hurling themselves into the gutter, the BMW would have run them over.

I watched, bewildered, as the BMW screeched to a halt right in front of me. The rear door was already opening as the car pulled up, and by the time it had stopped – with the engine still revving – the door was wide open. As I stood there, rooted to the spot, a calm voice called out to me from the back of the car.

'Can I offer you a lift, Travis?'

I'd never heard the voice before, but I was fairly sure who it belonged to. And as I leaned over and looked inside, my suspicions were confirmed. The man in the back of the car had short grey hair and steely grey eyes, and he was wearing the same dark suit he'd worn to the funeral.

There were two other men in the car. I didn't recognise

the one in the passenger seat, but the driver was the man with the shaved head who'd called himself Owen Smith. The man who'd come to the office and told Courtney that he was from an insurance company.

I heard raised voices then, people shouting, people running . . . the CIA agents.

The man in the car smiled at me and said, 'I'd say you've got about four seconds left to make up your mind, Travis. Get in the car and get some answers, or stay here and take your chances with the CIA. It's up to you.' He glanced over my shoulder. 'Two seconds . . .'

I stared at him, my mind racing.

There was no way I was getting into the car. I wasn't that stupid. The last thing I'd ever do was get into a car full of rogue security agents, one of whom had violated my parents' funeral, while another had already lied to me about who he was and what he was doing. I mean, how dumb would I have to be to even *think* about getting into a car with people like that?

I sensed rather than heard the movement behind me, and as Gough made a grab for me, looping his arm round my neck, I spun away from him, breaking his grip, and before I knew what I was doing, I'd thrown myself into the back of the car.

It took off like a rocket, flinging me against the back of the seat, and for the next thirty seconds or so, everything went crazy.

The BMW accelerated up through the gears, the

powerful engine screaming, and then almost immediately the driver hit the brakes and the car skidded to a stop again. The force of the sudden braking sent me flying forward, and as I half-rolled and half-slid into the back of the passenger seat, I heard two muffled bangs in quick succession – *bang! bang!* – like the explosive crack of fireworks. The sound seemed to come from the passenger seat, but as I wriggled around and tried to sit up to see what was happening, Shaved Head slammed the BMW into reverse, looked over his shoulder, and started reversing up the street at top speed. The sudden movement threw me off balance again and I fell back down to the floor. With the car still reversing, I twisted round, got hold of an arm rest, and pulled myself up onto the back seat. This time, when Shaved Head hit the brakes, I managed to stay upright.

And this time I could see what was happening.

We'd stopped right next to the CIA's Range Rover, and the man in the passenger seat of the BMW was leaning out of the window with a pistol in his hand. He aimed the gun at the Range Rover and quickly shot out both offside tyres – *bang! bang!*

'OK,' the gunman said, leaning back in and winding up the window. 'Let's go.'

Shaved Head swung the BMW round, mounting the pavement and knocking over a wheelie bin, then he put his foot down and we sped off down the street.

35

'Are you all right?' the grey-eyed man asked me.

Up close, I could see that he was older than I'd first thought. His stony face was lined with wrinkles, his grey hair was peppered with white. Although at first sight he seemed kind of tired and worn out, there was something about him, something indefinable, that simply exuded power and confidence. He was the type of man, I guessed, who was always in control and never needed to raise his voice to get anything done.

'Travis?' he said calmly. 'Are you OK?'

I nodded, glancing out of the car window at the passing fields and hedges. We were heading out of Kell Cross into the surrounding countryside.

'Where are we going?' I said.

'That's up to you,' Grey Eyes said. 'All you have to do is say the word and we'll drop you off wherever you want.' He smiled. 'Within reason, of course. I mean, if you asked to go back to the house in Kell Cross, I'd probably have to say no. But anywhere else – your grandparents' house, the office in North Walk . . . like I said, it's entirely up to you.'

'What if I don't want to go anywhere?'

He shrugged. 'We could just drive around for a while, enjoy the scenery, have a little chat about things.'

'What things?'

'I think you know the answer to that.'

I glanced at my watch. It was 7.55 a.m. Nan and Grandad usually get up around eight, eight thirty. So if I went home right now, I might just get in without them knowing I'd been anywhere. I looked around at the three men in the car. Shaved Head, the gunman, Grey Eyes. Was I safe with them? If it had just been Shaved Head and the gunman, I would have said no. I wouldn't trust those two to tell me the right time. But Grey Eyes was different. I was pretty sure that he was just as ruthless and dangerous as the other two, if not more so, but my instincts told me that underneath it all he was essentially a good and decent man.

The question was – could I trust my own instincts?

Should I take a risk in the hope that I might get some answers?

Or should I just go home?

Of course, there was always the possibility that Grey Eyes was lying through his teeth, and that he had no intention of taking me wherever I wanted to go. I looked at him, remembering Mum's advice about judging people by their appearance. Was I misjudging him? Was the decency that I thought I could see in him just a carefully crafted disguise?

'I'll talk to you on one condition,' I said to him.

'And what's that?'

'You tell me what you were doing at my parents' funeral. Agreed?'

He nodded. 'Absolutely.'

His name, he told me, was Winston – which I didn't believe for one second – and the reason he gave for being at the funeral was pretty much what I'd expected.

'We were aware of your parents' investigation into Bashir Kamal,' he explained, 'and we wanted to find out if anyone else knew about it. If they did, there was a chance they might show up at the funeral.'

'So you just turned up with a hidden camera and filmed everything.'

He looked at me. 'You spotted the camera?'

'Yeah,' I said coldly. 'I spotted the camera.'

Winston sighed. 'You must think I'm very hard-hearted.'

'I try not to think about you at all,' I said, unable to keep the bitterness from my voice. 'Did you see anyone interesting at the funeral?'

He shook his head. 'As far as we can tell, there was no one there who shouldn't have been there.'

'Apart from you.'

He didn't respond to that.

I said, 'Who did you think might turn up?'

'That's a good question.'

'Are you going to answer it?'

'Do you need me to?'

I didn't say anything, I just looked at him, waiting for him to go on.

After a few moments, he nodded slowly and said, 'There

are, as you know, a number of organisations who have an interest in the whereabouts of Mr Kamal.' He paused for a moment, gazing casually out of the window, then carried on. 'We know who most of these organisations are, and we're reasonably certain why they're looking for Bashir, and what they plan to do if they find him. But it's quite possible there are other interested parties out there who we don't know anything about, and who may well pose an even greater risk to Mr Kamal.'

'Who's "we"?' I asked him.

'I'm sorry?' he said, pretending to be puzzled.

'You keep saying "we this" and "we that", as if you represent some kind of official authority, but you haven't shown me any ID or credentials or anything.'

Winston looked thoughtfully at me. I didn't really expect him to tell me anything about Omega, but if I hadn't asked him he probably would have guessed that I hadn't asked him because I already knew about Omega. And I didn't want him to know that. I wasn't sure why I didn't want him to know. But as Dad once told me, you don't show all your cards unless you have to. It's always a good idea to keep your opponent guessing.

'Let me ask you something,' Winston said. 'Would it make you feel any safer if I showed you some ID?'

I shrugged. 'Not necessarily.'

'Did the people at your house just now show you their credentials?'

'Well, yeah . . . they told me they were CIA agents,

and they showed me their ID cards.'

'Did that make you think you could trust them?'

'No.'

'So despite seeing their ID, you still ran away from them.'

'Of course I ran away from them. They broke into my house and aimed a gun at me. What was I supposed to do? Offer them a cup of tea?'

Winston smiled. 'Would you have run away from them if they hadn't aimed a gun at you?'

'What's your point?'

'My point,' he said, 'is that it doesn't make any difference who anyone works for. MI5, MI6, the CIA, the FBI . . . they're all fundamentally the same. Their only real concern is for themselves. Just because someone can show you a badge or a government ID card, that's no guarantee of anything. It's certainly no guarantee of trust, is it?'

'If you say so.'

'You're here, aren't you?' he said. 'I'm not MI5 or MI6 or CIA . . . I don't have any credentials. But you're sitting here talking to me, aren't you?'

'That doesn't mean I trust you.'

He laughed quietly. 'Of course it doesn't. But you don't trust the CIA either, do you?'

'It's got nothing to do with trust. I just don't like people who break into my house and search through my stuff.' I looked at him, studying him carefully to gauge his reaction. 'I don't like people who ransack my parents' office either.'

Winston just stared at me, his face giving nothing away.

I said, 'So you're not going to tell me who you work for?'

'It's not important,' he replied simply. 'All you need to know is that *our* only concern, the *only* thing we care about it, is the safety and well-being of this country and its people.' He leaned towards me, looking me straight in the eye. 'I can't prove that to you. I can't *make* you believe me. You'll have to take my word for it.' He paused, looking even deeper into my eyes. 'We're the good guys, Travis. We do what's right.'

'No matter what it takes?' I said quietly, staring back at him.

He didn't answer me, he just carried on looking blankly into my eyes, as if my words meant nothing to him. But I'm pretty sure I saw his left eyebrow twitch. I held his gaze for a few more moments, then turned away and looked out of the window.

We were still out in the countryside, but we weren't driving away from Kell Cross any more. We'd circled around and were heading back towards Barton through the little villages and winding roads on the north side of town.

'What's your interest in Bashir?' I said, turning back to Winston.

He smiled at me again. 'What's yours?'

'I asked first.'

'Fair enough,' he said, nodding slowly, as if he was thinking about something. 'Although, in a sense, I've already answered your question. Mr Kamal is a British citizen. Our only concern is to defend and protect British citizens.' Winston shrugged. 'What else can I tell you?'

'Do you know where he is?'

'Do you?'

We just looked at each other in silence then, both of us wondering what the other one knew. We both had our secrets, and we both knew it.

'So,' Winston said nonchalantly, 'are you going to tell me why *you're* looking for Mr Kamal?'

'My mum and dad were hired to find him,' I said. 'They died while they were working on the case.' I paused, taking a breath to steady myself. I swallowed, cleared my throat, and went on. 'I'm just trying to finish off what they couldn't, that's all.'

'There's never anything meaningful one can say about the sudden death of a loved one,' Winston said, a look of genuine sympathy in his eyes. 'Not in my experience anyway. Words are never enough. Especially the words of a stranger. But I *do* know how it feels, Travis. Believe me. I know what you're going through.' He paused, staring into the distance. 'I lost both my parents at an early age. I was ten when they died, a little younger than you, but the circumstances weren't that dissimilar. They were driving at night, their car came off the road . . .'

'Your parents died in a car crash?'

He nodded. 'It was a slightly more understandable accident than your parents' . . . if "understandable" is the right word. They didn't just spin off the road and hit a tree for no apparent reason, they crashed because my father had been drinking. He was drunk. It was his fault, no question about it.' Winston looked at me. 'But having someone to blame doesn't make any difference. It doesn't change anything. And it certainly doesn't make you feel any better.'

There was no hint of pretence to him as he told me all this, nothing to suggest that he was making things up. But while I was fairly sure that he wasn't actually lying to me, I couldn't help feeling that something wasn't right. It was the kind of feeling that nags away in the back of your mind, telling you that you've missed something, something really important, but no matter how hard you concentrate, you just can't get hold of it.

I started going over what he'd said to me, replaying his words in my mind – *It was a slightly more understandable accident than your parents' . . . if "understandable" is the right word* – but that was as far as I got before Winston began talking again, and I was forced to turn my attention back to him.

'Listen, Travis,' he said earnestly. 'I admire what you're doing, I really do. And I totally understand why you're doing it. You want to finish the job your parents started. That's very commendable.'

'I'm so glad you think so,' I said sarcastically. 'I mean, your approval *really* means a lot to me.'

'OK,' he said, holding up his hands. 'I probably deserve that.'

'And now you're going to tell me to stop looking for Bashir, I suppose?'

'Not exactly, no.'

'What's that supposed to mean? You either are or you aren't. Not that it makes any difference to me anyway, because there's no way I'm going to stop—'

'Twenty-four hours.'

'What?'

'All I'm asking is that you put your investigation on hold for the next twenty-four hours. After that, you can carry on looking into things however you see fit, and you have my word that you won't see or hear from us again.'

All I could do while he was telling me this was sit there staring at him, pretending to listen to what he was saying, but the truth was that I could barely hear anything above the shouting and whooping in my head – *Twenty-four hours! TWENTY-FOUR HOURS! I knew it! I KNEW it! Tomorrow IS the last day!*

Forcing myself to stay calm, I said to Winston, 'What's so important about the next twenty-four hours?'

'I can't go into any more details, I'm afraid. All I can say is that if you don't comply with our request, you'll not only be putting Mr Kamal at some risk, you could also be putting yourself in danger.'

'Is that a threat?'

He sighed. 'I know you don't think very much of me, but I can assure you that I wouldn't stoop so low as to threaten you. All I'm trying to do is—'

My mobile rang then.

I took it out of my pocket and checked the caller ID. It was Grandad. My heart missed a couple of beats.

'You'd better answer it,' Winston said. 'He'll be worried.'

I looked at him, wondering how he knew . . .

'Go on,' he said, nodding at the still-ringing phone in my hand. 'It's not fair to keep him waiting.'

I didn't want to answer it, but I knew Winston was right.

I braced myself, then hit the answer button and put the phone to my ear.

36

'Hey, Grandad,' I said into the phone. 'Listen, I'm really sorry—'

'Are you all right?' he asked quickly.

'Yeah, I'm fine.'

I heard him let out a sigh of relief. Then, almost immediately, his anger kicked in. 'Where the *hell* are you, Travis? We've been worried sick.'

'I'm sorry—'

'Where are you?'

'I'll explain everything when I get back.'

'You're damn right you will. And when you've finished, I'll *explain* a few things to you.' He sighed heavily again. 'I trusted you, Travis. It's my own fault, I suppose. I should have known better—'

'I'm not a *child*, Grandad,' I said angrily.

'So why are you acting like one?' he snapped.

'That's not fair—'

'Do you think it's *fair* to promise me you'll stay at home and then go sneaking off without so much as a word?'

'Well, no—'

'Do you think it's *fair* to put your nan and me through hell again?'

His words cut into me like an icicle through my heart,

and for a moment I was too stunned to speak. I lowered the phone to my lap and stared blindly at nothing. I was too hurt to speak. I didn't know why. Was he right? Was I really that thoughtless? And why was I so angry? Was I angry at myself for treating Nan and Grandad so badly? Was I angry at Grandad for making me realise how thoughtless I was? Or was I angry at him for simply reminding me of the hell we'd all been through?

It was too much to think about.

It was all too much.

'Travis?' I could hear Grandad saying. 'Are you still there? Travis?'

I slowly raised the phone to my ear.

'Can you hear me?' Grandad was saying. 'Travis? Can you hear me?'

'Yes, Grandad,' I muttered. 'I can hear you.'

'Listen, Trav, I'm sorry, OK? I shouldn't have said that. I didn't mean it. It was just . . . well, you know—'

'I have to go, Grandad,' I said emptily. 'I'll be home soon. I'll see you later, OK?'

'Hold on, Travis,' he said quickly. 'Don't hang up—'

I hit the end key and turned off the phone.

As I put my mobile away and gazed blankly out of the window, I saw that we were approaching the North Road roundabout. My head felt drained and empty, and all I could do for a moment was watch the traffic streaming across the roundabout . . . cars and vans, lorries and buses, great lumps of coloured metal glinting in the morning sun . . .

'It's not easy, is it?' I heard Winston say.

'Hmm?' I said distractedly.

'Being a kid. It's not easy.'

I looked at him. Grey eyes, grey hair . . . a grey man. *What are you?* I found myself thinking. *I mean, really . . . what are you?*

'Are you OK?' he asked me.

'Can I go now?' I said. My voice sounded strangely distant, almost as if it didn't belong to me.

'Where do you want to go?' Winston asked.

I shrugged. 'Anywhere. I just don't want to be in this car any more.'

'Do you want us to take you to your nan and grandad's house?'

'No.'

'Do you want your bike?'

'The CIA slashed my tyres,' I told him.

He turned to Shaved Head and said, 'Stop the car. Pull in over there.'

Shaved Head did as he was told, slowing down and manoeuvring the BMW into a bus stop. As we rolled to a halt I saw Winston glance back through the rear window. I followed his gaze and saw a black Mercedes van pulling up behind us. There was no way of telling if it was the same van I'd seen in the background of the warehouse photograph, but I'd be willing to bet that it was. There were two men in the van. The driver, who was already getting out, was gaunt-faced and wore rimless glasses. I'd never seen him before. The man in the passenger seat was the guy with the goatee beard.

'What's going on?' I said to Winston.

He smiled at me. 'We pride ourselves on our customer service.'

'You what?' I said, frowning at him.

He nodded his head, indicating that I should look out of the rear window again. When I did, I realised what he meant. The driver had opened the side door of the van and was removing a bike from inside. It looked a lot like my bike. When he started wheeling it along the pavement towards the BMW, and I could see it more clearly, I realised that it *was* my bike. Brand-new tyres had been fitted to the wheels, and it even looked as if it had been cleaned.

'All right?' Winston asked me.

'Yeah . . .' I muttered. 'Yeah, thanks . . . but how—'

'We're very resourceful,' Winston said.

The gaunt-faced man had reached the BMW now and was just standing there on the pavement with my bike, waiting patiently.

'Off you go then,' Winston said.

I looked at him.

He smiled. 'It's been nice talking to you, Travis.'

I opened the car door and started to get out.

'Don't forget what I said,' I heard Winston say.

I paused, glancing back at him.

'Twenty-four hours,' he said, looking into my eyes. 'OK?'

I held his gaze for a second or two, and then I looked down and nodded in the direction of his left wrist. 'You need to tighten your watch strap,' I told him. 'It looks a bit loose to me.'

I watched as he looked down at his wrist, and I saw the flicker of surprise in his eyes as he noticed that his Omega tattoo was showing. As he turned back to me with a questioning look, I got out of the car and closed the door.

37

I wasn't entirely sure where I was going when I got on my bike and set off along the pavement. All I knew for certain was that I wanted to be somewhere where the Omega men couldn't see what I was doing. So rather than carrying on in the direction we'd been travelling, which would have made it quite simple for them to keep track of me, I headed off in the opposite direction, back the way we'd come.

That's why I passed the black Mercedes van.

And that's when I noticed the dent in its bodywork.

I wasn't even aware that I'd noticed it at first. I was concentrating on where I was going, scanning the layout of the roads and the roundabout up ahead, looking for any kind of route that was too narrow for cars and vans. It was only when I'd passed the van, and spotted a little footpath that led down into a pedestrian subway, that I suddenly realised what I'd just seen.

A dent over the front-left wheel arch of the Mercedes van.

It wasn't a massive dent or anything, and there was nothing particularly remarkable about it, and for a moment or two I had no idea why I was even thinking about it. It was the kind of minor crash damage you see on cars and vans every day. A dent in the bodywork, crumpled metal, scratched paint . . .

And then it suddenly dawned on me.

Crash damage . . .

Scratched paint . . .

I slammed on my brakes, skidded to a stop, and looked back at the bus stop. The van wasn't there any more. Neither was the BMW. The bus stop was empty. I looked along the road, and I thought I caught a glimpse of the black van in the distance, but it was so far away now that it didn't matter whether I'd seen it or not.

Hoping the memory was still fresh in my mind, I quickly closed my eyes and tried to visualise the moment I'd passed the van and seen the dent over the wheel arch. It was really hard to concentrate with the noise of the traffic filling the air all around me, but I did my best to block it from my mind and focus on what was inside my head. Eventually the image I was looking for came back to me. The jagged-edged dent in the shiny black metal, about the size and depth of an upturned fruit bowl . . . scrapes in the paintwork, flashes of silver showing through . . . and there, embedded in the crudely gashed metal . . .

Was I imagining it?

I held my breath and mentally zoomed in on what I thought I'd seen.

There wasn't much of it, and it was hard to make out with any real clarity.

But I wasn't imagining it.

There were definitely flecks of yellow paint embedded in the gouged-out metal.

Yellow.

The colour of Mum's car.

38

After fifty yards, turn right . . .

It felt kind of weird listening to Dad's sat nav while I was riding my bike. I couldn't actually see the sat nav – I'd put it in the top pocket of my T-shirt – so I didn't have a map to guide me, just the disembodied voice of a slightly odd-sounding woman (who for some reason pronounced the word 'roundabout' as 'roun-t'pout').

After one hundred yards, enter the roun-t'pout then take the second exit . . .

It also felt weird because I kept having this stupid idea that when the navigation satellites that the sat nav used realised I was riding a bike and not driving a car, they were going to instruct the sat nav lady to tell me off for misusing their services – *at the next lay-by, dismount from your bicycle and turn off the satellite navigation device, and DO NOT use it again unless you're driving a car.*

I *knew* it was a stupid idea. It was *beyond* stupid.

But I just couldn't get it out of my head.

Turn around if possible . . .

I wondered if my brain was making me think of stupid things in order to distract me from the things it didn't want me to think about. The complicated things, the painful things, the things that were too hard to think about . . .

Like Mum's car.

And the yellow paint on the Mercedes van.

And the possibility that maybe, just maybe, the two were connected.

I knew it was highly unlikely. The colour of Mum's Volvo may well have been quite distinctive, but that didn't mean she was the only person in the country, or even the county, to own a bright yellow car. There were probably thousands of bright yellow cars driving around, and any one of them could have been involved in a minor collision with the black Mercedes. The collision could have happened months ago. For all I knew, the Mercedes might not have hit another car at all. The dent could have come from anything – a wall, a bollard, a fence . . .

Recalculate . . .

The truth was, there was virtually nothing at all to suggest that the black Mercedes had anything to do with the car crash that killed Mum and Dad.

Just a few tiny flecks of bright-yellow paint . . .

Plus the inescapable feeling that was still nagging away in the back of my mind, the feeling that I'd missed something Winston had said, something really important . . .

Your destination is nearby . . .

I stopped pedalling, pulled up at the side of the road, and glanced across at the street sign on the corner. SOWTON LANE, it said. The sat nav had done its job. I took it out of my pocket and double-checked the address.

Sowton Lane, Barton BR10 6GG

The second-last address that Dad had keyed into his sat nav. I stared at the screen for a moment, imagining Dad entering the numbers and letters . . . then I turned off the sat nav, put it back in my pocket, and gazed around. I'd been reasonably sure that one of the addresses in the sat nav was going to lead me to the warehouse that Dad had photographed, but I'd had no way of knowing which one. The only reason I'd picked Sowton Lane first was that it was the next address on the list after Bashir's. But as I looked around now at the bleak industrial landscape, I felt fairly certain that I was in the right place. The street was situated on the outskirts of a busy industrial estate about three kilometres north of town. It wasn't completely deserted – I could see a few buildings with cars and vans parked outside – but most of the warehouses and small factories in the street were clearly no longer in use. There was a feeling of disuse and emptiness in the air – litter rustling quietly in the street, weeds taking over the pavement, wild grasses growing tall in stretches of wasteground.

It was the perfect place to hide someone away.

Or lock someone away.

As I carried on looking around, I spotted an official-looking poster fixed to some railings at the side of the road. I went over for a closer look. It was a typed message on a sheet of A4 paper in a clear plastic folder. The message read:

FINAL NOTICE OF
INTENTION TO DEMOLISH

Notice Is Hereby Given

That Barton Borough
Council intends to demolish
the properties listed in
the Schedule below (the
Properties). The reasons
for the intended demolition
are that the Properties are
located within the proposed
development scheme for
the regeneration of Sowton
Industrial Estate. The
proposed demolition date is
5 August 2013.

The Schedule

1 Sowton Lane, 1a Sowton
Lane, 2 Sowton Lane,
3 Sowton Lane, 4 Sowton
Lane . . .

The list continued all the way up to 38 Sowton Lane, which I guessed covered every building in the street. I looked at the date again – 5 August – and now I *knew* that I was in the right place. The warehouse *was* here. It was due to be demolished, along with all the other properties in the street, on 5 August. That's what the note on the back of Dad's surveillance photo referred to.

dem 5/8

Demolition, 5 August.

And now, at long last, I knew what the other part of Dad's note meant as well.

last day 4th?

If the warehouse was being demolished on 5 August, the last day it could be used for anything was the 4th.

It felt so good to finally get a definite answer to something that for a few seconds I forgot about everything else. It didn't take long for my sense of reality to return though, and I soon realised that solving the riddle of Dad's note didn't actually help me all that much. I still didn't really know anything.

I didn't know if Omega had Bashir. And if they did have him, I didn't know why. Maybe Winston had been telling me the truth, and Omega *were* just protecting him, defending his safety and well-being. But maybe they weren't. Maybe Winston was lying. And if he was lying about Bashir, maybe he was lying about everything else too.

Maybe this, maybe that . . .

I was letting myself get carried away.

I hadn't even located the warehouse yet. Until I'd done that, and found out if Bashir was actually there or not, there was simply no point in thinking about anything else.

Shielding my eyes from the sun, I began scanning the road up ahead, studying the layout, trying to work out the probable location of the warehouse and the best way to approach it without being seen.

39

I'd looked at Dad's surveillance photograph so many times that I practically knew it off by heart, so it wasn't too difficult to work out that the warehouse had to be on the right-hand side of the street. The tall chimneys I could see in the distance over to my left would definitely have been visible in the photograph if the warehouse was on the left-hand side of the street, and they weren't.

The warehouse had to be on the right.

Which meant that Dad must have taken the pictures from somewhere on the left-hand side of the street. I thought about that for a while, wondering if he'd just parked opposite the warehouse and taken the picture from his car, but that didn't seem likely. The street was too deserted for that. A parked car around here would stick out like a sore thumb. So he must have left his car somewhere else, somewhere nearby, and then . . .

And then what? I asked myself.

How had he got near enough to the warehouse to take photographs without being seen? And where had he taken them from? I gazed over at the buildings on the left-hand side of the street again, wondering if he'd used them as cover . . . and that's when I saw the pathway. A narrow dirt track, with buckled mesh fencing on either side, it ran all the way along the backs of the buildings.

From what I could see, it offered a fairly good view of the buildings across the street.

It wasn't hard to find the entrance to the pathway, and once I'd started wheeling my bike along it, I was pretty sure that this was the way Dad must have come. Although the view across the street was partially blocked by the buildings to my right, there were plenty of gaps to see through, so I was pretty sure I'd be able see the warehouse when I came to it. At the same time I was reasonably certain there was enough cover to see across the street without being seen.

I walked slowly, my head turned to the right, my eyes fixed on the buildings across the road.

It was a strange feeling, knowing that I was quite literally following in Dad's footsteps. My feet were stepping on the very same ground he'd stepped on – the same packed dirt, the same sun-baked grass, the same powdery dust. I was seeing the same things he'd seen, smelling the same smells, taking up the same space. It was a good feeling, in a way. It made me feel very close to him. But it also brought home to me the emptiness of the spaces he'd left behind . . . the spaces where he'd once been.

Him and Mum . . .

Empty spaces.

God, it hurt.

I stopped walking then. Stopped, blinked, and slowly backed up. I'd seen something. At least, my eyes had seen something. My mind had been somewhere else for a while. But now it was back. And now I knew what I was looking at. Directly in front of me, immediately to the right of the path, was an abandoned car-repair place. There were piles of tyres all over the place, a couple of ramshackle workshops, a rusty old car chassis propped up on bricks. The two workshop buildings were quite close together. A rubbish-strewn alleyway ran between them, with a low wooden fence at the far end, providing a tunnel-like view of the other side of the street. It was through this tunnel that I'd seen a flash of grey brick wall and a blur of wire-mesh fencing.

As I peered through the tunnel, there was no doubt in my mind that I was looking at the warehouse from the photograph. I could still only see a narrow strip of it, but that was more than enough. I'd know that grey brick wall anywhere. I closed my eyes for a second, picturing the photograph again, just to make sure. When I opened my eyes and looked over at the car-repair place, I not only knew that I was in the right place, I knew exactly where Dad had taken the photograph from.

I leaned my bike against the fence, squeezed through a gap in the buckled wire-mesh, and headed towards the workshop buildings. The sun was burning bright in the sky, and the hot air was thick with the smell of petrol and oil. As I approached the alleyway, other smells began drifting in the heat – the stink of old rubbish, rotten food – and I could hear the sound of flies buzzing around an overflowing wheelie bin.

I carried on down to the wooden fence at the end of the alley. It was an old fence, cracked and faded, and some of the boards were loose. It was about the same height as me, so I didn't have to stoop down to keep out of sight. But I guessed Dad must have had to. I could see him quite clearly in my mind . . . stooped over, keeping his head down as he approached the fence, his camera in his hands. I was *with* him now. I was right where he'd been. I was taking hold of the same loose board he'd taken hold of . . . we were it pulling it back together, jamming it to one side, looking through the gap, seeing the warehouse across the street . . .

It was exactly the same as it looked in the photograph. The grey brick walls, the blinds in the windows, the solid-looking doors, the small car park surrounded by a tall wire-mesh fence, the BMW and the Mercedes van parked in front of the warehouse. The only things missing were the three Omega men and the time and date printed in the bottom right-hand corner.

16:08 15/07/13

Eight minutes past four, 15 July.

The day before Mum and Dad died.

I looked at my watch. It was six minutes past nine.

3 August.

Today. Right now.

The day before the last day.

I sat down on the ground, facing the gap in the fence. I adjusted my position until I was satisfied I had the best possible view of the warehouse. Then I just watched and waited.

40

An hour and a half later, at just gone 10.40, I stretched the stiffness from my neck, got to my feet, and dusted myself down. I hadn't seen everything I'd wanted to see, but I could have sat there all day and still not seen everything.

And I didn't have all day.

I took a final quick look through the gap in the fence, then I turned round and headed back to the footpath.

I'd taken a few pictures of the warehouse on my mobile, but the camera on my phone isn't that great, and although the straightforward shots I'd taken weren't too bad, the ones I'd taken with the zoom were too blurry to show the details of what I'd actually seen. So as I rode back to Nan and Grandad's on my bike, I kept going over everything in my head, picturing time and time again what I'd seen, making sure that every little detail was safely lodged in my memory.

To make it easier to remember, I split the information into separate categories, and mentally numbered each different category.

1) The warehouse: it was a single-storey building, with a flat roof, a door at the front, and another at the back. I hadn't actually seen the door at the back, but I'd seen the

man with the goatee beard patrolling the yard at the rear of the warehouse, and he definitely hadn't come out of the front door. There were blinds in all the windows, and all the blinds were kept closed.

2) The surroundings: there were patches of waste-ground on either side of the warehouse, and the yard at the rear backed onto scrubby fields that stretched out into the distance. The fields were surrounded by hedges. The car park at the front of the building and the yard at the back were enclosed behind wire-mesh fencing that was approximately three metres high. The locked double gates that led into the car park were also about three metres high.

3) Sowton Lane: the street itself was barely used. In all the time I was there, I saw no more than a dozen passing vehicles, and no pedestrians at all.

4) The occupants: there were at least seven men in the warehouse. Winston (Grey Eyes), Shaved Head (the one who called himself Owen Smith), Goatee, the gunman (the one who'd shot out the tyres on the CIA cars), the gaunt-faced man, and two men I'd never seen before: a pale-skinned man with reddish hair, and a big muscle-bound guy with nasty-looking eyes. Three of them had come out of the warehouse while I was there. Goatee had spent five minutes patrolling the back yard; the big guy had come out and fetched something from the back of the van; and on two occasions Gaunt Face had wandered out and strolled round the car park smoking a cigarette.

The other four had stayed inside, but they'd all shown their faces at a window at least once, either peeking out from between the blinds or pulling the blind halfway up for a more thorough look around.

5) Conclusion: there was no real evidence that Bashir was in the warehouse. I hadn't seen him. I hadn't seen anything that actually proved he was in there. But I was 99 per cent sure that he was. Everything pointed to it. Dad's surveillance photograph, Omega's interest in Bashir, the behaviour of the seven men in the warehouse – patrolling the building, constantly on the lookout, keeping the blinds closed all the time. It all made sense if Bashir *was* in the warehouse.

There was still a lot that didn't make sense though. What was he doing there? Why did Omega have him? Were they protecting him? Or was he their prisoner? How long had he been at the warehouse? Had he been there when Dad had taken the photograph? And, if he had, why was he still there now? Why had he been there for almost three weeks, maybe even longer?

I didn't have any answers.

But it wasn't important now.

All I cared about now, as I carried on cycling back to Nan and Grandad's, was making sure I memorised everything. I could think about what it all meant later. The facts were all that mattered right now.

The facts.

The details.

I hit the rewind button in my head and started going over everything again. 1) The warehouse: single-storey building, flat roof, door at the front, another at the back . . .

41

I realise now that part of the reason I was so intent on memorising everything I'd seen at the warehouse was that it helped take my mind off what was going to happen when I got back to Nan and Grandad's. I really didn't want to think about that. It was bad enough knowing that they were going to be upset with me. What was worse was that I didn't know what that would mean. It would have been different if I'd been going home to Mum and Dad, knowing that *they* were going to be upset with me. I still would have felt anxious and worried, of course, but at least I would have known what to expect. The hurt in Mum's eyes, the quiet firmness of Dad's voice, their obvious disappointment in me . . . I would have *known* that. I would have known how bad I was going to feel.

But I wasn't going home to an upset Mum and Dad. I was going home to an upset Nan and Grandad, and I really didn't know what that was going to be like. Which, to be honest, was kind of scary. So rather than actually thinking about it, I suppose I just blocked it all out and concentrated on memorising things about the warehouse instead.

I don't think I was aware of what I was doing.

In fact, I *know* I wasn't.

Because I don't really remember riding back from the

warehouse at all. It was almost as if I was in a trance. I vaguely recall arriving back at Nan and Grandad's house . . . getting off my bike . . . putting it away in the shed . . . but I can't even remember if I came in the front way or through the back gate. I was so fixated on what I'd seen at the warehouse that I was still mumbling away to myself about it as I made my way from the shed to the back door – *How many men did you see? Seven. Who were they? Shaved Head, Winston, Goatee, Gunman, Gaunt Face . . .*

Then the back door opened, and I looked up and saw Nan standing there, her eyes brimming with tears. And suddenly everything became real again.

'Oh, Travis!' she cried, throwing her arms round me. 'Thank *God* you're back. We've been *so* worried. Where have you *been*?'

She was squeezing me so hard that I could hardly breathe, let alone say anything.

'It's all right,' she said tearfully, still hugging the life out of me. 'Everything's all right . . . you're OK now . . .' She suddenly let go of me, put her hands on my shoulders, and held me at arm's length. 'You *are* all right, aren't you, Travis?' she asked, staring intensely into my eyes. 'Please tell me you're all right . . . that's all I need to know—'

'I'm fine, Nan,' I told her. 'Honestly, I'm OK.' I wiped a tear from my eye. 'I'm *really* sorry, Nan. I shouldn't have—'

She grabbed hold of me again, pulling my head to her shoulder and holding me so tightly that this time I really couldn't breathe. But I didn't mind. With my face pressed up against her tear-stained skin, and her strong hand gripping the back of my head, I somehow felt like myself again – my *real* self – and just for a moment I didn't have to think about anything or try to understand anything. I didn't even have to know what I was feeling. All I had to do was feel it.

Whatever it was.

I couldn't hold my breath for ever though, and eventually I had to lift my head from Nan's shoulder and gulp down some air. That's when I saw Grandad. He was standing in the kitchen doorway behind Nan, staring quietly into my eyes. He looked tired, his face lined with worry and stress. But what struck me the most was the way he was looking at me. I knew that look. I'd seen it in Dad's eyes when he'd been upset with me. That strange mixture of disappointment and relief, pain and concern, despair and understanding . . .

I *knew* it.

And although that didn't make things any easier, it somehow felt OK.

'I'm sorry, Grandad,' I said, gently stepping out of Nan's embrace.

He nodded. 'I'm sorry too.'

'I don't know what I was thinking,' I said, shaking my head. 'Well, I *do* . . . but I just . . . I don't know . . .

it was just . . .' I let out a sigh, not really knowing what I was trying to say.

'Are you hungry?' Grandad said.

I looked at him, slightly surprised by the question. 'Well, yeah,' I said hesitantly, 'but I really need to talk to you about—'

'Oh, we're going to talk about things,' he said ominously. 'Don't you worry about that. We've got a *lot* of talking to do. But before we start, you need to get some food inside you.'

I wanted to tell him that there wasn't time for food, that I had to talk to him right now, before it was too late. But even as I opened my mouth to speak, and he angled his head and gave me a don't-you-*dare*-say-anything look, I knew it wasn't a good idea to start arguing with him now.

Besides, I *was* pretty hungry.

In fact, I was starving.

42

After Nan had made me some bacon and eggs and a big plate of toast, and I'd scoffed it all down as quickly as I could, I went into the sitting room and found Grandad waiting for me in his armchair. He gestured for me take a seat, and I sat down on the settee. I'd kind of imagined that he'd want to talk to me on my own, so I was a bit surprised when Nan came in and sat down next to me, but I was really glad that she did.

I looked at her.

She half smiled at me, then turned to Grandad.

'Nan knows what's going on,' he told me. 'I explained everything to her this morning.'

'Right,' I said.

'So from now on,' he continued, 'we're all in this together, OK?'

I nodded.

He glanced at Nan, then looked back at me. 'Listen, Travis . . . about what I said on the phone—'

'It doesn't matter—'

'Yes, it does. It was an inexcusable thing to say. Utterly selfish and thoughtless. I'm truly sorry for hurting you.'

'I deserved it,' I said. 'I *did* put you through hell again. If anyone was selfish and thoughtless, it was me.' I looked from Grandad to Nan, then back to Grandad again.

'I know I shouldn't have sneaked out without saying anything. I mean, I *know* it was wrong. I know it was really stupid—'

'You can say that again,' Grandad muttered.

'All right,' Nan said quietly, shooting a quick look at Grandad. 'Let's leave the recriminations for now, shall we?' She looked at me. 'You need to tell us where you went, Trav, OK? Forget about all the rights and wrongs, just tell us where you've been and what you've been doing.'

It was a lot to tell, but by the time I'd finished I was pretty sure I'd told them everything. The only thing I didn't mention was my suspicion about the yellow paint on the Mercedes van. And I only kept that to myself because it *was* just a suspicion, and a pretty vague one at that, and I knew what Grandad would say about it anyway. *I've seen the official police report*, I remembered him telling me. *I've spoken to the accident investigators. There's absolutely no evidence to suggest that anyone else was involved in the crash.*

As I began reeling off all the details I'd memorised about the warehouse, I couldn't help feeling kind of pleased with myself. I'd done a pretty good job, I thought. I'd been thorough, determined, patient. I'd behaved like a professional private investigator. Mum and Dad would have been proud of me.

But the comfort that gave me didn't last very long.

I'd only just begun talking about the occupants of the warehouse when Grandad brought me back to earth with a cold hard thump.

'I definitely saw seven of them in there,' I was saying, 'but there might be more. The seven I saw were . . .' I started counting them off on my fingers. 'The one who calls himself Winston, the one with the goatee beard, the one with the shaved head—'

'All right, Travis,' Grandad said. 'That's enough.'

'I haven't finished yet,' I said, carrying on. 'The man with the gun was there, the one who shot out the tyres, and the gaunt-faced man from the van—'

'Look at me, Travis,' Grandad said firmly.

I glared at him. 'I'm trying to tell you—'

'I know what you're trying to do,' he said calmly. 'But you need to stop it right now.'

'*Stop it?*'

He nodded. 'No more, OK? This has gone far enough.'

'What do you *mean*?' I said, frowning at him in disbelief. 'We *know* where Bashir is now. We know that Omega have got him. All we have to do now is—'

'We don't *have* to do anything, Travis. We're not *going* to do anything.'

'But if we don't—'

'That's *enough*!'

Grandad had never raised his voice to me before, and the sudden shock of it stunned me into silence. I stared at him, awed by the burning intensity of his eyes.

'Now you *listen* to me,' he said through gritted teeth. 'Just *listen*, OK?' He paused, taking a few moments to compose himself. 'This isn't some sort of game, Travis,' he said. 'You have to understand that. This is the real world. And the real world can be a dirty and dangerous place. You might think you can deal with it, but I can assure you that you can't. You were lucky today. *Very* lucky. You had a gun pointed at you. You outfought a man twice your size. You got into a car with three trained killers and they let you out when you asked them to.' Grandad looked into my eyes. 'Do you realise what *could* have happened? What probably *should* have happened? I mean, just *think* about it, Travis. Think about what *could* have happened to you today. Do you understand what I'm saying?'

I nodded.

'Life's tough enough as it is without taking unnecessary risks,' he continued, leaning back in his chair. 'The only people who go looking for danger are fantasists or fools.'

'What about you?' I said quietly.

'Me?'

'You were in the army. That's a dangerous thing to do, isn't it?'

'That's different.'

'Why?'

'It was my job. I was specially trained, I knew what I was doing.'

'Then you became a private investigator.'

'That's right.'

'Another dangerous thing to do.'

He just looked at me.

I said, 'No one *forced* you to be a soldier, did they? I mean, you chose a career that you knew was going to be dangerous—'

'It was my job,' he repeated calmly. 'Just as it was your mum and dad's job to find Bashir Kamal. But it *isn't* yours. That's all I'm trying to say, Trav. Whatever's going on with Bashir, whatever happens or doesn't happen to him . . . it's nothing to do with you. And even if you think it is, I'm *not* going to let you risk your life – or anyone else's – over something that doesn't concern us.'

'But we can't just leave Bashir at the warehouse.'

'Why not?'

'Because we don't know what's going to happen to him—'

'We don't *know* what's going to happen to anyone.'

I couldn't think of an answer to that, so I just scowled at him.

'I'm sorry, Travis,' he said, 'but all I care about is looking after you and Nan and Granny Nora. And right now the only way I can do that is by keeping the CIA and MI5 out of our lives. If that means leaving Bashir at the warehouse . . . well, I'm sorry, but that's how it has to be.' He leaned forward in his chair. 'Look, even if he *is* at the warehouse – and it's quite possible he's not – there's nothing we can do for him anyway. You said

yourself that there are at least seven Omega men there . . .'
He shrugged. 'What chance would we have against seven
trained men? Besides, if they *are* just protecting him from
the CIA . . . well, good for them.'

'Yeah, but what if they're not?' I said. 'What if they're
working for a terrorist group? I mean, just because Omega
claim they're working for the good of the country, that
doesn't mean they are, does it? You said yourself that no
one knows anything about them. They could be a bunch
of mercenaries for all we know, working for anyone who
pays them. What if the terrorists found out that Bashir
was an MI5 informant and hired Omega to kidnap him?
They could be keeping Bashir at the warehouse until they
hand him over.' I looked at Grandad. 'And they have to
hand him over tonight or tomorrow morning because
the warehouse is going to be demolished on Monday.
That's why Winston asked me not to do anything for
twenty-four hours.'

'Not necessarily,' Grandad said, without much
conviction. 'They might just be moving him somewhere
else. Somewhere safer. And anyway—'

'Why don't we call the police?' I said. 'If we're not
going to do anything to help Bashir, we should at least
let the police know what's going on.'

Grandad sighed again. 'You still don't get it, do you?'

'Get what?'

'The only safe thing for us to do is nothing. If we go
anywhere, talk to anyone, make any phone calls . . . if

we do anything at all that connects us to this case, we're going to have a whole load of people crawling all over us – the CIA, MI5, counter-terrorist units, Special Branch, Omega. If Omega *are* working for a terrorist group, and we start poking our noses into *their* business . . .' Grandad looked at me. 'Do you really want to take that risk?'

I reluctantly shook my head. I didn't like admitting he was right, but there was no getting away from the fact that he was. Everything he was saying made perfect sense. And I knew I just had to accept that. As I gazed down at the floor, feeling kind of deflated, I felt Nan's hand on my knee.

'I know it hurts, love,' she said tenderly. 'But we can't always follow our hearts, no matter how good our intentions are. Sometimes, whether we like it or not, we just have to do whatever's necessary to keep ourselves going.'

I wasn't exactly sure what Nan meant, but as I trudged up the stairs to my room – feeling physically and mentally exhausted – my only intention was to lie down and close my eyes and empty my head of everything.

I was through with thinking.

I'd had enough of it.

I just wanted to sleep.

43

After about ten minutes of doing what I *thought* I wanted to do – lying on the bed with my eyes closed, trying not to think about anything – I finally gave up and admitted to myself that it wasn't what I wanted to do after all. And even if it was, it wasn't going to happen.

You can't stop yourself thinking about something that means everything to you, can you? And if you can't stop thinking about it, you can't just close your eyes and go to sleep, no matter how exhausted you are. You have to keep going. Whether you like it or not, you just have to do whatever's necessary . . .

Was that what Nan had meant?

Probably not.

To be honest, I wasn't sure what anything meant any more.

It was two o'clock in the afternoon. I'd had about an hour's sleep the night before, and I'd been whizzing around doing all kinds of crazy stuff since six o'clock this morning. My legs were tired, my arms were sunburnt, my head was throbbing like a pneumatic drill.

How was I supposed to know what to do about anything?

How was I supposed to *know*?

Why couldn't I just accept that Grandad was right?

Why couldn't I just forget about Bashir Kamal? Of course I'd *like* to help him, but if helping him meant putting Nan and Grandad in serious danger, why should I take that risk? I didn't know Bashir, did I? I'd never even met him. So why did it seem to matter so much what happened to him? Why *did* it seem to mean everything to me?

It was only after I'd thought about that for a while that the ultimate truth finally dawned on me: Bashir Kamal *didn't* mean everything to me. Of course he didn't. He only *seemed* to. It was Mum and Dad who meant everything to me. They *were* everything. Everything I'd been doing, everything I'd been trying to do, was all for them. For their lives and for their deaths. That was it.

There wasn't anything else.

My mum and dad were everything.

I sat up, rubbed the back of my head, and looked around for my laptop. It was on the bedside table. I reached over and picked it up, turned it on, and logged on to the Internet. I knew what it was that I'd missed now. That nagging feeling I'd had that I'd missed something Winston had said, something really important . . .

I knew what it was.

At least, I thought I did.

It was something that wasn't there.

I opened Google and went looking for it.

The trouble with looking for something that isn't there is knowing how to tell if you've found it or not. You can keep looking for it in different places, keep finding it's not there, but how do you know it's not somewhere else? How many different places do you have to check before you can be 100 per cent sure it's not anywhere?

The answer, I suppose, is that you can never be 100 per cent sure.

You can't keep looking for ever.

But you *can* keep looking until you're 99 per cent sure.

It took me just over an hour.

And then, at last, I knew what I had to do. I had to go back to the warehouse. I wished there was another way, but there wasn't. I had to go back to the warehouse, and I had to do it tonight.

I spent the rest of the afternoon working out a plan of action. There was a lot to think about and a lot to be done, and I didn't have very much time. It was almost three thirty now. The sun would start going down in around five hours' time, and by nine thirty it would be dark. I had six hours to get everything ready.

First of all, I checked out the warehouse again on my laptop. Using a combination of Google Earth and Street View, I studied the whole area as thoroughly as possible – the surrounding fields, the pathway, the car park, the geography of the streets around Sowton Lane. The views weren't completely up to date, of course, but they showed me what I needed to know.

The next thing I had to work out was how to contact Mason Yusuf without anyone finding out. I didn't know for sure if our landline was being tapped (by the CIA, MI5, and/or Omega), but I got the feeling from Grandad that it probably was. Why else would he have used the telephone box when he'd called his contact the other day? As he'd also been reluctant to use my mobile, I had to assume that he didn't think that was safe either.

I went over to the window and looked down the street. The white van was still there, still in the same place. I wondered briefly if the CIA agents inside were the same ones I'd encountered at my house. Special Agents Zanetti and Gough, the giant-sized man I'd kicked where it hurts . . .

Probably not, I thought, turning away from the window and going back over to my bed. Not that it mattered. Whoever was in there, they'd see me if I tried to use the telephone box. They might even be monitoring it anyway.

Which left me a choice of either texting Mason or emailing him.

I knew that emails and texts can be traced quite easily once they've been sent, but I was less sure about whether they can be monitored *while* they're being sent. I guessed it wasn't impossible though. There are all kinds of ways of hacking into email accounts and mobile phones – viruses, malware, Trojan horses – and I knew it wasn't beyond the CIA or MI5 to have somehow gained access to my phone. If they could do it, so could Omega.

But what other choice did I have? I definitely couldn't phone Mason, and I didn't haven't time to go round and see him. So if I wanted to get in touch with him, I had to either text him or email him.

I thought about it for a while, trying to weigh up the pros and cons of both options, but there were so many unknown factors to consider that it was really hard to make a rational decision. So in the end I just went with my gut-feeling instead.

Text.

I took out my phone, found Mason's number, and got started.

It was a long and laborious process. First of all I had to explain the whole situation to Mason, tell him what I was planning to do, and ask him if he was willing to help me. Then after he'd texted back – *no prob. wot u wnt me 2 do?* – I had to spell out exactly what I wanted him to do. Then I had to wait while he made some phone calls, and after that we had to figure out *how* to do what we were planning to do . . .

I'd never texted so much in my life.

Finally, at 5.49 p.m., Mason's last message came through:

got 25ish def and 10or12 more poss ok?

I replied:

brilliant! cu at 10.

Then all I had to do was wait.

44

I'm not bad at waiting. I once sat in a parked car with Dad for three hours, just waiting for a man (who was falsely claiming compensation for a serious leg injury) to come out of his house and go jogging. On another occasion I spent nearly four hours on a park bench with Mum, just waiting to get a photograph of a recently sacked gardener who (the town council suspected) had been stealing koi carp from their ornamental pond.

So it's not as if I don't have any experience of 'just waiting'.

But that night it was almost too much to bear. As the early evening crawled into the summer dusk, and I waited for the sun to go down, the time seemed to pass so incredibly slowly that every minute felt like an hour. I looked at my watch so often that the exact timing of everything that happened is still seared into my memory.

6.32 p.m. I suddenly remembered that I'd arranged to meet Courtney in the office that morning, and that unless she'd called here and spoken to Nan or Grandad, she wouldn't know why I hadn't shown up.

I wondered if I should text her to apologise and explain.

And then I started wondering if I should let her know what I was planning to do with Mason, maybe even ask her to come along with us. I was pretty sure she'd like to be involved – or, at least, part of her would – and there was no question she'd be an enormous help. I just wasn't sure whether I could trust her or not. It wasn't that I doubted her loyalty. I knew she'd do almost anything for me. But I also knew that she felt responsible for me. So although the crazy-and-adventurous Courtney would love the idea of what I was about to do, the grown-up-and-responsible Courtney would quickly realise there was no way she could let me do it. If I told her what I was planning, she'd try to persuade me to change my mind, and then – having failed – she'd reluctantly call Grandad and tell him everything.

And that would be the end of it.

I couldn't let that happen.

6.56 p.m. Nan came upstairs to see how I was doing. I told her I was fine.

'Do you want anything to eat?' she asked me. 'We're just going to have sandwiches, but I don't mind cooking something if you're hungry.'

'I'm a bit tired, Nan,' I said. 'I think I'll just get some sleep, if that's OK.'

'Of course it is. Do you want me to make you some cocoa?'

'No, thanks.'

'All right,' she said, smiling. 'Well, I'll leave you to it then.'

7.02 p.m. I opened my laptop and started a game of chess.

But my heart wasn't really in it.

And neither was my brain.

Five minutes later, the game was over.

Checkmate in ten moves.

7.44 p.m. I went to the bathroom. As quietly as possible, I opened the window, leaned out, and double-checked the drainpipe. Could I reach it from here? Check. Did it go all the way down to the ground? Check. Was it sturdy enough to take my weight? Just about, I guessed . . . although it didn't look quite as secure as I'd thought.

Don't worry about it, I told myself, closing the window. *You'll be all right.*

I flushed the toilet, ran the hot tap for a while, then left.

As I was heading back along the landing, I heard Granny Nora calling out to me from her room.

'Travis? Is that you?'

For a second I was tempted to ignore her. Just pretend I hadn't heard her, go back to my room, and shut the door. But I knew I wasn't going to do that. I couldn't. It was Granny Nora . . . I couldn't *ignore* Granny Nora.

'Travis?' she called out again.

I paused for a moment, let out a sigh, then opened her door and went inside.

45

When Granny Nora's arthritis had started getting really bad, Grandad had fixed up the house to make things as easy as possible for her. He'd put in an en-suite bathroom so she didn't have to keep shuffling along the landing to the toilet, and although he'd rigged up a stairlift for her too, so she could still get downstairs even when her arthritis was really playing up, he'd also built a little kitchen area into her room, with a microwave and a mini-fridge and stuff, so she didn't have to come downstairs to eat if she didn't want to. Basically, her room was fitted out like a self-contained flat.

She was in her usual position when I went in that evening – sitting in her ancient armchair by the window. Her laptop and her mobile phone were in easy reach on the table beside her, together with a pile of crime novels, a packet of biscuits, and her iPod. A paperback book was resting in her lap, and her binoculars were on the windowsill. Granny Nora likes to know what's going on, and when she's not reading or listening to music or surfing the web, she's quite happy just sitting by the window watching the world through her binoculars.

'Hey, Granny,' I said, going over to her.

'What?' she replied, cupping her hand to her ear.

'Turn your hearing aid on,' I told her, tapping my ear.

'Oh, right,' she said, grinning as she fiddled with her hearing-aid controls. 'Silly me. I forgot again.'

'It's funny how you keep "forgetting" to turn on your hearing aid, but you never seem to forget anything else.'

'What?' she said, cupping her ear again.

'I said it's funny—'

She grinned again, and I realised she'd got me.

'Yeah, good one, Gran,' I said, smiling at her.

'I might be old and decrepit,' she said, 'but I'm still too quick for you.'

I've always loved the sound of Granny Nora's voice. She was born and raised in Dublin, and there's something kind of comforting about her strong Irish accent, something that never fails to lift my spirits. Even when she's moaning about things, which she does a *lot* – cursing about this, griping about that, effing and blinding about her 'stupid bloody arthritis' – I still love listening to her. She knows more rude words than anyone I've ever met. And unlike most adults, she doesn't stop using them when I'm around. 'They're only *words*, for goodness sake,' she'd told Mum once (although she'd used a *slightly* stronger word than 'goodness'). 'The boy's not a baby, is he?' she'd added. 'He's going to hear a lot worse in his time. He might as well get used to it.'

The memory of Mum trying to stifle a laugh at this brought a smile to my face. Mum and Granny Nora had always been really close, and although Gran was my dad's grandmother – and they didn't actually *look* anything like each other – there'd always been something about Gran that reminded me of Mum.

I looked at Granny now, trying to see my mum in her, but all I could see was something my mum would never be: an old woman. My mum would never be an old woman. She'd never be a nan or a granny. She'd always be thirty-seven years old.

If *that* wasn't unfair, I didn't know what was.

'Sit down, Travis,' Granny said gently. 'Talk to me for a while.'

I hesitated, not sure what to say. I loved being with Granny, but I didn't really feel like talking right now.

'Just sit with me for five minutes then,' she said, as if she could read my mind. 'I'm not *that* boring, am I?'

'You're never boring, Gran,' I told her, settling down in a cushioned wicker chair on the other side of the window. 'You might be really annoying sometimes, but you're definitely not boring.'

'Well, that's good to know,' she said.

'How are you feeling today?'

'You don't want to know how I'm feeling.'

'I wouldn't ask if I didn't.'

'Yes, you would. You're just being polite.'

I sighed, shaking my head. 'You wanted me to talk to you, Gran. That's all I'm trying to do.'

'I know,' she said softly. 'I'm sorry . . . I didn't mean anything.' She grinned. 'My default setting seems to be "grumpy old woman" these days. I don't even know I'm doing it most of the time. Just ignore me when I'm like that, OK?'

I didn't say anything. I just stared out of the window, pretending to concentrate on something outside.

'Travis?' she said. 'Did you hear me?'

'Sorry, Gran,' I said, turning round. 'I was ignoring you. What did you say?'

She nodded, smiling, and pointed a bony finger at me. 'That's one-all, I believe.'

It was nice having a joke with Gran, and just for a moment everything felt OK again, but we both knew it wasn't. As the moment faded, our smiles faded with it.

'Listen, Travis,' Granny said quietly, her eyes suddenly gentle and caring. 'There's nothing I can say to ease your pain, and I know you probably don't want to talk about it anyway. But if you do ever want to talk about it, or if you just want to talk about anything . . . well, you know I'm always here for you, don't you?'

I nodded.

'If you don't feel like talking,' she continued, 'you can always just come in here and sit with me if you want. And if you don't want to, if you want to be on your own, that's fine as well.' She leaned forward in her chair and looked into my eyes. 'At times like this, Travis, you just have to do whatever feels right for you.'

I looked at her. 'But what if it *only* feels right to me? I mean, what if I feel that I have to do something that everyone else thinks is wrong?'

'Do you care what everyone else thinks?'

'I care what Nan and Grandad think. And you, of course.'

'Ah, I see,' she said, nodding thoughtfully. 'Well, that's different, isn't it? That puts you in a bit of a tricky position . . .' She leaned back in her chair, her brow furrowed in thought, and I wondered then how much she knew about everything. Had Nan or Grandad told her what was going on? Had she worked it all out herself? Did she know a lot more than she was letting on?

'I can't tell you what to do, Travis,' she said. 'You know that, don't you?'

I nodded.

She smiled. 'I remember saying the very same thing to your grandad when he was a boy.' She gazed out of the window, her eyes lost in the memory. 'Joseph had just turned sixteen when he told me he was leaving home to join the army. He knew I didn't want him to, and I knew it pained him to go against my will. But for some reason – which I still don't understand – he was absolutely convinced it was the right thing to do. As far as he was concerned, he just *had* to join the army.' She sighed. 'He'd prefer to leave with my blessing, he told me, but in the end he was going whether I liked it or not.'

'What did you do?' I asked.

'Nothing,' she said emptily. 'What could I do? I wasn't going to lie to him and tell him he had my blessing, because he didn't. I despised the idea of him being a soldier. But I couldn't stop him. I couldn't lock him up, could I? All I could do was . . .' She shook her head. 'I couldn't do anything. I just had to let him go.'

'Do you still wish he hadn't joined the army?'

She looked at me for a moment or two, then said, 'There's never any point in wishing things were different. Things are what they are. Good or bad, right or wrong. You can't change the past, Travis. You just have to live with it.'

46

At 9.15, as the sun finally dipped below the horizon, I made one last adjustment to the pillows I'd stuffed under my duvet, then I went over to the bedroom door and studied my handiwork from there. I'd never actually seen myself asleep in bed, so it was hard to know whether the body-shaped lump I'd constructed under the duvet would fool Nan and Grandad or not. It obviously wouldn't stand up to close inspection, but if you were standing in the doorway, and you didn't turn on the light . . . well, it might just do the trick.

I nodded to myself.

It would have to do.

I picked up my trainers, opened the door, and paused, listening. The TV was on in the sitting room, and I could just make out the muffled sound of Nan's voice as she asked Grandad something . . . and a moment later he grunted something in reply . . . and then they were both quiet again.

With my trainers in my hand, I headed along the landing to the bathroom. I didn't try to keep quiet, I just tried to walk as normally as possible, as if all I was doing was going to the bathroom. It was a surprisingly difficult thing to do, and the more I thought about it, the more abnormally I walked. Eventually, worried that

I was going to burst out laughing or fall over, or both, I stopped thinking about it, and that seemed to work.

Inside the bathroom, I switched on the light, locked the door, put on my trainers, then stood still and listened again. Everything sounded the same. My abnormal hobbling didn't seem to have rung any alarm bells. I waited another minute, then flushed the toilet, ran the hot tap, and opened the window. After twenty seconds or so, I turned off the tap, switched off the light, unlocked the door, opened it, and then very quietly closed it again. There was nothing I could do about the lack of footsteps going back to my room. I just had to hope that Nan and Grandad didn't notice.

Moving very carefully, and as quietly as possible, I stepped up onto the windowsill, then crouched down and eased myself through the open window. The ledge outside was wide enough to stand on. I cautiously shuffled along it, inching towards the drainpipe.

The drainpipe was one of those big old metal ones, which had the advantage of being easy to climb down. But the closer I got to it, the more I started worrying that it might be too old to take my weight. It looked pretty solid – bolted to the wall with hefty metal brackets – but close-up I could see that the paintwork was peeling away, revealing thick patches of rust underneath.

Don't think about it, I told myself.
Don't think about anything.
Just do it.

I reached out my right arm, got a hold on the pipe, then stretched out my right leg and placed my foot on one of the brackets. I gave the pipe a couple of good shakes to test its strength, and then, satisfied that it seemed sturdy enough, I stepped off the window ledge, pulling myself towards the pipe, and grabbed hold of it with both hands. My heart stopped for a moment as my left foot missed the bracket and I felt myself slipping, but once I'd scrambled around and found the bracket with my left foot, I felt relatively secure.

I hung there for a second or two, waiting for my heart to get back to normal again, then I began climbing down.

For the first few metres or so, everything was fine. The drainpipe held steady, the brackets took my weight, the pipe was easy to hold on to. In fact, it was all so easy that I began to relax a little, taking my time, breathing in the cool night air, looking around at the view – the night sky, the street lights in the distance, the neighbouring gardens down below . . .

And then, with a rusty creak, a bracket gave way and the drainpipe lurched away from the wall. I'll never forget the momentary terror I felt, deep in my belly, as I felt myself falling backwards, still gripping onto the drainpipe, but suddenly aware that it was no longer connected to anything. Luckily for me the other brackets didn't break off immediately, and as the drainpipe held for a moment or two, groaning with the strain, I just had time to look down, see that I was only about two metres from ground, and jump.

It was an instinctive, split-second decision, so I don't really know if I was aiming to land in the big old lavender bush on the other side of the path, but that's what I did. And there was no doubt that it cushioned my fall. I just kind of dropped down into the bush, flopped around for a bit, then rolled off backwards into a flower bed.

Apart from a few scratches – and a horrible shaky feeling in my belly – I wasn't hurt.

I got to my knees, brushed myself down, and carefully peeked round the lavender bush at the house. The damaged section of drainpipe was leaning out at an angle from the wall, but now that it didn't have to support my weight any more, it didn't look as if it was going to get any worse. Inside the house, the kitchen light was on, but there was no sign of Nan or Grandad.

I waited a minute or two, then I crawled across to the shed on my hands and knees. Another quick look at the kitchen, then I got to my feet, opened the shed door, and went inside to get my bike.

As I wheeled it out and scooted off down the garden path, I checked my watch once again.

9.36 p.m.

I went out through the back gate, just as I had that morning.

It seemed like a thousand years ago.

47

The roads through the industrial estate were dark and quiet, and as I pedalled along Sowton Way – the approach road to Sowton Lane – the only sound I could hear was the rubbery hum of my brand-new tyres on the tarmac. It was a crystal-clear night, the air cool and fresh, and the sky was bright with stars. A pale crescent moon was rising over the distant chimneys, bathing them in an eerie grey light. The tall chimneys looked dark and stern, like faceless sentinels.

When I got to Sowton Lane, I cycled past it for another thirty metres or so, then pulled in at the side of the road beside a five-barred wooden gate. Mason was already there, waiting for me as we'd arranged. Big Lenny was with him, as usual. And as I got off my bike, I was pleasantly surprised to see that Evie Johnson was with them too. They were all wearing dark gear and black hoodies – Lenny wearing his under a long black coat – and they all looked ready for action.

'Thanks for coming,' I said to Mason, nodding at him and Lenny. I looked over at Evie. She was leaning casually against the gate, her hands in the back pockets of her tight black jeans.

'I thought we might need some help,' Mason said, glancing at Evie, then turning back to me. 'You don't mind, do you?'

'No . . .' I said, smiling at Evie. 'No, of course I don't mind.'

She smiled, pushed herself off the gate, and came over to me. 'What happened to you?' she asked, grinning as she glanced at my hair.

'What?' I said, reaching instinctively for my head.

'You look like you've been dragged through a bush.'

As I ran my fingers through my hair, bits of lavender bush started falling out. Leaves, purple petals, broken stems . . .

'Here, let me help you,' Evie said.

As she stepped close to me and began brushing her fingers through my hair, carefully picking out little bits of stick and stuff, I wasn't sure what to do. I felt awkward and slightly embarrassed, but I also felt kind of OK.

'It's lavender,' I told her, my voice oddly croaky.

'Yeah?'

I cleared my throat. 'I jumped off a drainpipe.'

'Right . . .'

I looked at her.

She smiled at me.

'It's a good job Jaydie's not here,' I heard Mason say.

Evie glanced at him. 'Who's Jaydie?'

'Travis's girlfriend.' Mason grinned. 'She'd smack you one if she caught you running your hands through his hair.'

'Jaydie's not my girlfriend,' I told Evie. 'She's Mason's little sister.'

Evie shrugged. 'Doesn't bother me who she is.'

'You think you're funny, don't you, Mason?' I said, giving him a sideways look.

'He's about as funny as a kick in the head,' Evie muttered, giving my hair a final ruffle. She stepped back and appraised her work. 'There, that should do it.'

'Thanks,' I said.

She smiled and bowed her head. 'You're welcome.'

As we all went over to the gate, I saw Evie give Mason a dirty look, warning him to watch himself. He tried to shrug it off with a carefree grin, but he didn't look quite as confident as he usually did. It was the first time I'd ever seen a lack of certainty in Mason, and for a moment or two I found myself wondering what it meant . . .

Then Evie said, 'Do you really think Bashir's in there?' And I refocused my mind, leaned on the gate beside her, and gazed out across the moonlit fields.

The warehouse was roughly a hundred metres away, over to our left, dimly visible in the darkness. There were no lights on at the back of the building, but a faint glow was showing from a small window in the left-hand wall, and I could just about make out the shapes of two vehicles in the car park at the front.

'Yeah,' I muttered, 'I think he's in there.'

'But you don't know for sure?' she said.

I shook my head. 'That's why I want to get in there.' I looked at Mason. He was busy studying the landscape ahead of us now, his eyes taking everything in – the warehouse, the fields, the fencing, the hedges.

'Are your people ready?' I asked him.

He nodded. 'They're in position, waiting for my signal.'

'How many did you get in the end?'

'About forty.'

'And they know what to do?'

'Make a lot of noise, chuck a few stones, but stay outside the fence.' Still studying the field, he said, 'Are you sure this is the only way in? I mean, if we head across the field to the warehouse from here, we're bound to be seen.'

'We're not going to head across the field, ' I told him. 'We're going to climb the gate and then follow the hedges round the edge of the field.' I indicated the hedge to our left, running along Sowton Way back to the corner of Sowton Lane. 'We follow this one down to the corner, then turn right and follow the other one to the fence at the side of the warehouse. As long as we keep in close to the hedges, we should be all right.'

All three of them were quiet for a moment as they contemplated the route I'd explained, looking down to our left, then over to the right. Eventually, one by one, they looked at each other and nodded.

'Any questions?' I said.

'I've got a few,' Mason said.

'Yeah, me too,' Evie added. 'In fact, come to think of it, I've got about a million questions.'

'How about you, Len?' I said, turning to Lenny. 'Have you got any questions?'

He didn't say anything, he just looked back at me for a moment, shrugged his shoulders, then shook his head.

'Right then,' I said, climbing up onto the gate, 'that's that sorted out. Let's get going.'

It was impossible to tell if we were being watched or not as we crept along the hedges towards the warehouse, but by the time we'd got to the fence there were no obvious signs that we'd been spotted. Of course, that didn't necessarily mean that we hadn't. But even if the Omega men *had* seen us, and were just waiting quietly to see what we did next, there wasn't anything I could do about it. So I didn't bother thinking about it.

We were crouched down in the corner between the hedge and the fence now, no more than fifteen metres from the warehouse. The car park was immediately in front of us, the warehouse over to our right. A rusty old skip full of rubble and bricks was parked in the corner of the car park, shielding us from the warehouse. As we gathered round behind the skip, Mason took a pair of wire cutters from his pocket and passed them to Lenny. Lenny shuffled over to the far end of the skip, settled himself down on his knees, and began cutting a vertical slit in the fence.

'All right, listen,' I said quietly. 'Before we go in, there's a couple of things you all need to know.' I looked at Evie. 'Has Mason told you what's going on here?'

'He's given me a rough idea, yeah. I mean, I know there's a bunch of guys in there who might or might not have Bashir. I know they might be protecting him from some bad guys, but they might be holding him against his will. And I know we're going to break into the warehouse and see if we can find him.' She smiled. 'Does that sound about right?'

'It's close enough.'

'So what else do I need to know?' she said.

'Well,' I said cautiously, 'at least one of the men inside has got a gun.'

'They're *all* going to have guns, Trav,' Mason said, as if it went without saying.

'Do you think so?'

'You said they were professionals, didn't you?'

'Yeah.'

He shrugged. 'So they'll have guns.'

'Right,' I muttered, wondering why I hadn't thought of that. 'Well, anyway,' I went on, 'I just thought you ought to know what we're up against before we go in . . . just in case you want to change your mind or anything. I mean, I don't expect they'll actually start shooting—'

'We live on the Slade, Travis,' Evie said matter-of-factly. 'We're up against guns every day. It's no big deal.'

'We eat guns for breakfast,' Mason added.

Evie looked at him.

'What?' he said, grinning at her. 'Come on, you've

got to admit that's pretty funny.'

She shook her head dismissively, but I could tell she was trying hard not to smile. Mason kept on grinning at her for a second, then he looked over to see how Lenny was getting on with the fence. The slit was about two metres high now. Easily big enough to get through, even for him.

'That'll do, Len,' Mason told him. 'Good job.'

Lenny stopped snipping and passed the wire cutters back to Mason. Mason slipped them in his pocket, then bumped fists with Lenny.

'So,' Mason said breezily, turning back to me and rubbing his hands, 'are we going to do this or not?'

'Just one more thing,' I said. 'I don't know if Bashir actually needs rescuing or not. Like Evie just said, they might be holding him against his will, but it's equally possible that he *wants* to be with them. We won't know which it is until we find him.'

'*If* we find him,' Mason said.

'Right. But if we *do* find him, and he tells us that he's not a prisoner and he wants to stay where he is, it's important that we just leave it at that, OK?'

'We take his word for it?' Evie asked.

I nodded. 'We don't say anything. We don't ask him anything. We just turn around and leave him to it.'

'What if he *is* a prisoner?'

'We get him out.'

'Just like that?' Mason said.

'Yep.'

'We just get him out?'

'That's right.'

'Then what?'

I shrugged. 'We'll think of something.'

Mason laughed. 'That's your plan? We'll *think* of something.'

'Have you got a better idea?'

He looked at me for a moment or two, not quite sure what to say, then he just shrugged one shoulder, as if to say, 'Ah, what the hell?' and reached into his pocket and took out his mobile. 'Just tell me when,' he said, thumbing the screen.

I looked at Evie and Lenny. 'Ready?'

They both nodded.

I turned back to Mason. His thumb was poised over the screen.

I nodded at him.

He pressed a key.

Almost immediately the silence of the night was broken by the sound of forty kids making as much noise as possible. Raised voices, shouts, the stomp of running feet. It came from across the road, and as I leaned to one side and looked through a gap in the hedge, I saw them emerging from the abandoned car-repair place where they'd been waiting for Mason's signal – a mob of tough-looking kids, most of them hooded up, some of them with scarves over their faces, all of them swarming across the road towards the warehouse. The noise rose and swelled as they got closer – chanting and whooping, banging dustbin lids – and as the mob approached the double gates, some of them started throwing missiles. Stones, rocks, bricks, fireworks. I heard the thud of bricks landing on cars, then car alarms going off, sirens wailing, lights flashing . . .

'Come on, let's go!' Mason hissed, grabbing my arm.

I looked round and saw that Evie and Lenny had already slipped through the gap in the fence and were hurrying round to the back of the warehouse. I followed Mason through the gap, and we set off after the other two.

With a bit of luck, the diversion I'd arranged with Mason would work, and all the attention inside the warehouse would be focused on the mob of kids out the front. Hopefully that was going to give us the chance we needed to sneak in without being seen, quickly find Bashir (*if* he was there), and then sneak out again. With or without Bashir.

And after that?

Well, when I'd told Mason that I didn't have a plan, I wasn't being completely honest. I had a plan. I knew exactly what *I* was going to do. But it didn't concern Mason. It didn't concern anyone except me and the man with the steely grey eyes.

48

'It's locked,' Evie announced as Mason and I joined her and Lenny at the back door of the warehouse. 'Bolted shut from the inside.'

'No keyhole or anything?' Mason asked, studying the solid wooden door.

'Nope.'

'It's not an electric lock, is it?' he said, looking around for an entry-code box.

'I just *told* you, Mase,' Evie sighed. 'It's bolted shut.' She looked at me. 'What about trying one of the windows?'

I glanced along the rear wall, checking out the windows. 'They're too small,' I told her, shaking my head. 'You and me could probably just about squeeze through, but Lenny and Mason would never make it.' I looked at the door. 'We'll have to break it down.' I turned to Lenny. 'Can you smash it in without making too much noise?'

Lenny thought about it for moment, then looked at Mason.

'He'll do his best,' Mason said, answering on Lenny's behalf.

'OK,' I said, nodding at both of them. 'Do it.'

As Evie moved out of the way, and Lenny lumbered

up to the door, I crossed my fingers and hoped that the racket the estate kids were making would drown out the sound of Lenny breaking the door down. That was if he *could* break it down, I suddenly thought. Maybe it wasn't *just* bolted shut on the inside? Maybe it was secured with heavy-duty industrial bolts, or reinforced with steel bars or something? Or maybe—

Thud!

The door was open.

While I'd been busy thinking about it – worrying about this, fretting about that – Lenny had just gone up to the door, looked at it for a moment, then slammed it open with his shoulder. He'd hit it just hard enough to wrench out the bolts but leave the door swinging on its hinges, and he'd hardly made any noise at all.

'Top man, Len,' Mason said, patting Lenny's arm as he headed for the open door.

Lenny just nodded.

Mason stepped through the doorway and paused for a moment, looking around. A wide corridor stretched out in front of him, a pale light glowing at the far end. In the shadowy light I could make out a bare concrete floor, metal cupboards lined against the wall, and another corridor immediately to the right of the door.

'Come on, then,' Mason whispered, beckoning us to join him. 'What are you waiting for?'

*

Inside the warehouse it was all breezeblock walls, plywood roofing, and plasterboard partitions. It looked to me as if someone had started converting the building into offices or a small business or something, but either they'd never got round to finishing it or they'd just done a really bad job.

The main corridor in front of us led to the front of the building, while the one to our right – which was much narrower, and unlit – headed along the rear wall at a right angle to the central corridor. There were doors along both corridors. All of them shut.

'Which way do you want to go, Trav?' Mason asked, keeping his voice low.

I looked to my right, then straight ahead.

'Maybe we should split up,' Evie suggested. 'Two of us take one corridor, the other two take the other one.'

'No,' I whispered firmly. 'We all stick together.'

'But it'd be quicker—'

'Splitting up is a bad idea,' I said. 'I mean, they always do it in thrillers and horror films, don't they? And it *never* works out very well.'

'That's true,' she agreed.

'OK,' I said, heading off towards the narrower corridor. 'Let's start with this one.'

'Why this one?' Evie asked, following along beside me.

'I don't know. I've just got a feeling about it . . .'

*

A few minutes later we were back where we'd started from. After checking out one room, and finding it empty, we'd then discovered that the corridor was a dead end. We hadn't realised it before because it had been too dark to see, but the corridor was sealed off about twenty metres along by a breezeblock wall.

'That's the trouble with having a "feeling" about something,' Evie said quietly to me as we trudged back the way we'd come. 'It's fine if it turns out to be right, but you look kind of stupid if it doesn't.'

I looked at her.

She was grinning.

'Thanks for pointing that out,' I said.

'You're welcome.'

As we started searching again – moving cautiously along the central corridor, checking every room we came to, keeping our eyes and ears open all the time – I found myself wondering why we hadn't come across any Omega men yet. Why hadn't there been anyone guarding the back door? Even with all the mayhem going on outside – and I could hear that it was still going strong – why hadn't they put someone on the back door, just in case? I mean, they were professionals – ex-army, ex-security services. They were supposed to know what they were doing, weren't they? So how come the four of us had got in so easily? It was almost as if . . .

Shut up, Travis, I told myself. *You're over-thinking*

everything again. Worrying about this, fretting about that.
Why don't you take a leaf out of Lenny's book and just get
on with it?

'Hey, Travis,' I heard Mason say.

I looked over at him. He'd stopped beside a pair of
swing doors on the right of the corridor. The doors had
small plastic windows in them, and Mason was peering
through one of the windows to see what was on the other
side.

'There's another corridor through here,' he said. 'Do
you want to take a look?'

We were about halfway along the main corridor now.
All the rooms we'd checked out so far had either been
empty or so stacked full of stuff you could barely get into
them. One room had been piled to the roof with office
furniture – desks, chairs, tables – another had been jam-
packed with cardboard boxes full of files and papers and
stationery. The rooms themselves were as badly built as
the rest of the building – cheap fittings, bare flooring,
wafer-thin plasterboard walls.

There'd been no sign of Bashir anywhere, no evidence
to suggest that he'd ever been here at all.

'Travis?' Mason said. 'What do you want to do?'

I looked back at him, suddenly feeling incredibly
tired. *I don't know what to do*, I felt like saying. *I don't*
know anything. I'm beginning to think that this whole idea
was a big mistake.

And then, just to make things worse, Evie tugged at

my shirt and said, 'We've got company.'

I looked round at her. She was staring straight ahead, her eyes hard and cold. I followed her gaze and saw two suited figures standing together at the far end of the corridor. One of them was the gaunt-faced man, the other one was Goatee.

They weren't moving, just standing there staring at us.

'What do you reckon, Evie?' Mason said. 'Two of them, four of us . . . do you fancy our chances?'

'Piece of cake,' she replied, without taking her eyes off Goatee and Gaunt Face.

Then Goatee reached inside his jacket and pulled out a pistol, and a moment later Gaunt Face did the same.

'Ah,' Evie said calmly. 'That evens things up a bit.'

The two men began walking towards us, holding their guns down at their sides.

'Uh-oh,' Mason said, looking back down the corridor. 'Here comes another one.'

I turned round and saw the muscle-bound guy lumbering towards us from the other direction. He had a gun in his hand too. His eyes were even nastier-looking than I remembered.

'Where the hell did he come from?' I muttered.

'Who cares?' Mason said, shoving open one of the swing doors and ushering Lenny through. 'Come on, quick,' he said to Evie and me. 'Come *on*, let's go!'

Evie grabbed my hand and we ran for the doors.

49

The corridor on the other side of the swing doors had whitewashed walls and a white stone floor. Fluorescent strip lights hummed and flickered, and as we ran along the corridor, our distorted shadows circled weirdly around our feet. Everything was beginning to feel oddly unreal now, as if it wasn't really happening, or it was happening to someone else. At the same time I was acutely aware that it *was* happening, it *was* real, and it was happening to *me*. *I* was running. *I* was scared. *I* could feel *my* heart hammering.

'Which way, Travis?' Mason called out. 'You want to keep going or should we try one of these doors?'

I studied the corridor up ahead. We were approaching two doors – one on the right of the corridor, one on the left – both of them closed. The one on the right was marked *STORES*, the other one said *OFFICE*. Twenty metres further along the corridor was another pair of swing doors. There were no windows in these doors, so I couldn't see what was behind them, but if the corridor continued on the other side, there was a chance it might lead us to another exit. And that's all I was thinking about now. Finding an exit, getting us all out in one piece. That's all I cared about.

'Keep going!' I called out. 'Head for the swing doors!'

The words were barely out of my mouth when the swing doors crashed open and Shaved Head came striding through with a pistol in his hand. We all stopped suddenly at the sight of him, and then almost immediately we all looked round as the swing doors behind us flapped open and Goatee and Gaunt Face appeared at the other end of the corridor.

Mason cursed.

'This way!' I said quickly, stepping over and opening the door marked *STORES*.

I went inside and turned on the light, and as the other three hurried in after me, I rapidly checked out the room. There were no windows, no other exits. It was just another shabby little room full of discarded office furniture and cardboard boxes.

'There's no lock on here!' Mason said as he slammed the door shut behind him. 'We need to block it with something.' He looked around, searching the room. 'Lenny, get that cabinet. Trav, Evie, give me a hand with this desk.'

As Lenny went over and grabbed hold of a big metal storage cabinet and began heaving it across the room, the rest of us manhandled a heavy old desk away from the wall and jammed it up against the door.

Lenny lumbered over with the storage cabinet.

'On top of the desk, Len,' Mason told him.

Lenny dropped the cabinet on top of the desk and started manoeuvring it into position against the door.

'Leave it, Len,' Mason told him. 'We'll do that.' He pointed across the room. 'You go and get that other cabinet.'

As Lenny strode off, I helped Mason and Evie push the cabinet against the door. Just as we got it nice and tight, the door handle rattled and someone gave the door a shove. It gave a little at the top, but the lower part didn't move at all.

'Mind your backs,' someone said in a big soft voice, and I turned round to see Lenny looming over us with the other storage cabinet cradled in his arms. It'd been so long since I'd heard him say anything that I'd almost forgotten he could speak. But I didn't have time to be surprised. One of the Omega men was trying the door again now, only this time he was *really* trying, slamming his hands against it. *Thump! Thump! Thump!*

'*Now*, Lenny!' Mason yelled, and we all got out of the way as Lenny lurched forward and heaved the metal cabinet on top of the other one.

The barricade covered the whole door now, making it much more solid, and when the Omega man gave the door another hard thump, it not only barely moved at all, but we also heard a satisfying grunt of pain from the other side.

'Nice work, Len,' Mason said. 'That should hold them for a while.'

'It won't hold them for ever though, will it?' I said.

Mason looked at me.

The door went *thump* again, much harder this time.

'That's probably the muscleman,' I said to Mason. 'You know they're going to get in eventually, don't you?'

'We'd better hurry up and think of something then, hadn't we?'

'We're trapped, Mason,' I said, sighing. 'There's no way out.'

Mason smiled. 'There's always a way out, Trav. You've just got to find it.'

As Mason began pacing around the room, searching for any possible way out – glancing up at the ceiling, stamping on the floor – I went over to Evie and asked her how she was doing.

'I'm all right, thanks,' she said, looking at the door as it took another big *thump*.

'Listen,' I started to say, 'I'm really sorry I got you into all this—'

'You didn't get me into anything. I wanted to come along.'

'Yeah, I know. But—'

'Hey, lighten up,' she said, giving me a playful punch on the arm. 'I'm *glad* I came. I haven't had so much fun in ages.'

I frowned at her. 'You're *enjoying* this?'

'It's better than hanging around the estate all night, bored out of my mind.'

Another shuddering *thump* rang out then, and this

time part of the door frame splintered off.

'It's not going to last much longer,' Evie said, looking at the door again. 'It's too cheap and flimsy, that's the trouble.' She glanced around, shaking her head. 'It's like this whole place was made on the cheap . . .'

I heard a tapping sound from across the room then, and even as I turned round to see what it was, I was struck by a sudden thought. And when I saw Mason rapping his knuckles against the far wall, I knew that he was thinking the same. The front and side walls were solid breezeblock, but the far wall . . .

'It's just plasterboard, isn't it?' I said to Mason.

He looked over at me, a glint of realisation in his eyes, and then – grinning to himself – he turned round and hammered his fist into the wall. It went straight through, the thin plasterboard giving way as easily as cardboard. He withdrew his fist and big chunks of bare plasterboard broke off, leaving a football-sized hole in the wall. Mason peered through the hole.

'Looks like another empty room,' he said, beckoning us over.

A massive *thump* hit the door. The frame cracked and one of the hinges flew off.

Mason started attacking the wall, ripping away at the hole, kicking big lumps out of the plasterboard, and we all ran over and joined him. It took us about five seconds to smash out a hole big enough for us to get through. As we squeezed through into the darkened room next door,

I could already hear the door behind us beginning to give way.

Once we were all safely through, we didn't waste any time. There was enough light coming in through the hole to see the door in the opposite wall, and as the sound of splintering wood and crashing metal grew louder behind us, we just ran for the door and yanked it open.

It brought us out into another corridor. More whitewashed walls, more flickering fluorescent lights. The corridor led off to our left, and to our right was another breezeblock wall.

We turned left and ran.

50

As we raced along the corridor I began to think that maybe we were going to make it after all. It was hard to be sure which way we were going now, but I got the feeling we were heading away from the main corridor towards the far side of the building. There was a junction up ahead, and if my feeling was correct, a right turn would take us back towards the rear of the warehouse, and a left turn would take us up to the front. More importantly, either way might lead us to an exit door. And even if we didn't find a door, we were bound to find a window.

We were nearly at the junction now. Evie was out in front, with Lenny just behind her – he was surprisingly quick on his feet – and Mason and me bringing up the rear.

'Left or right, Trav?' Evie called out.

She was glancing over her shoulder as she spoke, so just for a moment she wasn't looking where she was going, which is why she didn't see the three men coming round the corner in front of her. I recognised them instantly: the gunman from the BMW, the pale-skinned man with reddish hair, and Winston, the man with the steely grey eyes.

'*EVIE!*' I yelled. '*LOOK OUT!*'

But I was too late, and before she could do anything

about it she'd run straight into them. Red Hair immediately made a lunge for her, and although she managed to get away from him, she couldn't get away from the Gunman. As he grabbed her from behind and clamped her arms to her sides, Lenny charged head first into Red Hair, knocking him off his feet. As he went down, and Mason launched himself at Winston, I went after the Gunman.

He'd backed up against the wall now and was struggling to hold on to Evie. She was lashing out at him like a crazy thing – twisting and writhing, stomping on his feet, flinging her head back into his face. When he saw me coming, he suddenly let go of her and pushed her away and started reaching into his jacket for his gun. But instead of moving away from him when he shoved her, Evie quickly spun round and hammered her fist into his chin. It was a perfect left hook, and it caught him right on the sweet spot. His eyes rolled, he staggered to one side, then his legs turned to rubber and he toppled over and slumped to the floor.

I watched him for a second to make sure he wasn't getting up, then I looked up at Evie.

'Are you OK?' I asked her.

'Fine,' she said, smiling.

I held her gaze for a second, then turned round to see how Mason and Lenny were getting on.

I was just in time to see Lenny finishing off Red Hair, effortlessly slamming his head into the wall. But when I looked over at Mason I could see that he was in trouble. He was still on his feet, and still squaring up to Winston, but he'd obviously taken a bit of a beating. His mouth was bleeding, he was swaying a bit, and his left arm was hanging down at his side. He lurched towards Winston and threw a punch at him, but there was no power or speed in it, and as Winston stepped back, the punch missed him by a mile and Mason stumbled forward and almost fell over.

Winston could easily have finished him off then, but he seemed reluctant to do anything. He just stood there, calmly watching Mason stagger around. I started running then, and as Winston glanced over and saw me coming, he didn't hesitate for a second. He moved so fast that I wasn't even sure he'd hit Mason until I saw Mason double over and drop to his knees, grimacing with pain and clutching at his side. And by the time I'd reached Winston, he was already moving towards me, holding his hands up, as if trying to strike a truce.

'Hold on, Travis,' he said quickly. 'Just listen to me—'

I launched myself at him, swinging a right hook at his head, but he saw it coming and batted my fist away.

'For God's *sake*, Travis,' he spat. 'I just want to—'

I went for him with another right hook, only this time, as he went to fend it off, I ducked down and hit him in the belly with a shuddering left uppercut. He groaned and doubled over, and I hammered my fist into the back of his head and then brought my knee up into his face.

It was a vicious combination, and he should have gone down. But he didn't. He staggered back a couple of steps, holding his face in his hands, then he straightened up, wiped a stream of blood from his nose, and smiled at me. His lips were all smashed up and bloody.

'Not bad,' he spluttered, nodding his approval. 'Not bad at all.'

I glanced quickly at Mason. He was trying to get up now, but he was clearly in a lot of pain. From the way he was leaning awkwardly to one side, I guessed he had a broken rib or two.

I looked round, wondering where Lenny and Evie were, and when I saw them standing side by side, staring back down the corridor, I knew it could only mean one thing. With a sinking heart I looked down the corridor and saw Shaved Head, Gaunt Face and Muscleman moving rapidly towards us.

As Lenny and Evie stood there waiting for them, I turned back to Winston.

I'd only been looking away from him for a moment or two, but I'd forgotten how fast he could move. And when I turned back he was standing right in front of me, his bloodied face staring right into my eyes.

I don't know what he hit me with. I didn't even see him move. At least, I don't remember seeing him move. All I remember is a sudden impact, a black light exploding in my head, and then nothing.

51

The first thing I saw when I opened my eyes was a young man in a black tracksuit sitting on a white settee. He had a longish face, short black hair, and hauntingly dark eyes. Mason and Lenny were sitting on the settee with him, and Winston was standing just to one side. Mason and the young man were talking about something, but the settee was on the other side of the room and I couldn't hear what they were saying.

I didn't understand it.

I didn't know where I was.

I didn't know why my head was throbbing.

And I didn't know why the young man in the tracksuit seemed so familiar.

I closed my eyes and tried to think about it, but nothing would come to me. Nothing at all. I just couldn't get hold of anything. My head was all fogged up.

I didn't want to open my eyes again.

I didn't want to see things I didn't understand.

It was too confusing.

But then I felt a hand on my arm, and a gentle voice whispered my name, and I opened my eyes and saw Evie peering into my face.

And all at once everything came back to me.

*

The room we were in was a lot more comfortable than the other rooms in the building. It had two small settees (one of which I was sharing with Evie), an armchair, a table, a good-sized TV. There were rugs on the floor, a couple of cupboards, a little kitchen area. Evie wasn't sure exactly where the room was located. She'd been brought here at gunpoint with Mason and Lenny, she told me, and I'd been carried here by Muscleman. So she'd had other things on her mind at the time, and she hadn't really paid that much attention to where she was being taken. But she thought we were probably somewhere near the front of the warehouse.

'Winston's explained everything to us,' she told me. 'And Bashir's confirmed it.'

I looked across at Bashir Kamal. He was still sitting on the settee across the room with Mason. I saw Mason smile at something he said. He said something back to Bashir, miming a punch, and Bashir laughed quietly.

Winston had noticed that I was awake now, and when he saw me looking at him, he nodded at me. It reminded me of the time he'd nodded at me in the church car park after the funeral. And it was probably the memory of that that prompted me to glance at his suit jacket now and realise that the middle button looked slightly different from the other buttons, just as it had at the funeral.

He was wearing the hidden camera again.

As I thought about that, I gazed around the room. Shaved Head was leaning against the wall by the door, and Goatee was sitting in the armchair with his legs crossed, staring idly at his mobile.

The door to the room was open.

There were no guns in sight.

Everyone seemed very relaxed.

It didn't feel right to me.

Nothing felt right.

'Why's it so quiet?' I asked Evie. 'Why aren't the kids outside making any noise?'

'Mason called them off.'

'Why?'

'We don't need them, Trav,' she said softly. 'We never did.'

'She's right, you know,' I heard Winston say.

I looked up and saw him coming towards us. Bashir was with him, and as they both stopped in front of us, I got the impression that they were reasonably comfortable in each other's company.

'How are you feeling, Travis?' Winston asked. 'I'm sorry I had to hit you . . .' He grinned, pointing to his battered face. 'But you didn't really leave me much choice, did you?' He turned to Bashir. 'Travis does a bit of boxing himself.'

'Yeah?' Bashir said, nodding his head at me and glancing at Evie.

I stood up.

Bashir turned back to me and held out his hand. 'I hear you've been looking for me.'

I shook his hand, not sure what to say.

He grinned. 'Well, here I am.'

'Right,' I said.

'And as you can see,' he went on, 'I'm not tied up or chained to a radiator or anything. The door's open. I could walk out of here right now if I wanted to.' He shrugged. 'It's like I told your friends, I'm *not* a prisoner, OK? I mean, I appreciate your concern for me and everything, but I don't need rescuing.'

As Bashir smiled at Evie and sat down on the settee beside her, I turned to Winston.

'The British security services treated Bashir like dirt,' he explained. 'He risked his life for his country, but as soon as MI5 had no more use for him, they just threw him out into the cold. The only reason they want him back now is because the CIA are after him, and MI5 will do anything to stop the CIA interrogating one of their informants, whether *they* value him or not.' Winston looked at me. 'The CIA think Bashir's a terrorist.'

'I know.'

'If they were to get hold of him, there's no knowing what they might do.'

'I'm aware of the situation,' I said. 'What I want to know is—'

'No, Travis,' he said firmly, 'you're *not* aware of the situation. If you were, you wouldn't be here.'

'I had to make sure Bashir was safe.'

'He *was* safe,' Winston said, sighing. 'We had it

all under control. No one knew where he was, he was guarded around the clock, and we were in the final stages of arranging a new identity and a new place for him to live. We've also been gathering evidence to prove beyond doubt that, far from being a terrorist, Bashir was in fact an MI5 asset who'd successfully infiltrated a terrorist cell.' Winston stared at me. 'Do you get it now? Once we convince the CIA that Bashir's not a terrorist, he's no longer of interest to anyone. He's free to start a new life without having to keep looking over his shoulder all the time. If it wasn't for you, Travis, he would have been starting that new life tomorrow.'

'What do you mean, *would have been*?' Bashir said, suddenly concerned.

Winston looked at him. 'I'm sorry, Bashir, but our operation's been compromised.'

'*What?*'

'Earlier tonight emergency services received an anonymous call about a serious disturbance in Sowton Lane. The good news is that the call was intercepted by one of our contacts, who managed to bury it before any action was taken, so we don't have to worry about the police showing up.'

'What's the bad news?' Bashir asked.

'The CIA have contacts in the local police force too. They intercepted the call *before* it was buried.'

'So what?' Bashir said, frowning. 'I mean, the CIA don't know we're here, do they? So why does it matter if they know about a bunch of kids kicking off in Sowton Lane? There's no *reason* for them to connect that to us, is there?'

'We have a contact in the CIA.'

'So?'

'So we know they're not stupid. They monitor everything, they analyse everything. Their agents are trained to take particular notice of anything out of the ordinary. And forty-odd kids from the Slade Lane estate besieging a supposedly empty warehouse is definitely out of the ordinary.' Winston glanced at me, then turned back to Bashir. 'According to our contact, within two minutes of the emergency call being received, a CIA agent was dispatched to investigate the disturbance. He arrived at the scene ten minutes later, spent a further ten minutes getting close enough to the warehouse to see inside, and then quickly reported back to his bosses.'

'He couldn't have seen me,' Bashir stated, shaking his head.

'He didn't,' Winston told him. 'But he didn't have to. He saw one of my men. He recognised him from an altercation we had with the CIA at Travis's house in Kell Cross this morning. I'm sorry, Bashir, but the CIA know you're here.'

Bashir said nothing, just stared intently at the floor.

'They've got the building surrounded,' Winston said quietly. 'There's at least a dozen agents out there, maybe more.'

Bashir slowly gazed up at him, a look of disdain on his face. 'You promised you'd look after me. You gave me your *word*.'

Winston shrugged. 'These things happen.'

'So that's it, is it?' Bashir said. 'You're going to give up without a fight? Just throw me to the wolves?' He laughed scornfully. 'You're no better than the rest of them.'

'We're heavily outnumbered,' Winston said patiently. 'We wouldn't stand a chance if we tried to fight our way out of here. The only option we have is to negotiate.'

'*Negotiate?*' Bashir sneered.

'Why not? I know we still don't have *undeniable* proof of your innocence, but we have enough circumstantial evidence to at least give the CIA something to think about. If we show them what we have right now . . . well, who knows? By the time they've processed and analysed the evidence we've given them, it's possible we'll be in a position to give them all the proof they need.'

'And what do you think the CIA are going to do with me in the meantime?' Bashir scoffed. 'Put me up in a five-star hotel?'

'Well, that's one of the things we can negotiate—'

'They're *Americans*!' Bashir hissed, spitting out the word as if it sickened him just to say it. 'You don't *negotiate* with Americans.'

His burst of anger took me by surprise, and as I turned and glanced at him it was hard to believe the sudden change in his demeanour. The easy-going young man who'd sat down on the settee a few minutes ago had gone, and in his place was a hate-filled fanatic seized with venom and rage – his face livid, his eyes unbalanced, every muscle in his body strained to breaking point.

Evie had clearly noticed the change too, and without making it obvious she was quietly edging away from him.

For the next couple of seconds, everything seemed to happen in slow motion.

I saw Winston moving towards Bashir, a consoling look on his face. As he began to bend down and reach out, intending – I assumed – to give Bashir a reassuring pat on his shoulder, I wondered why the look in Winston's eyes didn't match the look on his face. His face was a picture of sympathy – comforting, soothing, encouraging. But his eyes were ruthless and razor sharp.

He leaned over a little more, extending his hand towards Bashir's shoulder.

His jacket was unbuttoned. It opened at the front as Winston leaned over, revealing an automatic pistol in a shoulder holster.

I looked at Bashir.

He was already reaching for the gun.

I opened my mouth to say something, but all of a sudden everything speeded up. Bashir's hand flashed in and out of Winston's jacket, and before anyone had a chance to do anything, he'd grabbed Evie around the neck, dragged her to her feet, and was holding the gun to her head.

52

'What the hell—' Evie gasped.

'Shut up!' Bashir hissed.

I'd jumped to my feet as soon as he'd grabbed her, and Mason and Lenny were already halfway across the room, but there was nothing any of us could do. Bashir was holding Evie in front of him, the gun jammed to her head, his left arm curled tightly around her neck.

'Get *back*!' he snapped at Mason and Lenny.

They stopped in their tracks.

'Over there,' he said, jerking his head to the left. 'Against the wall.'

They backed up slowly and stopped at the wall.

'You, sit down!' he barked at me.

I slowly sat down.

Bashir turned to Winston. 'If anyone moves, I'll kill her,' he said simply.

Winston didn't say anything, he just stood there, looking back at Bashir and casually buttoning his jacket as if he didn't have a care in the world. I glanced over to see what Shaved Head and Goatee were doing. They were both on their feet, both watching Bashir's every move, but they weren't doing anything to stop him.

What's the *matter* with them? I thought.

Why aren't they *doing* anything?

And what the hell's Bashir up to anyway?

I looked at Evie, desperate to help her, but I didn't know what to do. I just didn't understand *any* of this.

Bashir was approaching the doorway now. I saw him glance quickly over his shoulder to see how close he was, and as he did so a familiar muscle-bound figure appeared from the corridor and stepped quietly into the doorway, blocking his exit. Bashir glared at Muscleman for a moment, then tightened his grip around Evie's neck and jammed the gun harder into her head. Evie winced, grimacing at the sudden pain, but she didn't cry out.

Bashir turned back to Winston. 'Tell the musclehead to move, *right* now, or I swear I'll pull the trigger.'

'It's all right, Evie,' Winston said softly, looking her in the eyes. 'You're going to be OK. I promise. Nothing's going to happen to you.'

'You think I'm *bluffing*?' Bashir spat.

Winston ignored him for a moment, concentrating on Evie, silently asking for her trust. She calmly held his gaze, the message in her eyes saying – *go ahead, do what you have to do*. Winston turned his attention to Bashir. 'No, Bashir,' he said, fixing him with an icy stare, 'I don't think you're bluffing. I think you're perfectly capable of shooting an innocent girl in the head.'

Bashir hesitated, momentarily confused.

'You see, we know who you *really* are,' Winston told him. 'We've known all along. What you are, what you've done, what you're planning to do.' Winston smiled. 'Do you really think we'd let a man like you get anywhere near a *loaded* gun?'

Bashir grinned coldly. 'Nice try. Now tell the big guy to get out of the way or I'm going to put a hole in the girl's head.'

Winston sighed, looked down at the floor, then looked up again and began walking deliberately towards Bashir.

'I mean it!' Bashir warned him. 'Come any closer and I *will* shoot her.'

Winston kept walking. 'Go ahead,' he said casually. 'Pull the trigger.'

As Bashir stared back at him, desperately trying to decide what to do, I couldn't take my eyes off Winston. Was he telling the truth? Was the gun really empty? Or was he calling Bashir's bluff?

It was impossible to tell.

Winston's face was a mask.

He was about three metres away from Bashir when Bashir made his decision. Without letting go of Evie, he suddenly straightened his right arm and levelled the pistol at Winston's head. Winston stopped and stood perfectly still, his eyes never leaving Bashir's. Bashir paused for just a moment, then steadied his arm and pulled the trigger.

The gun clicked emptily.

I breathed out.

'It's over,' Winston said quietly to Bashir. 'Let her go.'

Bashir slowly lowered the gun, but he didn't let go of Evie.

'Let her go, Bashir. *Now.*'

Bashir dropped the gun. But he still didn't let go of Evie.

Winston had had enough. He glanced over at Shaved Head and Goatee, and they began moving towards Bashir.

Bashir smiled. 'It's never over, Winston,' he said ominously. 'You of all people should know that.' In one swift movement he let go of Evie's neck, grabbed her arm and twisted it up behind her back, while at the same time reaching round to the back of his trackpants and whipping out a short-bladed kitchen knife.

'Tell your men to move back against the wall,' Bashir ordered Winston, holding the knife to Evie's throat.

Evie choked back a cry.

'Do it,' Winston told them, staring at Bashir.

Bashir waited while Shaved Head and Goatee cautiously moved back, then he turned to Winston again. 'Now tell the big guy to join them.'

Winston nodded at Muscleman, and the big man reluctantly moved away from the door and crossed over to the far wall.

Bashir looked over at the three of them. 'Lie down,' he barked, 'face down on the ground, hands on your heads.'

They glanced over at Winston. He nodded. They got down on the ground. Bashir shot a look at Mason and Lenny, who'd both moved away from the wall, and they held up their hands and moved back.

Bashir looked around, making sure he was safe, then he started edging back towards the doorway, taking Evie with him. 'I'm walking out of here now,' he said. 'If anyone tries to stop me, if anyone follows me, the girl's dead. Understand?'

'No one's going to follow you,' Winston assured him.

'They'd better not.'

I stared helplessly at Evie, wanting to help her, wanting to go after Bashir, but I didn't dare move. As long as he had the knife to her throat, I knew I couldn't take any risks. All I could do was sit there and watch as he dragged Evie out through the doorway . . .

The arm that flashed out from somewhere behind him moved so fast that at first I didn't even realise what it was. I just saw a blur of movement and a shape snaking out of the shadows. But then, as Bashir's knife hand was suddenly jerked away from Evie's throat and yanked to one side, I saw the figure behind him. It was a man, an old man . . . with a grizzled old face and grimly determined eyes . . .

'*Grandad?*' I heard myself whisper in disbelief.

He was twisting Bashir's right hand now, bending it back at the wrist to make him drop the knife. Bashir's face was screwed up in pain, but he was doggedly holding on to the knife. Grandad drew back his left arm and started hammering his fist into Bashir's side. *Thud! Thud! Thud!* Bashir groaned, and Grandad yanked on his right arm again, and this time the knife dropped to the ground.

Bashir let go of Evie then, and as she took her chance and ran back into the room, Bashir spun round to his right, swinging his left fist at Grandad. Grandad leaned back to dodge the punch, but he wasn't quite quick enough and Bashir caught him square on the chin. As Grandad staggered backwards, momentarily dazed, I was already on the move, jumping to my feet and running towards the doorway. But as Bashir moved towards Grandad, his fist drawn back, ready to hit him again, I knew I wasn't going to get there in time.

'Grandad! I shouted out, trying to warn him. '*GRANDAD!*'

I knew it was hopeless. Grandad was half dazed, and I was still a good couple of metres away from him, and Bashir was about half a second away from smashing his fist into Grandad's head . . .

Courtney Lane must have made some sound as she came racing along the corridor, but I swear I didn't hear anything. One moment there was nothing, and then she just streaked into view, speeding towards Bashir like a missile. She was moving so fast that Bashir never even saw her. I watched, awe-struck, as she launched herself at him, leaping off her feet and slamming her shoulder into his back. The air exploded from his lungs and he flew face first into the breezeblock wall, crashing into it with a sickening thud. He slid down the wall and slumped to the ground like a broken doll. Courtney was onto him in a flash, leaning over him with her fist drawn back, ready to finish him off, but it was clear that he wasn't going to get up again. He was out for the count.

Courtney stooped down and put two fingers to his neck, checking his pulse, then she straightened up, let out a relaxing breath, and looked over at Grandad to make sure he was OK. He gave her the thumbs up, then turned to me.

He was still a bit unsteady on his feet, but his eyes were clear, and for a wonderful little moment we just stood there looking at each other as if nothing else in the world really mattered.

Someone said something then. I don't know who it was or what they said, but it broke the silence, and a second later everyone else started talking. Winston and the Omega men, Mason and Lenny and Evie, all of them muttering away in quiet relief. I let out a long sigh of relief myself and watched as Grandad went over to where Bashir was lying and stood there gazing down at him.

'I thought he was supposed to be the good guy?' Grandad said to me.

'Well, yeah . . .' I replied. 'He was.'

Grandad frowned. 'So what happened?'

'That's what I'd like to know,' I said, turning to Winston for the answer.

Winston smiled tightly at me, then looked at Grandad. 'It's somewhat complicated, Mr Delaney. Might I suggest we deal with a few practicalities first? And then I'll be more than happy to explain everything to you.'

53

'Bashir Kamal is a key member of a terrorist network known as al-Thu'ban,' Winston told us, 'which roughly translated means "the Snake". As far as we know, Bashir was recruited by al-Thu'ban operatives at the age of eleven for the specific purpose of infiltrating British security services. It was a long-term mission. It took almost five years of indoctrination, re-education, conditioning, and training before al-Thu'ban finally thought he was ready. Two days after his sixteenth birthday, al-Thu'ban put their plan into operation.'

'The suicide bomb in Islamabad,' Grandad said quietly, shaking his head in disbelief.

Winston nodded. 'It was made to look as if Bashir's brother was a random victim of the bombing, but the ugly truth is that Saeed Kamal was actually the target. He was murdered by al-Thu'ban in order to provide Bashir with the perfect cover for infiltrating the intelligence services.'

'Hold on,' I said, frowning at Winston. 'You mean al-Thu'ban murdered Bashir's brother just to make it *look* as if Bashir had a genuine reason to hate terrorists?'

'Exactly,' Winston said.

'Did Bashir *know*?'

'We think so.'

'God,' I muttered, 'that's unbelievable.'

'It is,' Winston agreed. 'And that's precisely why it worked. No one would ever suspect that Bashir's hatred for his brother's killers wasn't genuine. Why should they? And from MI5's point of view, he *was* the perfect undercover agent. A young British Pakistani with a profound hatred of terrorism, ready and willing to work for them . . . what more could they ask for?'

It was past midnight now, and there were only the four of us left in Bashir's room. I was on the white settee with Grandad and Evie, and Winston had pulled up a chair and was sitting in front of us. Courtney had taken Mason to the hospital to get his ribs checked out, and Lenny had gone with them. Bashir had been carried off by Shaved Head and Muscleman, and I guessed he was being held somewhere in the warehouse. Presumably the other Omega men were either guarding him or getting on with whatever they had to do.

'So when did Omega find out that Bashir was a double agent?' Grandad asked Winston.

Winston furrowed his brow. 'Omega?'

Grandad glared at him. 'I'm not in the mood for games.'

A brief flash of irritation flickered in Winston's eyes, but he quickly composed himself and carried on. 'We began to have our doubts after MI5 broke up a terrorist cell in Stratford that Bashir had infiltrated. The cell was supposedly planning an attack on the American Embassy in London, and on the surface it seemed as if MI5 had successfully foiled their operation. They certainly thought they had. But there were some strange inconsistencies about the case, odd little things that just didn't add up. The more we looked into it, the more we began to suspect that something wasn't right.'

'Did you share your suspicions with MI5?' Grandad asked.

'Would *you* have?'

'Probably not,' Grandad admitted.

'They had too much invested in Bashir. They wouldn't have listened to us. We had no proof anyway.'

'So what did you do?'

'We went looking for proof.'

'Did you find any?'

Winston waggled his hand. 'We found some, but it was mostly just bits and pieces. It was more than enough to convince *us* that Bashir was a double agent, but we knew we needed a lot more to convince MI5 that their security was compromised.' Winston took a deep breath and let it out slowly. 'You see, that's exactly what it amounted to. Britain's national security service had been fatally compromised by a double agent. An al-Thu'ban terrorist had infiltrated MI5. We *had* to deal with that.'

'I'm surprised you didn't consider neutralising him,' Grandad said.

'Oh, we did. And if we'd thought it was the best option, we would have gone ahead and done it. But then we realised that if we could prove to MI5 that Bashir was a double agent, there was a chance they could turn him. They could make him into a *triple* agent.'

Grandad nodded knowingly. 'So al-Thu'ban would *think* he was their inside man at MI5, pretending to be an informant but passing on information to them, whereas Bashir would actually be working *for* MI5, passing on false information to al-Thu'ban and gathering real information about them to pass on to MI5.'

'That's right,' Winston said.

Evie nudged me. 'Do you understand a single word of all this?'

I smiled. 'Sort of . . . but it kind of hurts my head trying to think about it.'

'Probably best not to think about it then.'

I would have liked nothing more than to stop thinking about it. I was so tired now that I could barely stay awake, let alone think about anything. But there was no way I was giving in to exhaustion just yet. I still had unfinished business with Winston.

'So anyway,' he continued, 'while we were redoubling our efforts to prove that Bashir was an al-Thu'ban operative, his MI5 handler got himself involved in an idiotic scandal, and MI5 made the *ridiculous* decision to stop using Bashir as an informant. Fortunately it didn't make any fundamental difference to the situation. Bashir was still a double agent, and he was still a potential triple agent. We assumed he was told by al-Thu'ban to lie low for a while and wait for MI5 to realise their mistake and take him back.'

'So he left London and came to Barton,' Grandad said.

'And we continued with our investigations. Then the CIA started poking their damn noses in, and that changed everything. They had no idea what Bashir really was, or even what he was pretending to be. They just thought he was a terrorist, or he *might* be a terrorist. If they'd got their hands on him they would have whisked him away to some hellhole and we'd never have seen him again. On top of that, when MI5 found out about the CIA's interest in Bashir, that got them interested in him again.' Winston sighed. 'So we *had* to step in. And we had to do it quickly.' He gazed around the room. 'Hence this place.' He looked back at us. 'Bashir knew the CIA were after him, and that if he went back to MI5 they might give him up to the Americans, so we offered to keep him safe while we arranged a new life for him – relocation, a new identity, financial security, everything.'

'And he fell for that?' Grandad asked.

'He's arrogant. He thought he was taking us for a ride. Besides, we're very good at what we do.'

'So I've heard.'

'We would have preferred *not* to have made a move so soon. It was far from ideal having to hide Bashir away from the CIA and MI5, and we knew it wouldn't take them long to find out that he hadn't gone to Pakistan to look after his sick grandmother.' Winston shrugged. 'It was the best cover story we could come up with at such short notice.'

'Why did Bashir's parents go along with it?' I asked.

'They were protecting him.'

'Do they know he's a terrorist?'

Winston shook his head. 'They think he's a hero.'

'Why?'

'We told them he was a key witness for the prosecution in a gang-related murder case, and that because the defendant was a violent criminal with a history of witness-intimidation, Bashir was being kept under police protection for his own safety until the case came to trial.'

'No wonder Mrs Kamal was so frightened,' I muttered.

'We had to give them *some* explanation for the sudden disappearance of their son,' Winston said. 'It was a difficult situation. It became even more difficult when John Ruddy hired Delaney & Co to find out what had happened to Bashir.' He paused for a moment, looking at Grandad. 'But as I'm sure you know, Mr Delaney, in our line of work you don't dwell on the negatives, you always look to turn the situation to your advantage.'

'You've got what you needed now, haven't you?' Grandad said without hesitation. 'You've got everything that's just happened tonight on tape.' He looked around the room. 'I'm assuming the CCTV cameras in here are hidden?'

'They're state of the art, incredibly good quality. I was

wearing a button camera as back-up. We actually tried tricking Bashir into revealing himself before, but he didn't go for it. This time though . . .' Winston glanced at me and Evie. 'Well, you and your friends did everything for us really. Once we'd let Bashir see that your attempt to rescue him was genuine, it was relatively easy to convince him that the CIA were on to us, and that we were about to hand him over to them.'

'You used us,' I said wearily. 'You *wanted* Bashir to take your gun, you let him take it on purpose. You *let* him threaten Evie with it—'

'It wasn't loaded. She was never in any danger.'

'She didn't know that, did she?' I snapped. 'And what about the knife?'

'Well, yes, that was unfortunate,' he said, without so much as a glance at Evie. 'But it proved beyond doubt the kind of man that Bashir really is. And we have it all on video.' He shrugged. 'It's probably not enough on its own to convince MI5, but once they see everything else we have on him, it should seal the deal.'

'Do you really think MI5 can get him to work as triple agent?' Grandad asked.

'There's no guarantee of anything,' Winston admitted. 'But they've been trying to infiltrate this kind of terrorist group for years without success, so if they *can* turn Bashir, it'll be a massive step forward.' He looked at me. 'Sometimes we have to make short-term sacrifices for the sake of potential long-term benefits. A life risked today might save a thousand lives in years to come.'

'You knew I'd come looking for Bashir tonight, didn't you?'

'I didn't *know* anything, Travis. I was just trying to maximise our opportunities. In an operation like this, you have to be prepared to deal with all kinds of contingencies.'

'Right,' I said, looking him in the eye. 'And what about my mum and dad? Were they just another *contingency* you had to deal with?'

'I'm sorry,' he said, looking confused. 'I don't understand.'

'They knew you were here.'

He didn't say anything, just carried on looking puzzled.

I said, 'I don't know how he did it, but Dad found out about this place. He found out you were here. He took surveillance photographs from across the road.'

'He took photographs?' Winston said.

'He also knew that MI5 were interested in Bashir. That's why he was driving down to London with Mum. They were going to see someone at MI5.'

Winston glanced at Grandad. 'Did you know about this?'

Grandad ignored him, turning to me instead. 'Go on, Travis.'

'I think you knew where my parents were going that day,' I said to Winston. 'I think you tried to stop them.

In fact, I think you *did* stop them.'

'No,' Winston said firmly, shaking his head. 'We knew your parents had been hired to find Bashir, and I'm not denying that we had them checked out and were keeping half an eye on them. But I can assure you that's all there was to it. If they were meeting with MI5 that day, we certainly didn't know about it.'

'So why were you at their funeral?' I asked him.

'I told you. We were aware of your parents' investigation and we wanted to find out if anyone else knew about it.'

'But you just said you were only "keeping half an eye on them".'

'That's right.'

'You filmed their funeral with a hidden camera. That doesn't sound like "keeping half an eye on them" to me.'

He just shrugged.

'And you went to all the trouble of arranging a riot so you could search through their offices without anyone knowing. I mean, if they were of no real concern to you, what were you looking for?'

'Look,' Winston said, beginning to get edgy. 'I really don't think—'

'How did your van get damaged?' I asked.

'What?'

'The Mercedes van. It's got a dent over the front-left wheel arch.'

'So?'

'There are flecks of yellow paint in the dent.' I stared hard at him. 'Mum's car was yellow.'

He laughed quietly. 'I'm sorry, Travis, but this is really getting a bit too much now. Just because one of our vehicles has a little scratch on it—'

'How did you know that their car had spun off the road and hit a tree?'

'I'm sorry?'

'When you were telling me about *your* parents' car crash, you said, "They didn't just *spin off the road* and hit a tree for no apparent reason, they crashed because my father had been drinking."'

He frowned. 'I'm not with you.'

'How did you know my parents' car had *spun* off the road?'

'I don't know,' he said dismissively. 'I suppose I read it in the newspaper reports—'

'No, you didn't,' I told him. 'Earlier this evening I spent an hour on the Internet checking through every newspaper article about the crash I could find. Not one of them mentions anything about the car spinning off the road.'

Winston shrugged. 'I expect I probably got it from the police report then. We have contacts in the police, it's not difficult to get hold of the official reports—'

'I don't believe you,' I said. 'I think you know their car spun off the road because you were there at the time. You *saw* it spin off the road. You knew they'd found out about the warehouse, you knew they were going to talk to someone at MI5, and you didn't want that to happen. So you drove them off the road.'

'No.'

'You killed them.'

'No, you're wrong. I can *prove* you're wrong.'

I stared at him.

He said, 'I can show you something right now that will prove beyond doubt that neither myself nor my colleagues had anything to do with your parents' death.'

I'd been so sure that I was right, and Winston seemed so confident of his proof that I wasn't, that I didn't know what to say. I just sat there, watching him as he got to his feet and took a mobile from his pocket.

He put the phone to his ear, waited a moment, then said, 'It's me. I need those files. Are they still in the ops room?' He listened for a second, then spoke again. 'No, it's all right, I'll get them.' He ended the call and put the phone away. 'I'll be two minutes,' he said to me. 'OK?'

I nodded, and he turned round and walked out of the room.

'You should have talked to me, Travis,' Grandad said quietly.

'I tried to.'

'You should have tried harder.'

I looked at him. 'Sorry.'

He shook his head. 'It's not your fault.'

We sank into silence then, all three of us just sitting

there, staring at nothing, lost in our own little worlds.

I don't know how long it was before it dawned on me that Winston wasn't coming back. Five minutes, maybe. Perhaps a little longer. It wasn't a gradual realisation, I just suddenly knew that he wasn't coming back. He'd tricked me. Tricked us all. There were no files. There was no proof of anything. He'd gone. They'd all gone. Him, Shaved Head, Muscleman, the rest of them. They'd taken Bashir, got in their cars, and quietly driven away.

I turned to Grandad and saw that he knew it too.

'Sorry, Trav,' he said, annoyed with himself. 'I should have guessed.'

'What's going on?' Evie asked, yawning.

Grandad sighed. 'I've been out of this game too long.'

54

We checked the rest of the warehouse before we left, just in case we were wrong about Winston, but there was no sign of life anywhere. And when we looked in the car park and saw that the BMW and the Mercedes were no longer there, we knew there was no point in looking any further.

They'd definitely gone.

It was time for us to go too.

Grandad had left his car a couple of streets away. I didn't really feel like talking, so I let Evie sit up front with Grandad while I sat in the back, and as we drove across town and then on towards the Slade, I just closed my eyes and let myself drift away.

It didn't take long to get to Evie's flat.

As she thanked Grandad for the lift and got out of the car, I opened the back door and got out too.

'I'll walk you back to your flat,' I said to her.

'You don't have to,' she told me.

'I want to.'

'My flat's just there,' she said, grinning as she pointed at the building right in front of us. 'I mean, if you *really* want to walk me the two metres to my door . . .'

'Well, I suppose not . . .' I muttered, feeling kind of stupid.

She surprised me then by putting her arms round me and giving me a hug, and then she surprised me even more by giving me a kiss on the cheek.

'Thanks for a great night out, Trav,' she said.

I smiled. 'You're welcome.'

'Give me a call sometime, OK?'

'Yeah . . .' I mumbled, watching her walk away. 'Yeah, OK . . .'

'She's a nice girl,' Grandad said as we drove away from the Slade.

'Yeah.'

He waited a few seconds, then said, 'How old is she? Fifteen, sixteen?'

'I don't know,' I admitted. 'Does it matter?'

He glanced at me. 'I was only asking. There's no need to get funny about it.'

'I wasn't getting funny about anything.'

'Well, that's all right then.'

'Yeah.'

We went quiet again then. It was a slightly awkward silence, but somehow it felt kind of OK. There was nothing too uncomfortable about it.

After a few minutes had passed, I said, 'You weren't fooled by the pillows under the duvet then?'

'I might not be as sharp as I used to be,' Grandad said wryly, 'but I haven't lost all my marbles yet.'

'How did you know I'd gone to the warehouse?'

'It wasn't hard to guess. I mean, where else would you go?' He glanced at me. 'You didn't clear the browsing history on your laptop either.'

'So you knew I'd been checking out Sowton Lane on Google Earth.'

He nodded. 'I saw all the other stuff you'd been looking at too – the newspaper reports about the crash.'

'I had to find out, Grandad. If the newspapers didn't say anything about Mum's car spinning off the road, how did Winston know?'

'He *could* have found out from the police report. It wouldn't be that hard for him to get hold of a copy.'

'Does the police report say the car spun off the road?'

'I can't remember. I'll look at my copy when we get back.'

'But even if Winston was telling the truth about that—'

'I know,' Grandad said. 'It doesn't mean he *wasn't* there when the car went off the road.'

'Do you think he was?'

'I think . . .' He hesitated. 'I think it's quite possible, yes.'

'Really?'

He glanced at me. 'I was wrong, Travis. You were right. What we have to do now is start working together to *prove* that you were right.'

I couldn't help smiling. 'We're going to work together?'

He gave me a stern look. 'As long as you realise

that working together means no more climbing out of bathroom windows and running off on your own.'

'I'm sorry, Grandad,' I muttered. 'But I just couldn't—'

'And if I *do* decide to keep the agency open,' he continued, 'and if your nan says it's all right for you to help me out—'

'You're going to keep the agency open?' I said excitedly.

His face softened slightly. 'Well, I haven't made a final decision yet. I had a quick word with Courtney about it earlier on, and she's really keen to give it a go, but I still need to talk it over with Nan and Granny Nora. Even if they're OK with it, there's still a lot to consider. Our financial situation, my health, what kind of work we'd take on, whether we'd specialise or not . . .'

As Grandad carried on talking, it was perfectly clear to me that his mind was already made up. He was going to re-open Delaney & Co. We were going to keep Mum and Dad's business alive. And that meant so much to me that as I leaned my head back against the car seat, everything that had been driving me on over the last few weeks – the intensity, the blind determination, the desperate need to know . . . it all seemed to float out of me, and for the first time since my mum and dad died, I felt like I wanted to sleep.

As I closed my eyes and let myself drift away, I wondered how it was possible to feel so sad and so happy at the same time.

Look out for Book Two in the

series

Publishing in September 2014

Read the opening chapters here . . .

1

It was just gone three thirty on a cold and wet Friday afternoon when Kendal Price came up to me and said he'd like a quiet word. I'd just finished a double period of PE – half an hour's fitness training, another half-hour of football practice, followed by two twenty-minute seven-a-side games. I was covered in mud, tired out, and although I was still dripping with sweat, the icy wind blowing around the playing fields was beginning to bite into my bones. So all I wanted to do just then was get into the changing rooms, get out of my muddy football gear, and have a quick shower. And that's exactly what I told Kendal when he caught up with me just outside the changing rooms and said he wanted to talk to me about something.

'Just let me get changed first, OK?' I told him, rubbing my arms. 'It's freezing out here.'

'Now would be better,' he said.

'I'll only be ten minutes. Can't it wait?'

'No,' he said simply, 'it can't.'

If it had been anyone else, I probably would have stood my ground. 'If you want to talk to me,' I would have said, 'you'll just have to wait.' But this wasn't anyone else, this was Kendal Price.

Kendal is the kind of kid that every school has – the

all-round superstar who's naturally brilliant at everything. Captain of the school football and cricket teams, a straight-A student, sophisticated, popular, attractive. The teachers all love him, and constantly hold him up as a 'shining example' to the rest of us. The girls all love him because he's tall, blond, and handsome. And the boys all love him (or envy him, at least) because he's not only really good at football and cricket, but he's tough and courageous too, both on and off the field. So even though he's a straight-A student who's loved by all the teachers – which normally might make him a prime target for bullying – no one ever messes with Kendal Price. Not if they know what's good for them anyway. In fact, Kendal's such an all-round superhero that even the genuinely hard kids – the ones who claim to hate his guts – go weak at the knees in his presence.

Personally I've never really had any strong feelings about him either way. I don't worship the ground he walks on, but I don't despise him or envy him either. He is what he is, and he does what he does, and as long as that doesn't affect me, I'm really not that bothered. Mind you, having said that, I'm pretty sure that if Kendal had come up to me last term and asked if he could have a quiet word with me, I probably would have been just a tiny bit thrilled.

But a lot can change in a few short months, and so much had happened to me during the summer holidays that I was a completely different person now. My world had been turned upside down, my outlook on life changed for ever, and I'd found out the hard way that most of the stuff we spend our time worrying about doesn't actually mean anything at all.

So when Kendal approached me that afternoon, I wasn't thrilled or overawed or flattered. I didn't care that merely by talking to me he was boosting my reputation and making me look cool. I couldn't have cared less about 'looking cool'. That kind of stuff just didn't mean anything to me any more.

So why didn't I tell Kendal that if he wanted to talk to me he'd just have to wait?

Because I was curious, that's why. And curiosity was one of the things that still meant something to me.

Questions: Why on earth did the almighty Kendal Price want to talk to me? What could he possibly want? And why was he so insistent on talking to me *before* I went into the changing rooms?

Questions had kept me going through my recent summer of hell, and I wasn't going to stop asking them now.

2

'I'm sorry about your mum and dad,' Kendal said. 'It must have been really hard for you.'

It had been four months since my parents had died in a car crash, and I'd got so used to condolences now that my response had become automatic – a nod of acknowledgement, and a look that said, 'Thanks, I appreciate your kindness.'

Kendal's initial reaction was the same as most people's – a sombre nod, followed by an awkward silence. I let the silence hang in the air and gazed out over the playing fields. We were sitting on a bench at the edge of the little car park in front of the changing rooms, and I could see all the way across to the girls' changing rooms on the other side of the school grounds. There were three full-size football pitches, another area marked out for five- and seven-a-side games, and a running track that wouldn't be used now until next year. A fine November rain was drifting across the fields, and a few kids in wet and muddy football gear were hurrying back to the changing rooms, desperate to get out of the cold.

Kendal was still wearing his football kit too – he'd just finished playing for the Under 15s in a match against a visiting French school – but although he was just as sodden and caked in mud as everyone else, it didn't seem to bother him at all. Or if it did, he was really good at hiding it.

'Your parents were private investigators, weren't they?' he asked casually.

I looked at him, slightly surprised that he hadn't changed the subject. Most people, once they've offered their condolences, quickly start talking about something else. But, as I've already said, Kendal wasn't like most people.

'Yeah,' I said. 'My mum and dad ran a private investigation business called Delaney & Co.'

'What's happened to the business now?'

'My grandad's taken it over.'

'Right,' Kendal said thoughtfully. 'So you're still involved in the investigation business yourself?'

'Yeah,' I said cautiously, 'I'm still involved.' I looked at him. 'Are you going to tell me what this is about, Kendal? Because I don't know about you, but I'm getting *really* cold out here.'

'Before I tell you anything,' he replied, 'I need you to promise me that you'll keep it to yourself. It's really important that none of this goes any further.'

I shook my head. 'I can't promise anything.'

'Why not?'

'I don't know what you're going to tell me, do I? I mean, for all I know, you might want to confess to a murder or something.'

Kendal smiled. 'That's not very likely, is it?'

'Even superstars are capable of murder,' I said, grinning at him.

I thought he might take offence at that – he probably wasn't used to being mocked about his status – but, to his credit, he took it pretty well. I don't think he liked it very much, but he didn't make a big deal of it or anything. He just gave me one of those condescending looks that adults use when they think you're being childish. Which might sound a bit odd, given that Kendal wasn't an adult. But although we were both the same age – fourteen years old – there was no doubt that in lots of ways Kendal was years ahead of me. He was much taller than me, for a start – at least five feet ten – and he was also a *lot* hairier. Hairy legs, hairy arms, hairy upper lip, sideburns. His voice was deep, his face rugged and knowing, and he had an air of self-confidence about him that I could only dream about.

Compared to Kendal, I *was* just a child.

Which was the kind of thing that used to bother the hell out of me.

But not any more.

'All right,' Kendal said in a businesslike manner, 'how about this – you give me your word that you'll keep quiet about this conversation *unless* I tell you something that puts you in a legally compromising position. Is that acceptable?'

'Perfectly.'

He gave me a look, making sure I was taking him seriously, and then he finally started telling me what it was all about.

3

The petty thieving from the boys' changing rooms had started in October, Kendal explained. The first time it had happened was at an Under-14 football match between our school – Kell Cross Secondary – and Barton Grammar, our biggest rivals. Then a couple of weeks later it had happened again during an Under-15 game against Seaton College.

'To be honest, we didn't take it very seriously at the time,' Kendal said. 'Partly because the items that went missing didn't have any great value, and partly because the kids who owned them weren't even sure they *had* been stolen.'

'What kind of stuff was going missing?' I asked.

Kendal frowned. 'Well, that's the weird thing. The first time it was a graphic novel, and the next time it was a hat . . . you know, like a baseball cap. That was it. No money was taken, no mobiles or watches or anything. Just a comic book and a hat. So, like I said, we didn't really give it much thought—'

'Who's "we"?'

'Mr Jago and me. I mean, the kids reported it to Mr Jago first, of course, and then he told me about it.'

John Jago was the senior PE teacher. As well as being in charge of all the school's sporting activities, he

9

personally coached the football and cricket teams from Under-14 level upwards. He was almost obsessed with the sporting reputation of the school, and he spent a lot of time working with the most gifted athletes. Kendal was one of his protégés, and he treated him like a trusted lieutenant.

'Anyway,' Kendal went on, 'when the thieving started again straight after the half-term break, and it quickly became more frequent, we realised we had to do something.'

'Was the same kind of stuff being taken?'

He nodded. 'A book, a scarf, another hat . . . it still happens mostly when we're playing another school, but earlier this week a kid's belt went missing during a normal games period.'

'Any thefts from the girls' changing rooms?'

'Nothing's been reported.'

'The changing rooms are locked when they're not being used though, aren't they? I mean, we can't get in until someone's keyed in the entry code.'

'Yeah, and the code's changed every day.'

'What about the door inside that connects the home and away dressing rooms?'

'Unless there's a reason for it to be opened, it's always kept locked. Mr Jago has a key, and there's a spare one in the headmaster's secretary's office.'

'Has there been any sign of forced entry?'

'We haven't found any.'

'No broken windows or forced latches?'

'Nothing.'

'Have the police been informed?'

'No.'

'Why not?'

Kendal just looked at me, as if the answer was obvious.

'The Twin Town Cup?' I said.

'Exactly.'

The Twin Town Cup is a school football tournament that takes place every two years. Four teams from Barton – the town where I live – take on four teams from the two towns that Barton is twinned with: Wetzlar in Germany and Rennes in France. The venue for the tournament changes each time it's played, and this year Kell Cross was hosting it for the first time. It was a pretty big deal for the school, with all kinds of sponsorship and press coverage and stuff.

The semi-finals were being played on Monday, and the final was on Wednesday. Kell Cross had finished top of their group and were playing the runners-up from the other group in the semi-final.

'We don't know who's responsible for these thefts,' Kendal told me. 'It could be a pupil at Kell Cross, it could be someone from outside the school. Until we know for sure, we'd prefer to deal with it ourselves rather than calling in the police.' He looked at me. 'I mean, imagine how embarrassing it would be for the school if the police showed up and arrested someone in the middle of a Twin Town Cup game. We'd never live it down.'

'Why don't you just put a guard on the changing-room doors?' I suggested. 'Two teachers, or two Year 12s, one on each door at all times. Then no one can get in.'

'That's precisely what we've been doing. But it hasn't made any difference.'

'Stuff's still going missing?'

'Yeah.'

'How the hell are they getting in?'

'That's what we want you to find out.'